Everything you ever wanted to know
—and more—
about

WORLD'S MOST ELIGIBLE BACHELOR

Kieran O'Hara

Occupation:	"Agent of the Black Watch—a secret government organization."
His Reputation:	"Some would call me a gentleman, due to my aristocratic background and my somewhat old-fashioned manners when it comes to women. Others would call me...a scoundrel."
His Code:	"To never let anything get in the way of completing my mission. Not even the most desirable of women."
Marriage Vow:	"There's no place for a bride in my dangerous line of work. But ever since I met Beau Anna Cahill, I wish I was in a position to love, honor and cherish...."

Dear Reader,

Thanks for returning for another WORLD'S MOST ELIGIBLE BACHELORS novel. This brand-new twelve-book series is all about men—and gives you all the romance you've come to expect from Silhouette Books.

Each of these delectable heroes has been named a World's Most Eligible Bachelor by *Prominence Magazine*—a fictitious publication we editors created just for you! These compelling stories, written by some of your most beloved authors, focus on to-die-for bachelors, with plenty of juicy details about how they finally succumb to marriage.

Bestselling author BJ James brings you a hero no woman could resist, Kieran O'Hara. This dedicated *Agent of the Black Watch* is on a secret mission to protect an innocent beauty...but will Kieran's heart need the real protection? You won't want to miss this exciting story, which is also part of BJ James's THE BLACK WATCH miniseries.

And next month be sure to look for an exciting CODE OF THE WEST story from popular author Anne McAllister. Who'll be able to resist this *Cowboy on the Run?* Surely not the woman who had his secret child!

Until then, here's to romance wishes and bachelor kisses!

The Editors

Please address questions and book requests to:
Silhouette Reader Service
U.S.: 3010 Walden Ave., P.O. Box 1325, Buffalo, NY 14269
Canadian: P.O. Box 609, Fort Erie, Ont. L2A 5X3

World's Most
Eligible Bachelors

BJ James

Agent of the
Black Watch

Silhouette Books

Published by Silhouette Books
America's Publisher of Contemporary Romance

For Mother.

 SILHOUETTE BOOKS

ISBN 0-373-65028-0

AGENT OF THE BLACK WATCH

Copyright © 1998 by BJ James

This edition published by arrangement with Harlequin Books S.A.

® and TM are trademarks of Harlequin Books S.A., used under license.
Trademarks indicated with ® are registered in the United States Patent
and Trademark Office, the Canadian Trade Marks Office and in other
countries.

Printed in U.S.A.

A Conversation with...
Award-winning author
BJ JAMES

What hero have you created for WORLD'S MOST ELIGIBLE BACHELORS, and how has he earned the coveted title?

BJ: Kieran O'Hara is an agent of The Black Watch, a fictitious agency that comprises my Silhouette Desire miniseries THE BLACK WATCH. A man of The Black Watch is supremely loyal to his country; completely dedicated to his work; honorable, without peer, in thought and deed. He is a man of great strength, great integrity and even greater compassion. Kieran is Mr. Normal and Mr. Nice Guy rolled into one. Yet he is as competent as a brigade of agents, and as dangerous. And his prestigious and wealthy background makes him more than intriguing....

What modern-day personality best epitomizes a WORLD'S MOST ELIGIBLE BACHELOR?

BJ: The men I admire most are everyday people who go about their lives with honor, not for fame or glory, but because it's the right thing to do. Men who are kind, compassionate and heroic when the need arises, simply by reason that such values are in their makeup. Though he hasn't been an eligible bachelor for many years, my husband fits this description better than anyone I know. Charles N. James, M.D. Better and fondly known as Buck, the most caring and dedicated physician his fortunate patients have ever known.

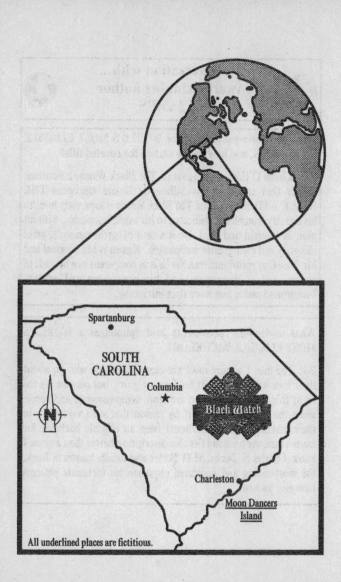

Spartanburg

SOUTH
CAROLINA

Columbia

Black Watch

N

Charleston

Moon Dancers
Island

All underlined places are fictitious.

Foreword

In desperate answer to a need prompted by changing times and mores, Simon McKinzie, dedicated and uncompromising leader of The Black Watch, has been called upon by the president of the United States to form a more covert and more dangerous division of his most clandestine clan. Ranging the world in ongoing assembly of this unique unit, he has gathered and will gather the elite among the elite—those born with the gift or the curse of skills transcending the norm. Men and women who bring extraordinary and uncommon talents in answer to extraordinary and uncommon demands. They are, in most cases, men and women who have plummeted to the brink of hell because of their talents. Tortured souls who have stared down into the maw of destruction, been burned by its fires, yet have come back, better, surer, stronger. Driven and colder.

As officially nameless as The Black Watch, to those few who have misfortune and need of calling on their dark service, they are known as Simon's Chosen...Simon's Marauders.

Prologue

*G*od.
A young man prayed.
And the wind ceased screaming.
Please.
He wept.
And daggers of rain turned to mist.
Hear me.
In ominous peace a storm passed slowly.
And in the black of night, prayers turned to anger.
No!

* * *

"No! Damn you, not Anna!"

The cry of Roderick Beaumont Cahill was bittersweet. A keening of love and despair, shattering a deathly hush. A melancholy echo of the storm ravaging the land. Grief that would never be silenced as the wind was silent, never stilled as the rain in an eye of false calm.

Yet, as he reviled the fates that returned his only love too late, as he damned the chaos that would take her forever, the eye began to pass. The wind began to wake.

Rising with a low moan, it skittered among the eaves making known its return in shudders and creaks and the clatter of a shutter ripped away. With an angry howl it gathered strength, driving the lash of rain and towering tide before it. Ancient oaks thrashed, limbs stripped bare clawed at wall and window. Palmetto and palm quaked, slinging fronds turned to rapiers to impale anything in their path.

The storm seethed. A neophyte discovering its monstrous power, it vacillated, stalled, churning in place, feeding on its own malevolent power. Gorging, spawning. Then spawning again to wreak its worst over Moon Dancers Island and the plantation known as Cahill's Grant.

But in the torment of his bedside vigil, Beaumont Cahill didn't care. His world was here, with life and death embraced in a single room. The room where every Cahill of his lineage had come into the world. Where his tiny daughter had been born this night. Too soon.

Where Anna Lee Bonnet, his beloved, would perish.

"Too soon."

Burrowing his head in his hands, he sat as still as death, while the wind howled its song of madness. This savage despot of nature, saving the cruelest of its havoc for last, descended again on the manor. Battered walls ravaged, The Bluff, the old house that had known life as well as death, only moaned. Sobbed. Yielded.

As for more than a century, in yielding, it stood.

Another hour passed. The storm altered. A subtle veering, a meager decline. A sliver of hope.

Beaumont Cahill roused, prayer and anger ceased. He listened, a seasoned islander calculating, determining. As a man catching a toehold in an escape from hell, he lifted his tortured gaze from the wraith-like figure in his bed.

"Tabby." His voice roughened with strain as he spoke to more than the ears of God for the first time in hours. "Tabitha?"

The old woman straightened, throwing off the mantle of age and fatigue. From her post apart, her clouded eyes sought him. "I'm here."

"The storm is easing. If..." His voice broke. With desperate effort he regained his composure. "If we could make it to the mainland, surely there would be help. Transfusions. Surgery to stop the bleeding."

"No," Tabby said, dashing a mad dream. "The storm has eased, but it isn't done. Even so, no seaworthy vessels are still in the harbor." Her face, timeworn into a maze of wrinkles, crumpled into regret. "If there were a hundred crafts, if the journey were possible, nothing could be changed. No one can do more for Anna than we've done."

"Don't say that. I won't hear it." His red-rimmed eyes blazed in denial.

Tabby let his anger flow over her, feeling it fill the room tainted with the coppery scent of blood. In a moment of respite, she closed her eyes in sorrow, a grizzled crone bearing the lifelong burden of knowing. When she spoke, it was into the muted passion of the storm. "Beaumont."

"No." He turned his face from her, denying the truth. "Damn you, Tabby. No!"

Rising, she tottered to him. Touching his shoulder, feeling him cringe, she murmured, "Be angry. Damn me for what I know, but hear what I say."

As she had since he was a boy, she waited for wisdom to become reason. With her fingertips she felt tension lessen. She heard his sigh of resigned despair. He would not like the truth, but he would accept it.

"Anna Lee Bonnet has loved you all the days of her life." Tabby spoke softly, remembering. "First in the worshipful innocence of a child. Then, with the strength of a woman, she loved you more than her own name, more than her life. Defying her father, renouncing convention, she left all she believed and held dear to come to you. Her time with you was short, but without regret. Without doubt. Tonight, she's given you the most selfless and precious gift of that love. Now you must be as selfless.

"We'll never know why she was in the garden by the oak, nor why it fell in the first stirring of the storm. Charter Oak stood on that ground from the day it was planted by the first Cahill who came to the island. For more than a century it was a symbol of strength. Yesterday its strength failed, and Anna was grievously hurt."

Tabby's fingers strayed over the solid muscles of his shoulder. In a familiar gesture, a palm as hardened as it was soothing rested at his cheek. "Her legs are crushed, with the hemorrhaging she's lost too much blood. There's nothing anyone can do.

"When you pray, let it be that she never wakes. For it would be to incredible agony." Beneath her consoling touch, she felt his body clinch in agony as he recognized the truth. "Let her go. Let her go in peace."

Taking her hand away, Tabby waited. Beaumont Cahill was a strong man whose greatest virtues were truth and compassion. She harbored little doubt what choice he would make.

With a long breath drawn, then released with the calm of profound grief, he nodded, and turned back to the bed. Back to Anna, who slept and, if his prayers were answered, would never wake.

Tabby, who had been a part of his life since she'd taken him from his mother's body, had never seen him more alone. With love and suffering so complete, it could be no other way. In her tottery step she returned to her post, until she would be needed again.

The night passed. Anna grew weaker, and beyond the walls of Cahill's Bluff the storm grew stronger. Then, tiring of its macabre game on this playground, it began to move.

It had come to the island slowly, it would take leave as slowly.

Hours of tumult passed before Beaumont whispered a broken goodbye. There were no tears, he didn't say the terrible words. But Tabby knew.

Anna was gone. Lost to him and their newborn child. "She never saw our daughter."

Certain this would be the lasting anguish, Tabby chose her words with care. "Not with her eyes. But for the months she carried her, Anna saw her as every woman sees her child…in her dreams and in her heart."

Someday he would find comfort in her words, but now he hardly heard. His face was a mask. With eyes as empty as a ravaged soul, he asked a single question. "Why?"

Tabby made no offer of compassion he neither wanted nor needed. Hands gripped in her lap, lips drawn in misery, the old woman shook her head. "I don't know."

She looked away, for even in her nearly blinded sight, his stony desperation was too much to bear. "For my sins, it isn't always given to me to see."

"Perhaps for all our sins. Mine," Beaumont murmured as he turned again to Anna, "more than any of yours."

Ancient, ageless, a legend on the island for more than half a century, Tabby had been part of every factor of his life. In one of fate's cruel twists, as with his daughter, it was Tabby who had taken him from his mother as she lay dying on this very bed. Tabby who helped raise a motherless child, sharing his laughter, walking with him through grief. He knew it was her cross to bear that her gift of sight was never what she wished to see, but only what was "given" to her.

Tabby's cross. As losing Anna Bonnet for years as a young boy, and again, forever, as a man was his.

With an unsteady hand, he stroked the dark, wildly curling mane from the pale face grown paler in death. Anna. His beloved Anna, injured in a caprice of the storm, weakened beyond hope by the onslaught of labor and the premature birth of their child.

"Anna."

Taking an icy hand in his, lacing his fingers through hers as she liked, he kissed a bruised knuckle. "I've loved her all my life."

Tabby nodded, grim lines in her face easing in remembrance. "She was your shadow from the time she could walk."

"Until our fathers quarreled and hers forbade us to see each other ever again." An old, never forgotten bitterness coiled deep within him. "When we disobeyed, he shipped her to Switzerland."

"You were certain she would defy him and refuse to go."

"Yes."

"When she didn't, couldn't, you were cruel."

With a ragged moan, Beaumont remembered how, in his hurt, he had lashed out at the young Anna.

"She was just sixteen, beautiful and untamed. But for all that, except in matters concerning you, she was an obedient daughter. Her courage was young and untried, Beaumont, but never weak."

"I know that now, Tabby. I knew it then, too late. I had driven her away. When the fog of anger cleared, I understood, and I hoped she would. But when weeks turned to months, then years, and I didn't hear from her, I thought I'd lost her forever."

"So you went on with your life. If you couldn't have Anna, you chose a wife who was nothing like her in temperament, but could pass for her twin."

"A wife who hated the island and my attentions so badly, she deserted our marriage bed after a single night." There was no regret in his heart for his errant bride. Never any love.

"She'll be back."

"No!" Beaumont's head reared back, his look fierce.

With her failing vision Tabby couldn't see, but she knew the man the boy she raised had become. She knew the fire that smoldered in him. She heard the rage. But she knew the honor as well. "Fionna Elliott Cahill will return to Moon

Dancers Island after the storm. This time she will come to stay.''

"She won't! She wouldn't dare."

As if he hadn't spoken, Tabby continued with the monotony of a chant, "She'll dare. And this time she'll stay."

"Never! Do you think that after Anna…" His voice broke as he struggled to keep a tenuous control. "Dear heaven, why would I want her after Anna, when I didn't before?"

"Didn't say you would want her," Tabby insisted doggedly. "But she'll stay. For a while, if not forever."

"After nearly a year? You're babbling like an old fool. Why would Fionna come here now? Why would she stay even a while, when, before, a night was too long?"

"Not a year." Tabby ignored the rebuke. "Yet time enough."

"Enough!" he snarled.

"Yes." The old woman stood her ground.

Beaumont started to protest, but before Tabitha's certainty, his scathing rejection was suddenly tempered. "What have you seen? What has been 'given' to you? Tell me what reason would I have to let Fionna stay?"

"I think that's better left for you to discover."

"I think it's better you tell me."

Tabby's thin lips pursed. "In due time you'll know. Then you'll do what's right."

"What's right would be that Anna never left me. That she be whole and vibrant, the beautiful person she was. Fionna?" He spat the name, hating her for being alive, for being his wife when Anna could never be. "I promise, as long as I draw breath Fionna will never set foot in Cahill's Bluff."

"Hush!" Hands flying, fingers twisting, Tabby made a sign to ward off any spirits who might insure that his word be kept. "Don't make bold promises you can't keep."

"Save it for the tourists, Tabby," Beaumont said grimly as he saw the familiar gesture. "You're an educated woman. My grandfather and his father saw to that. I won't question how you've reconciled your education with your beliefs. I know the visions you're given are very real. But I refuse to believe there are good or bad spirits waiting to take me to task for something I've said."

"Don't!" Fanatic fingers made another sign. "Do as I taught you. Take care in what you say, Roderick Beaumont Cahill!"

Beaumont's anger escalated. "Dammit, Tabby! I'm not a boy to be scolded…"

With the roar of a maddened creature incensed by his disbelief, a blast of wind buffeted the house. Rain drenched the slate roof in a thunderous downpour, slashing drops thrummed against brick and tabby walls. The latch of a second shutter broke.

With this final squall, the storm came to its end on Moon Dancers Island. Ending with it, Beaumont's anger at Tabby and a wife who no longer mattered. What remained of the night was given up to silent brooding, a final goodbye to the only woman he would ever love.

Dawn came with a clear and golden sunrise. But Beaumont couldn't conceive that there was still beauty. Still hope. His gaze turned to the horizon, his thoughts on love and loss, he listened as Tabby left the room. When she returned, without abandoning his sightless stare, he asked, "What now, Tabby? How do I go on? Why should I?"

"You do as every Cahill before you. You survive."

"I can't forget."

"No."

"Yet I should go on." He spat the words. "You haven't told me how."

"I won't tell you." Tabby stepped in front of him. The child she held only a ripple in the shawl that bound her. "She will."

"No." Beaumont would have refused her, but Tabby wouldn't allow it. Before he could react, the baby was in his arms. He shoved the child back. "Take her."

Tabby backed away. "I'm too old for babies."

"You're too old for God."

"Perhaps." She moved toward the door.

"Dammit, Tabitha!"

"Hush. Good daddies don't talk such."

"Maybe I won't be a good daddy."

"You will."

"Maybe I don't want to be."

"Humph!" Clouded eyes narrowed. Dark brows arched, wrinkled lips pursed. "Bit late for doubts. That poor babe didn't ask to be born." With a tilt of her head, she muttered words intended to shake a foolish young man to his soul, "She didn't kill her mother. Lot of things did. Lots of folk had a hand in it, but not this sweet babe."

"Dammit! I didn't...I wouldn't." He stopped, turning a hollow-eyed stare down at his tiny daughter as the horror of an unrecognized truth scoured his soul. "God forgive me," he whispered, drawing the baby close. There were tears on his cheeks as he turned an appalled gaze to the old woman. The first and last tears he would shed for Anna, for himself, for their child.

"Help me, Tabby. Tell me what do I do?"

"What do you do? You love her, as you loved Anna." Opening the door, Tabby stepped through it.

"Wait," Beaumont cried. "What will I call her?"

Reflecting on how history repeated itself, especially with the Cahills, Tabby smiled at the child who would be his salvation. As he had been his father's. "You call her Beau Anna, as her mother wished." Her smile grew thoughtful. "She will be a wondrous child, this Beau Anna Bonnet."

The door closed with a satisfied thump. Beaumont was alone with his child, and the mother she would never see. Unfolding the shawl because he could think of nothing else to do, he was astounded. She was tiny, exquisite, a replica of Anna.

He was amazed by the softness of her skin, enchanted by the sweet shape of her lips. When her eyes opened, her fathomless regard locked on his face. His heart lurched, and Beaumont Cahill found a reason for living.

"Beau Anna," he said the name, the sound of it strange on his tongue.

"Beau Anna Bonnet." A name with music in it, but not

quite right. Looking down at her, he saw, not a child, or a daughter, but a precious gift.

Shifting her in his arms, he went with her to his chair by the bed. For a long while he sat there silently by Anna. Anna, brave and kind, as lovely in death as life. "You won't be forgotten," he said quietly. "I promise."

Cuddling the child closer, his cheek brushing her shock of dark hair, he murmured, "Let me tell you a story, sweetheart, of the woman who loved us. She won't be around to show you how much, so, I'll love you enough for both of us."

He kissed a tiny cheek, then he smiled. This time the name he said was perfect.

"Beau Anna...Beau Anna Bonnet Cahill."

One

"No man alive should look like that."

And it was doubly unfair to the other half of the human race, the female half, that any of the Chosen should, Callie McKay decided. Especially this one.

It made little difference that she'd been a topnotch agent with The Black Watch, before becoming Simon McKinzie's assistant. Familiarity had done nothing to breed immunity to the type. "Nope," she smiled wickedly. "Not when they make them like the Nomad."

A manicured fingernail drawn down the line of a masculine jaw strayed over lips curved in a grin. As familiar tension curled through her, she imagined the feel of the stubble of his beard, the heat of his skin.

"There oughta be a law." Her voice drifted into a sigh, as footsteps approached her desk. She didn't need to look up to know whose footsteps. She would have known even if she hadn't been expecting him.

Breathless, she waited, playing her little joke and barely keeping a leer from her face. When he paused at her desk, she kept her attention riveted on the glossy page and the striking photograph.

A second ticked by.

Two.

He didn't disappoint her.

Calloused hands slapped the desk, brawny arms framed hers. As he leaned close, there was the tantalizing scent of soap and sea air that always clung to him.

"Reading trash these days, sweetheart?" His breath was warm on her cheek, his lips brushed her hair.

Keeping the excitement he always sparked in check, she answered solemnly, "You know the old cliché."

"What cliché would that be?" he drawled, straightening in a move of inborn grace.

"Oh, you know. The one about one man's trash being another man's treasure." In spite of herself she smiled as she looked up at a face as handsome as the photograph, and into eyes as blue. A lingering survey proved an unnecessary reminder that his body was as lean and sexy as it had been in what was left of torn and soot streaked business attire. A hero in the remnants of a three piece suit, still very much a hero in faded jeans and denim shirt. With mischief creeping into her tone, she amended, "Or should I say another woman's?"

"Yeah, sure." He turned away. But not before she saw the uncommon frustration. "Just what I needed, my face and half-naked body spread over those chic little pages like some sort of..." Sucking in an angry breath, grasping for his trademark calm, he growled, "Like some centerfold."

"Kieran," Callie chided. "*Prominence Magazine* isn't *Playgirl.*"

"I didn't think so. Until now."

"Not so much has changed. All those pages detailing your accomplishments and charm should be a compliment." She was enjoying this rare moment when Kieran the invincible, discovered some things were beyond his control. That bit of frustration made him even more attractive. "Having your photograph...ahh...*photographs*...filling these pages doesn't mean you're a centerfold."

"Might as well," he tossed back at her. "What with every woman I meet..."

"Don't stop now." Hands folded over the magazine and Kieran O'Hara in all his half-naked glory, she prodded, "Every woman... What?"

"Hell! I don't know." Leaving the desk he went to the window. Head bent, dark hair glittering in the light as it tumbled over his forehead and curled against his neck, he stared at the street below. The workweek in the nation's capital was drawing to an end. The entire city seemed to be moving by. Bedlam en masse, everyone eager to begin the weekend. "I don't know anything except that my life hasn't been my own since that damned article."

"Two whole days of torture." Though her sympathy was suspect, Callie had weathered a bit of his dilemma as she stopped by a newsstand to pick up a reserved issue. The publication enjoyed good sales, now it flew off the shelves. Only a warning that her hands were registered lethal weapons discouraged a zealous young woman from engaging in a tug of war over the last copy the vendor had.

By tomorrow, Kieran's heroic photograph would adorn thousands of bulletin boards in thousands of offices, and even more high school lockers. For further inspection, it would certainly be tucked beneath a pillow in countless bedrooms. She was sure the chance of that particular notoriety hadn't occurred to him. He would be horrified when it did.

Biting back another smile, she made a pitying sound. "It must be difficult being one of the world's most eligible bachelors and a hero in the bargain."

He met her bland look grimly. Laying a palm against his nape, he kneaded the taut muscles. An unconscious repetition of the photograph he found so offensive.

Sneaking another look at the magazine, Callie wondered how many times she'd seen that gesture, except, to her regret, always fully clothed. "Poor baby! It was just your bad luck to be born wealthy and gorgeous and heroic."

"Take your tongue out of your cheek, McKay. What my family has is no accomplishment of mine. I'm not gorgeous. As far as that specific photograph is concerned, I was doing my job, and you know it."

"I don't think dashing into an exploding building, getting your shirt burned off, being nearly overcome by toxic fumes, then taking a rafter across the shoulder as you guided people to safety is part of your job description."

"My job description is to do the job," he snapped, irritation certainly not abating as she teased him. "That's all I did."

"Umm-hmm," Callie agreed. "In typical Kieran O'Hara—never recognizing the impossible, no matter the cost to himself—sangfroid."

This was the quality causing the furor about him. As much as the sex appeal, the success, the wealthy background. Well, almost as much as the sex appeal, she admitted, opting for honesty.

Reiterating her own point, her appreciative gaze strayed, then narrowed on his shoulder. With the photograph as vivid reminder, she knew there would be a wound beneath the denim. "How is your shoulder, by the way?"

"The shoulder's fine. Fine and dandy," Kieran began in clipped tones, then catching her look of concern, his voice softened. "It's almost healed, thank you. The doctor expects minimal scarring."

"That's a relief." Callie shifted, not so subtly bringing the magazine into view. "We wouldn't want the gorgeous body of one of the world's most..."

"Dammit! Callie. Don't say it." A hand raking through his hair added to the dishevelment that made him more attractive.

"Wouldn't think of it." She touched her mouth. "My lips are zipped."

"You're paying me back, aren't you?" Kieran said as she lost her battle with a chuckle. "For all the times I've teased you."

"Maybe I just like seeing a handsome, most eligible bachelor get his due." Without pausing, she asked, "Just for the record, was your great-great-grandfather really a baron?"

"Callie..."

A buzzer signaled Simon McKinzie was ready for Kieran.

"My summons to the lion's den?" His scolding cut short, he grinned at Callie. "I don't suppose our leader finds this so amusing."

"As a matter of fact, he does."

"You're joking, right?"

"Joking?" Callie looked up in an innocent stare. "When was I ever joking?"

"He isn't going to have my head for this breach of security?"

"What breach?"

The buzzer sounded again, in staccato blasts.

"Still impatient," Kieran observed. "That much hasn't changed."

"Never will," Callie agreed as she ushered him to Simon's office. "That, you can be sure of." Waiting until he stepped through the door of Simon's Sanctum, quoting the caption beneath her favorite photograph, she drawled, "Try 'the killer smile of a hero and a heartbreaker.' Maybe Simon will be charmed."

As the door closed, Kieran waited for the explosion. But the man whose opinion he valued second only to his father's gave no indication that he'd heard, nor that he knew of the hapless compromise of security.

Beyond a wave drawing the younger man into the room, and to a seat across from him, there was no communication. Simon sat as if carved of granite, letting Kieran feel the weight of his scrutiny.

Among his colleagues in Washington there were many who had felt the piercing stare. Many who felt the Scot was, indeed, granite. Body, soul, heart. These were the sycophants who knew him only in his persona as the perennial Presidential advisor whose rare common sense and sometimes undiplomatic expertise transcended party lines.

Only the informed insider knew the bull-shouldered Scot, a veteran of years of covert activities, had conceived and brought to fruition the most proficient and covert government agency in history. Among the latter, only those recruited to be part of the nameless organization saw the true man. Only they knew the spectrum of his temper, the enduring quality of honor, the depth of compassion.

In the time he'd worked for the organization unofficially referred to as The Black Watch, Kieran had been certain he'd experienced all of Simon's moods and temperament. But something lurking in the unwavering stare warned he was about to experience another facet of a complicated personality.

Minutes passed, Simon said nothing.

Wondering what game the older man was playing, and what mischief he saw there, Kieran waited with the patience and tenacity that defined Kieran O'Hara.

Simon was first to speak. "I was sitting here thinking how fortunate The Watch has been to have you."

Startled, Kieran had no quick answer. Before he could voice his acknowledgment, Simon moved on.

"How is your shoulder?"

"Better. Thank you." A logical question, but not what Kieran expected.

"Healing as it should?"

"Yes, sir." Something the exacting leader of The Watch would know from the detailed medical report Kieran knew would be lying on his desk.

"A good piece of work, the Meecham project." Blunt fingers joined in a steeple to rest Simon's chin. "Identifying the saboteur, minimizing the destruction. Saving lives."

"Part of the job."

"Modesty?" Simon tilted a fuzzy brow. Hammerlike hands unfolded. Spinning his chair, he took an unmistakable object from a drawer. "Must be hard, after this." He tossed it on the desk.

"Prominence," Kieran growled in distaste.

"I take it you aren't happy with your recent fame."

Kieran shook his head, frustration growing. "Would you be?"

Simon chuckled, an unexpected reaction. "If it were me? No. Since it's you? I couldn't be more pleased."

Kieran was seldom caught off guard, but Simon had managed it deftly. "You're pleased with this?"

"Quite."

A gesture speaking volumes of contempt accompanied Kieran's scowl. "With this frivolity and the publicity?"

"Especially the publicity."

"I don't know what sources provided the information, but

there's little that was left out. It's like discovering you live in a fishbowl. It wouldn't surprise me if someone out there knows what brand of toothpaste I prefer.''

"Most of what's here is easily obtained. The rest you provided." Simon riffled pages, turning to the image of Kieran dressed in trousers, meager tatters of a shirt, sweat, soot, and little more. "This—doing your job—added to the attraction, making you newsworthy.''

Another riffle closed the magazine. Simon turned a steady gaze to him. "Some girl's heart goes pitty-pat when she discovers you happen to like the same toothpaste. That sort of publicity does no real harm. And it might help.''

Suddenly it was all clear. The ever ingenious Simon McKinzie had found a way to turn adverse publicity to an advantage. Kieran laughed. "You have something up your sleeve. I assume it involves my…uh…recent fame.''

The leonine head inclined, the hooded gaze never strayed. "A fair assumption.''

"I assume, as well, that you're going to explain that remark.''

"I have an assignment for you." Humor vanished. Eyes that flashed with mischief turned cold as winter rain. "A series of murders on a private island off the coast of South Carolina. Could be a serial killer. Could be drug related. Could be neither.''

"What does that leave?" Kieran asked.

"That's for you to discover. A lot of peculiar things are going on. Things even the resident seeress can't explain.''

"The resident seeress?" The younger man didn't bother hiding his skepticism. Not because he didn't believe such power existed, but because he knew it did. Once in a rare while.

"She isn't one of your Eastern mystics, and she makes no claims, but she's one to reckon with. The lady must be nearly a century old, and her powers have been proven by time.''

"Even with her powers, The Watch has been asked to intervene?''

An incline of a silver head underscored Simon's reply. "We've been asked."

"By whom?"

"For the time being, it's best that only I know."

A strange turn of events, but Kieran had learned early in his days with The Watch, that its leader acted only with reason, and never ever without purpose. "This person, or persons will know me, but I won't know them."

"You'll know."

"When?"

"Soon enough."

In the closed society of a small island, he would hardly be inconspicuous. "What reason will I have for coming to the island?"

"This!" Simon slapped a palm over the cover of *Prominence Magazine*. "You'll go as yourself. A successful businessman, unhappy with the notoriety this dubious honor caused."

"What will I hope to accomplish in this exile?"

"For some time you've questioned the direction of your life. The article brought your dissatisfaction to a breaking point. A friend has offered you a place on the island for the summer."

"This friend's name?"

"Norris Selkirk Candler, the third. Norrie to you. The land on the island is entailed. No one can own it except members of the family to whom the original grant was made. The Candlers and families like them have perpetual leases on small oceanfront tracts. No commercial renting is allowed, but Norrie graciously agreed to lend his cottage.

"You'll find all you need to know about your host here." Simon stacked an envelope on the magazine. A second envelope, considerably thicker, joined the stack. "Callie prepared a history of the island in general. The particulars, the in-depth studies of the people with whom you will be most concerned, I did myself."

"Because of the secrecy."

Leaning back, Simon laced his fingers over his flat stomach. "All our investigations are conducted in secrecy. But this one must be taken a step further. The Watch has an agent in place in the area. The slightest breach could mean his life."

"So he'll know who I am, but I'm not to know his identity."

Realizing Kieran had focused on his use of the masculine pronoun, Simon smiled. "Sharp. Just be that way on the island. When the time comes, he will identify himself."

Simon gathered together the envelopes and handed them to Kieran. "Read these. When you've finished, buzz Callie. She'll know where to find me. If you have questions, I'll answer them then.

"Take your time." The last was a command, given unnecessarily. Kieran was nothing, if not thorough. "I'll have Callie bring in a pot of coffee. After that, no one will disturb you."

Simon strode from the room, leaving Kieran to ponder the strange beginning of what could prove to be a mission as strange.

"All right." Opening the thicker of the envelopes first, he drew out a sheaf of paper and scanned the first page. "Mr. Roderick Beaumont Cahill and Miss Beau Anna Bonnet Cahill, let's discover what Simon has to say about you and the mysteries of your island."

An hour would pass. Callie would come and go unnoticed. Coffee would grow cold in the carafe before Kieran O'Hara, the man called Nomad, laid down the last page and stabbed the button to summon Simon. While he waited, choosing a marked page, he read it again.

"Beau." He laid the page aside. "Beau Anna Bonnet Cahill of Moon Dancers Island."

An unusual name, an unusual woman.

Perhaps a woman in danger.

TWO

"Beau Anna."

Tabitha Hill peered at the rigging of the ship though her eyes could distinguish nothing more than a hulking shape. No one knew how she directed herself so unerringly over the island's far-flung paths. But no one ever escaped when she was determined to find them.

"Beau Anna!" The frail throat strained to raise its harangue above the lap of the tide and the crack of sails. "It's time you came down from there."

"Just a minute, Tabby. I've almost got it." The voice was low, intent. A pleasant contralto with an edge of contained exasperation. "Or I will have."

The reply floated from the far side of a sail. Kieran, who stood a pace behind the elderly Tabby, but towered a foot over her, hadn't realized anyone was aboard. Even now, as he searched among the sails, he could see only a bare foot braced precariously against a mast, a mop of dark hair flying in the breeze, and the intriguing curve of a behind barely contained in faded cutoffs.

The old woman wouldn't be put off. "You promised you'd meet the noon launch."

"I know! I will! I'll even dress for the role of island chatelaine. In glorious elegance. Though, heaven knows, we have more serious problems to concern ourselves with than some discontented man too good-looking for his own sake. Probably dresses like he owns Savile Row, too." The last was muffled, delivered through gritted teeth.

Gritted around a dagger, no doubt, Kieran thought.

Attention riveted on fluttering sails, he waited for a glimpse of more than a leg, or shapely hip. Letting his imagination fly, he wondered if there would be a scabbard for the dagger cinched at her waist. Perhaps, this lady of the unusual name wore a scarf knotted about her head and a patch over one eye.

Amused by the direction of his thoughts, he gave himself up to the moment, the time, the place, the pleasure. The shore was his home, his place of renewal. As the second son and second child of the incomparable Keegan and Mavis O'Hara, love of the sea, for its wonders and enchantment, was part of life.

In time, the love and fascination of a child became the love and fascination of the man. The first diminishing little in the years since his nomadic and adventurous childhood. The latter flourishing, mature and refined. No matter where his assignments took him, when his work was done, it was to the sea he ultimately returned.

Whether teeming port, exotic atolls, or the shores of common barrier islands such as this, in the meeting of land and tide, he found strength. From it he drew a measure of peace.

He was discovering that Moon Dancers Island was more than the typical island. Far from commonplace. It was a sea island paradise, replete with blooming yucca, palmetto and palm.

The road Tabitha Hill had walked with him, meandered at will beneath a canopy of oak and Spanish moss. Lilting birdsong and the rhythm of the distant tide marked the cadence of every step, whispered accompaniment for every word. Following the seemingly endless track, like a wizened bird in a colorful turban and a dress of multihued scarves, she'd led him into the wild. Taking him where the world was green and still. A vacuum of muted sound far removed from sea or sky.

Yet, one last twist, a divided path, a climb over sea oats studded dunes, and the sandy beach of a narrow bay glittered in the sun. Beyond the boundary of the shifting ribbon of white lay the sea, as blue and unfettered as the sky.

Sea, sand, sky. The scents, the sounds, the feel of the sun on his skin. Always familiar, always the same, no matter the country, whatever the sea. The brigantine, a seaworthy replica of the "tall ships" of the nineteenth century was the unforeseen.

The brigantine and the cute behind of Beau Anna Cahill, Kieran amended.

"Beau Anna Cahill," Tabitha scolded seriously now. "You mind your aunt Tabby and bring you sassy behind down from that rigging this minute. Time you quit playing pirate and behaved."

There was silence as Kieran turned to stare at the ancient black woman. Not because she referred to herself as the stubborn Miss Cahill's aunt, but for the eerie sensation that she had plucked his thoughts from his mind.

He was beginning to believe this would be an interesting case. Perhaps more interesting than any before.

"You hear me and do as I say. Skip Hayes and your brother done busted their heads falling out of that rigging, pretending to be Blackbeard and Bonnet. Israel would've too, except he's always smarter." As Tabby tottered closer to the ship, Kieran moved apart to watch.

"Three grown men acting like children is enough. You ain't got time for fool games. You got obligations to meet." An empathic tilt threatened to dislodge the turban. "Promises to keep."

"I know," the voice agreed in resignation. "What I don't understand is why Norrie insisted I meet Mr. Wonderful at the dock and escort him to the cottage. Even a fool and a mainlander could find the way."

The foot disappeared. With it, the rest of Beau Anna Cahill.

"Don't you go hiding. Won't change nothing."

"I couldn't hide among sails, if I wanted to. Or anywhere else if you were determined to find me. So, don't scold anymore, Tabby." Beau's voice was muffled by yards of snapping sailcloth determined to defy her efforts to catch it. "I said I'd meet the launch."

"But…"

"Please, Tabby. No more." The loose sail was captured and contained, but no Beau Anna was revealed.

Kieran assumed she'd scrambled around the mast to secure another line. Surprised by a frisson of concern, he waited. Not as amused.

"Tell you what, Tabby." The strain in Beau's voice was replaced by laughter. "Just for you, I'll be so beguiling Mr. Wonderful won't know what hit him." Giving a grunt of satisfaction as the sail stayed in place, she stepped into view, keeping her back to them she clambered down.

Moving easily in her precarious descent, she tossed comments over her shoulder. "By the way, I do need to get by the wharf. The mail boat was to bring the current copy of *Prominence Magazine*. Want to get a look at the newest heartthrob before he arrives. To immunize myself, so I don't swoon at his feet."

The last was delivered with sly sarcasm. Tabby turned toward Kieran, shrugged, then chuckled, but made no effort to stem the tide.

"Might constitute a disaster if I swooned at the same time he tripped over his own feet admiring himself in a tidal pool." Beau Anna paused, and searching out the final loop of the ladder, gained purchase with practiced skill. The distance left was dispatched with an agile leap that brought her to the deck. Obscured by the ship's wheelhouse, her return to the polished wood was followed by a moment of silence, then broken by a yelp.

"Ouch!" Then, in disgust, "Damn! I got a splinter." Another stretch of quiet was punctuated by the squawk of a curious gull and an exasperated moan. "I can't get it."

"Humph!" Tabby folded her arms beneath sagging breasts and her lips pursed as she nearly lost her battle to keep her stoic dignity. "Splinter's better than a broken leg. Though, with my eyesight, I could come nearer setting a bone than taking out a sliver.''

"Feels more like a tree than a sliver, but I suppose there's no help for it here." With her hands gathering her hair in a futile effort to control it, Beau Anna Cahill stepped into view. Preoccupied, as she limped down the gangway and over the dock, she grumbled, "If he doesn't faint at the sight of blood, maybe Mr. Wonderful will take it out for me."

Stopping, she turned, scanning the dock and the steps. "What did I do with my shoes? I tied the strings together so I wouldn't keep losing one. So now I lose both."

"If you'd wear your glasses, you'd see." This time Tabby's scolding was delivered fondly, in a frequent point of contention. "Sometimes I suspect you're blinder than me without them."

"I've told you the glasses are for distance, Tabby. Great distance," she underscored as she gave up on her hair and searched among coils of rope and fishing gear.

No gesture betrayed Kieran's presence, but something akin to glee softened Tabby's frown. "Don't appear to me you can see so well close up either."

"My eyes are fine once they adjust."

"Ruined 'em with all that reading."

"My eyes aren't ruined, and reading didn't do it." A single deck shoe that might fit Big Foot appeared out of a mass of rope and was discarded. "There's a word for the condition. Just like there's a word for sneakers that hide."

"Looking for these?" Though he was enjoying the conversation and the view, spying the worn sneakers, Kieran abandoned his vantage and moved into the friendly fray.

"I beg your pardon?" Pausing in her scrambling search, Beau stared at the shoes.

"They're small, the strings are tied together," Kieran said dryly, as he glimpsed a bit of tanned forehead that was, as he'd imagined, banded by a scarf tied at a rakish angle. Though securely fixed to keep her hair from her eyes, the scarf did nothing to contain the wild, ravishing mass that flew about her shoulders, inviting a smoothing caress. Tempting Kieran.

Reining in errant thoughts, he inched the shoes closer. "They fit the description, so, I thought they were what you're looking for?"

She made no move to take them as her head tilted and eyes the color of a stormy sea lifted a dreamy, unfocused gaze to his. Blinking against the brilliance of the sun, she rose in loose-limbed and effortless ease.

Shoes and Tabby forgotten, she stood peering at him. A small woman with the hair of a fey gypsy, dressed like a tattered tomboy rather than the elegant chatelaine she'd promised. Her face was smooth, without any nuance of expression, until the faint line of a puzzled frown appeared between her brows. Dark lashes drifted down, veiling her eyes. When they lifted again, her gaze sharpened, focused. The dreamy look replaced by uneasy concern.

For a second time she stared at him, eyes solemn and studious, then stunned by turns.

"Oops," Beau muttered, half aloud and half to herself, as she continued to stare. She didn't need an introduction to know who he was. At least, if he wasn't the man she assumed, *Prominence* had missed a sure bet. "Mr. O'Hara, I presume."

Kieran bowed in acknowledgment. "In person and at your service, Miss Cahill."

His gallantry went unnoticed.

"You weren't due until noon." Her softly accented words bore an accusation.

"I caught an earlier plane."

"But the first launch isn't until…"

"The mailman gave me a lift."

"Ohh."

"Sorry." Kieran shrugged and smiled. "It isn't noon, but I'm here."

Frown lines deepened. "Yes you are."

"I can leave and come back," he suggested, with a trace of irony. "At a more convenient time."

"There isn't one. I mean…" He'd put her at a disadvantage and she was babbling. There was nothing she hated more than babbling. Silently, she counted to ten, then back to one. Sighing, she faced what she must. "I don't suppose I should fool myself into thinking you didn't hear every word just now?"

Kieran's gaze never turned from hers. "My hearing's twenty-twenty."

The allusion to her conversation with Tabby didn't miss its mark. Hoping he would think the heat in her cheeks was from wind and sun, she suggested tentatively, "I don't suppose an apology would help."

"No."

His blunt answer took her by surprise, until she recognized the humor in his eyes. His gorgeous eyes. But then, she admitted after another slow perusal, they simply matched the rest of him. He was gorgeous all over, from the shaggy, windblown hair as black as her own, to the tips of his spanking new deck shoes.

An unquestionable trendsetter in elegantly tailored casual chic. Fashionable, gorgeous, charming. And mischievous, she added to the lot. But she could deal with that. She had for most of her life. Her own brother was the most gorgeous and charming tease she'd ever known.

Until today.

"No apology," she agreed, determined to make the best of an awkward circumstance. "I didn't think so."

Kieran waited. The next move was hers.

"In that case, I won't try." Taking the shoes from him, she tossed them over her shoulder. Leaving one to dangle down her back and the other over her breast, she offered a hand. "Shall we start again? A truce, Mr. O'Hara?"

"Mr. O'Hara? That's twice you called me that." A brow arched, lips curled, flashing a dimple at the edge of his mouth. "I've been demoted?"

The flush deepened and there was no chance it could be mistaken for a touch of sun. Standing tall, she brazened it through. "I thought you would prefer it."

Tearing his attention from her face, Kieran studied her hand. An interesting hand, tanned, delicately formed, but he wouldn't be foolish enough to doubt its strength. "I prefer Kieran, the name my friends call me."

His speculative gaze trailed over her in a lingering study before lifting again to hers. Holding her with a magnetism that was inescapable, he spoke in a voice as soothing as a whisper. "We're going to be friends, you know."

Hearing a serious note beneath the teasing, Beau said nothing as the tide lapped at the shore, the wind danced among sails, and Tabby stood listening.

Kieran moved closer, concentrating intently on her mouth, ignoring her proffered hand. "Friends, Beau Anna?"

Jerking back as her fingers touched his belt, she was acutely conscious of every nuance in his look and his voice. A part of her was drawn to him, a part wanted to retreat. Gathering her wits, she held her ground.

He was a charming one, with an irresistible grin and an elegant old-world gallantry. Beau didn't question that he knew exactly how charming. How elegant. How gallant. But he was only here for the summer, and she could deal with that, too.

"All right." With an attitude meant to be nonchalant, she accepted the challenge. "I won't make promises, but we can try."

"I can't ask more than that." Catching her hand, he enveloped it in his. His grip was considerate, but his palm was hard and ridged against hers as he kept it with a subtle pressure. "No promises. For now."

Releasing her, he retreated a step. He'd been teasing her, as he'd teased his younger sisters all his life. But his responses weren't what he expected.

He'd come to the island well versed in its history, and in the lives of the Cahills. But a dossier and random photographs hadn't done Beau justice. The first listed the accomplishments of an intelligent woman, the latter revealed that she was beautiful.

Cold facts and sterile beauty recorded on paper. That, on a glance, had little to do with the intriguing hoyden he'd discovered. Beau Anna Cahill was many things—Doctor of Psychology, island chatelaine, scaled down pirate for a scaled down brigantine—but most of all, she was a woman.

One whose life might be at risk.

"It's a short walk along the beach to the cottage. I can take you there, if you'd like. You must be tired...."

Kieran scarcely heard her as a rush of fury shook him. Fury that a murderer stalked the shores of Moon Dancers Island. Fury that there could be such evil in paradise. Such evil threatening Beau Anna.

"No!" The word was a snarl.

Shocked by the change, Beau stopped in mid-sentence. "I'm sorry, I thought after your trip you might be anxious to see..."

"The cottage?" He finished for her, shaking off his anger.

"If there's something you'd rather do." She let the suggestion dangle, waiting for Kieran to fill the void.

"There's nothing I'd rather do," he assured her, recovering from his unexpected reaction, but filing it away for consideration. "Though there's something I should do first." Taking up a small valise, he slid the zipper down and took out a glossy magazine. "The mailman asked me to deliver this."

"*Prominence,*" Beau guessed with a sinking feeling.

"With the latest heartthrob. Mr. Wonderful himself."

Beau's mouth drew down in a grimace. "You heard that, too?"

"Umm-hmm." Offering the magazine, he grew suspiciously solemn. "Since we'll be walking along the shore, shouldn't you glance at it. To immunize yourself, so you can save me when I trip into a tidal pool."

"When you said every word, you meant every word."

"...every word," he said in unison with her. He was grinning again. That heart stopping rogue's grin with the dimple dancing. "As a rule, I'm not into eavesdropping, but it was hard not to hear. While you were speaking to Tabby, I was standing beside her."

Beau groaned and lifted her face to the sun, wishing she could move it back an hour and begin all over again.

"If you wore your glasses," Kieran suggested kindly, "maybe you wouldn't get into these predicaments."

"I haven't worn my glasses in years. But they wouldn't fix the problem, and I don't make a habit of getting into these predicaments." From babbling she'd gone to blustering.

"Of course you don't, Beau Anna."

"Don't patronize." Snatching the magazine from him, she backed away, her hands lifted, warding off his mocking sympathy. The pages of *Prominence* rippled in the wind, revealing subtly colored photographs. Too briefly to be recognized, yet, with each fluttering sound, adding a mockery of their own. "I'm sorry I didn't meet you. Sorry if I insulted you. Sorry I took the time to work on the 'brig.' But I think best when I'm busy."

"And this morning you needed to think," Kieran suggested.

"Yes, I needed to think." *Prominence* and mockery were forgotten.

"You're worried about the murders."

"You know?" she exclaimed abruptly. As abruptly surprise turned into disgust for the guileless remark. "Of course, you know. The whole southeastern seaboard knows! The papers were full of it. We're so insular and isolated, that I forget what goes on here isn't always private."

"Murder seldom is."

Beau looked at him curiously. "You knew about the trouble and danger, and you wanted to come here?"

Kieran didn't hesitate. "I wanted to come."

Beau glanced at the magazine, the pages captured tightly

in her grasp. "You must truly hate what this article has done to your life."

"Let's say it was the finishing touch. The straw that brought down the whole haystack. As you did with the brigantine, I needed a place to think. Norrie was kind enough to offer his cottage as sanctuary and meditative retreat."

"But the danger!"

"There's danger everywhere, Beau Anna."

"Not here."

"Everywhere, always. Even on Moon Dancers Island."

"But not murder," she insisted.

Washed by an ominous rogue current, the brigantine pitched and turned, tugging at its mooring and bumping against the dock. Masts creaked and sailcloth snapped sharply as it rocked. A look told him the repaired sail held in the freshening breeze.

Turning from a concerned survey of sea, ship and sky, he found her watching intently, waiting for his answer.

"No," he relented, saying what she needed to hear. "Not murder."

Tabby had stood aside listening with quickening interest, more to the tone of their voices than to words. With an awareness that owed nothing to her fabled "sight," she knew Beau Anna would be safe with Kieran O'Hara. Now, and in the dreadful days a somber sense of foreboding warned were coming. But for this day, she was pleased and happy for the motherless girl child she'd taken as her own. Hiding a snaggletoothed smile, she said with a mock severity, "If you two can proceed without me, I'm due at the village."

"Tabby!" Beau whirled toward her, forgetting she intended to be cross for the trick she'd been played. "I wasn't thinking. This is the day you tell fortunes at the Island Tea House." Taking the sneakers from her shoulder, and laying the magazine aside, she recklessly plucked out the offending splinter and put them on. "I'll walk back with you."

"You'll do no such thing!" Tabby declared. "Another

mile or so and you could be at the cottage. There's no reason
you shouldn't go now, to help Mr. O'Hara settle in.''

"I'm in no hurry," Kieran assured her. "We can both
walk back with you. I can settle into the cottage later."

"Don't need nobody walking me nowhere!" The old lady
bristled. "Been walking this island near a hundred years, and
ain't needed no one."

Beau finished tying her shoes, and went to her. "Of course
you don't need us, but wouldn't you like company on the
way back?"

"Had all the company I need for the day." Tabby took a
step in the tottery gait that took her everywhere. "Don't need
no more. You two go on with the business at hand, and I'll
go on with mine.

"Beau Anna, you explain to Mr. O'Hara about the 'gators.
I 'spect he knows, but explain anyway." The last was tossed
over a skinny shoulder as Tabby crossed the shore and
climbed the dune. "When you get all that done, if you're a
mind to, I'd like it if you'd come by the Tea House about
six for a glass of wine."

"I'll be there," Beau promised.

"And I." Kieran added, "If I'm invited."

"'Course you're invited." Tabby huffed. "I ain't so old I
forgot my manners."

"About six, then." Kieran waited until Tabby crossed the
dune in a flutter of color and scarves. She was beyond his
vision before he turned to Beau. "Her speech changes when
she's angry."

Beau laughed. "The children of the island have always
used it as a barometer. The angrier she is, the more her
speech reverts to the island patois of her childhood."

"A hundred years?" A brow arched, lending a rakish look
to his expression.

"No one knows that for certain. But, there's no one who
can remember when Tabby didn't live on the island."

"She was born here?"

"Yes, but there's no proof. The Cahills were notorious for

keeping records, but some are missing. No one knows why or how. We assume it was during the lost time that she was born.''

"She speaks with an educated voice—when she isn't angry.''

"She speaks very well when she wishes, thanks to an education she was given on the island.'' Crossing the dock, Beau gathered the tools she'd used on the brig. "Over the centuries the Cahills have been guilty of many sins. But their strongest and most consistent family virtue has been their belief that it is their duty to provide an education for every islander. The tradition was begun by the first Cahill to settle on the island. And, in part, is responsible for its name.''

When the last tool had been returned to its proper place in a weathered sea chest, Kieran was there, kneeling beside her to take the lock and key from her.

As she looked up, saying her thanks, she was acutely aware of the brush of his fingertips over hers. But Kieran was completely absorbed in the intricacies of the lock, and Beau's suspicions of mischievous intent were quieted.

When he rose to stand over her, she took the hand he extended, accepting the courtesy and kindness as part of a gallantry as natural to him as the jut of his jaw and the wickedness of his smile.

"You were saying?'' he prompted, keeping her hand when she would have taken it from him. "About Tabby.'' Catching her look of surprise, he laughed quietly. "You'll grow accustomed to it. I'm like a snapping turtle, I don't let go of a subject until the sun goes down.''

"Or until it thunders?'' Beau quoted another version of the cliché.

"Maybe.''

"Meaning that you like every subject discussed thoroughly.''

"That's about the size of it.''

"And every problem solved.''

"Touché." Kieran bowed to her perception. "You know me pretty well for short acquaintance."

"More accurately, I know the type."

"A gentleman friend?"

Taking back her hand, Beau evaded the question, and wondered why. "About Tabby," she began, returning to a safer subject. "Though there were opportunities, she's never left the island. I doubt she ever will. This is her world." A gesture included sea and sky and sandy shore. "It's all she wants. It's all most of us want. The peace, the quiet. The mainstay of our lives, broken only once a year by the Moon Dancers Carnival.

"Only once a year, before the murders," she amended.

Lines of distress reappeared between her brows, and Kieran wanted to smooth them away with a kiss. Instead, he turned the subject back to the island's near-centenarian. Their mutually accepted neutral ground. "So, Tabby never felt the need to leave. Nor to learn more than the island offered. But you did."

Her look was quick and sharp, with none of the dreaminess he'd seen before. "How could you know that?"

Kieran realized he'd made a mistake. A rare happening for him. Proof of her fascination, but a mistake he mustn't repeat.

"Norrie told me." He spoke the lie with bland skill, and a twinge of guilt. "He taught me quite a lot about the island and its people." Another lie, as cover for the next slip. He'd never met Norrie Candler. It was likely he never would. What he knew about the man came from the same sheaf of dossiers as his knowledge of Beau and the island.

"Norrie is certainly one who could tell you about the island and our family. He could tell you more than you ever want to hear about the younger Cahills."

"I doubt that." Kieran moved closer, drawn by a need he didn't understand. But being Kieran O'Hara, the analytical, he would. Towering over her, feeling an instinctive protectiveness he knew she would resent, he allowed himself one touch.

The back of his hand drifting across her cheek startled her. Instinctively, she caught his wrist intending to push him away. But something in his look stopped her. Curious, she asked, ''What?''

''Sand.'' The small lie came easily. And another, as he took his wrist from her grasp. ''Here.'' Hardened fingers glided with incredible tenderness from her cheek to her chin and throat. ''And here.''

The pulse at the hollow of her throat throbbed in an uneven rhythm beneath his touch. As desire wakened like a hungry tiger, he knew he was moving too fast, too soon.

''Sand from a gust driven before the storm.'' Another brush of his fingers over frown lines and he moved away. ''There. No more sand.''

''Thank you.'' He's lethal, Beau thought. Gorgeous and lethal. Not a good combination, if she were vulnerable. ''Which I'm not.''

''Pardon?''

''What?''

''You were saying?''

She wasn't aware she'd spoken. ''Just wondering aloud.''

''About?''

He wasn't going to let her off with the ambiguous explanation. Walking away, giving herself space to deal with her responses, she studied the horizon.

The sky was an astonishing silvered blue, blending with an ocean as silver, as blue. No line of demarcation separated one from the other. No clouds roiled and tumbled and the sun continued its passage undimmed. The tide, with another rogue wave nowhere in sight, whispered and rippled, barely disturbing the glassy surface of the sea. A spectacular day, with no hint of change.

A perfect day. Yet, with an islander's instinct honed by the years, she'd known for hours a storm was brewing.

Kieran O'Hara knew, as well.

Facing him, she noted the darkened skin, remembering the hard ridges of callus on his hands. ''It's a beautiful day.''

"Yes," Kieran agreed, letting her take the exchange where she would.

"Perfect."

He nodded, agreeing again. "Yes."

"But you know that's going to change."

"Yes, again." He glanced at the sky, then back at Beau. "But sooner than I realized."

"How do you know?"

"Gut feeling. If you want it a little prettier, instinct."

"You aren't clairvoyant like Tabby?"

"No more than you are." Relenting, he explained, "My family traveled a lot, but our home was…is," he corrected, "on the Chesapeake. I suppose I learned to interpret the moods and changes of the sea exactly as you have. By osmosis and trial and error of experience. I was caught in a few storms before I learned to recognize my feelings, and heed them."

"As we should now."

"It won't be a matter of a mad dash, but we should both heed, indeed." The last was accompanied by another grin.

Beau wasn't surprised that he knew the sea. Nor that the chic togs were more than a fashion statement. She was even willing to admit that it wasn't the clothing that made the statement, as much as the way he wore them.

The brig rocked again, sending storm warnings of its own. The creaks of its mast turned to a low groan, as gusts of wind snaked among its rigging. She considered taking down the sails, then decided the squall posed no real danger to the ship, and only a careful check of its mooring was needed.

Kieran was there before her again, leaping nimbly to the deck, seeing to the ropes and the anchor. When he finished he glanced at the sky, still bright with unbroken sunlight. "This shouldn't amount to much. A small blow and a good hard downpour. She's in for a rough ride, but she'll be safe with the cove serving as buffer." He spoke of the ship as a woman. His fingertips roving over her glossy wooden surfaces were loving. "She'll fare better than either of us, if we don't hurry."

Through the brilliance of the day, a change in the air told a tale Beau Anna recognized all too well.

"The village, Beau Anna? Or the cottage?" Kieran asked as he returned to her side.

"The village if you don't mind a good soaking."

"And if I do?"

"The cottage."

"Then it's settled." Once again he offered his hand, and as before, Beau accepted the gallantry. "Ready?"

Strangely, Beau knew she was. The summer had proven tragic, and her heart wept for the lost lives of two women. But, for no reason she could explain, as she took his hand she felt a nuance of hope.

Three

The storm broke sooner and unlike Kieran or Beau supposed.

As if the god of errant sea storms stepped from the legends of the island to prove the folly of human premonition, the shore was swiftly transformed. In one great rush the heavens opened, sending down seething clouds. Threads of cool air laced with warm, wrapping everything in its path in mist.

A harbinger of the deluge to come.

Breaking off discussion of points of interest along the shore, Beau Anna lifted a palm, catching the mist itself. "So much for the wisdom of sea pups."

As he turned, Kieran found her watching him. An illusion wrapped in clouds, her skin gleaming with translucent pearls, and her hair with black diamonds. Matching his pace to hers, delighting in the look of her as much as her company, he teased, "Did you plan this?"

Beau laughed, a whimsical note. "Sorry. My name's Beau Anna, not Mother Nature."

"Don't be sorry." With certainty innate to Kieran O'Hara, he knew whatever the outcome of his sojourn on Moon Dancers Island, he would never regret this moment, or this woman.

Dragging the band from her forehead, she shook her head, sending her hair flying about her shoulders. "I'm not."

"An honest woman." A conclusion he'd drawn from her manner at the brig.

"For the most part."

"Then you won't deny you're enjoying this."

As she sidestepped a crab scurrying to safety, Beau made no attempt at denial. "I like walking in the first of the rain."

"I'm sure you do."

"You are?"

A snowy egret wading in a tidal pool watched cautiously, then glided to the sea. A regal male at the end of breeding season, with long plumes cascading. A handsome fellow, grace in slow motion, retreating again. Then, squawking irritation at this intrusion on his stretch of beach, he lifted from the surf, abandoning the search for one last morsel before the rain. With spindly black legs and golden slippered feet held stiffly, he soared toward the horizon. As graceful in flight as stalking the shore.

Pausing by unspoken consent, the intruders watched. The angry egret was a tiny flutter of white against the leaden sky before Kieran looked away.

Reading her pleasure in a sight that never grew old, returning to their conversation, he rephrased her question. "Am I sure you like walking in the rain? Maybe you didn't plan this, but you like it. Especially today. With me."

"Oh?" Beau left her study of the egret and the sky to meet his gaze. Had she misjudged him? Was he that arrogant? Wondering why it should matter, she asked wryly, "How did you arrive at this conclusion with such certainty?"

"I have two sisters." He made the remark cheerfully, undaunted by the frost in her response. In explanation, he elaborated, "Two younger sisters, both of whom have enjoyed putting me in unusual situations. As a manner of evening up, so to speak."

"For revenge." Beau had been guilty of that with her own brother.

"If the shoe fits," Kieran agreed. "Or the word."

His honest and engaging manner made it impossible to stay aloof. Succumbing once more, Beau chuckled. "After the fiasco at the brig, I admit it makes strolling the beach with one of the world's most eligible bachelors a little less intimidating when he's soggy and disheveled."

And as splendid as ever, she could add to the list. But she didn't. She didn't intend to keep noticing either.

In the distance a foghorn sounded, its mournful knell keeping rhythm with the winking beacon of a buoy. Safeguards marking the channel to the harbor, guiding sailors home. Beau wondered what safeguards there were for her.

As the vapor over the sea thickened to dense fog and moved to shore, Kieran closed the distance between them. Her subtle and uncommon fragrance, a delicate blend of flowers and lingering sunlight, wafted on the heavy air.

"You've no reason to be intimidated by me, Beau Anna."

"I'm not," she retorted, regretting he'd sensed her capricious mood. "I wasn't."

"Then why are you so guarded?" The question trailed away, the empty void saying more than words.

If he wanted his own revenge by having what he knew spelled out, Beau decided he would have it. "You could call it a prickly conscience, for how I've behaved."

"How have you behaved?"

"You do like things explained, don't you?"

"Sorry."

She stopped his apology. "Don't be."

"All right, then I won't."

He plainly had no intention of letting her slide by with a vague admission. "All right." Unconsciously parroting him, she cataloged her sins for his pleasure. "How about rude, for starters? Grumpy? Sarcastic? That leaves tacky and shabby, just to list a few."

Kieran wouldn't have applied any of those descriptions to the fetching creature who flitted over a ship's rigging and the sandy shore like a light-footed sprite, splinter and all. But he wouldn't correct her. Not now. "You've quite a list."

"Believe it or not, I don't make a practice of greeting the islander's guests dressed in scruffy work clothes. I don't usually suffer from such an acute case of foot-in-mouth disease." With a disparaging shrug, she added, "There I was, a total idiot and a mess, and you looked so...so..."

"Like I own Savile Row?" Kieran prompted.

"Great blue herons!" Beau moaned the peculiar oath. "Did you miss anything?"

"Not much." The dimple was there, playing hide-and-seek. "I make that a practice. It keeps life interesting. And then some." There was amusement in his tone as his voice dropped to a whisper. Hoping to see the flush that turned her eyes from storm silver to sea green, he let his gaze slide deliberately and provocatively over her again.

Beau Anna Cahill was a lovely woman. Not beautiful by popular interpretation, but with qualities that made her unforgettable. An exquisite and beguiling mix of patrician and tomboy set her apart. And with it a radiance and magnetism guaranteed to fascinate the men she would meet.

Even a seasoned agent of The Black Watch standing on crumbling sand, watching as mist continued to gather in her hair.

Especially this seasoned agent, he amended, as mist turned to a lazy drizzle, and black diamonds to rivulets tumbling from black silk. As the soft heat he'd waited for brushed her cheeks and throat, he searched for and found the rare, elusive green in her gaze.

Beau conquered the impulse to turn his attention from her with some flippant remark. Instead, she stood passively, accepting the reflective scrutiny of his piercing gaze. She would hear him out. The courtesy Tabby had drummed into her demanded that she should.

Kieran knew the effort required in allowing oneself to be analyzed by a complete stranger. With no thought to tease, but simply because he couldn't help himself, he smiled, recalling an image imprinted in his mind. His first glimpse of her...the cutoffs worn paper-thin. Hair like a night heron's wing flying in the wind. A bare foot braced against the mast, gathering splinters.

Who was this magical creature, who, with a look and a smile, had captivated him completely?

"An idiot?" Returning to her judgment of herself, his

question was complete rhetoric. "Hardly. A thorn in Tabby's schedule? Maybe. I suppose even a pirate." His smile quirked fondly at the indelible memory, and there was no time nor tide, no sky nor shore. Only Beau Anna, rapt and still beneath his riveting intensity.

"A lady?" His smile faded into solemnity as compelling as charming mischief. "I would think, always. Tabby wouldn't let you grow up to be anything else.

"A mess?" He turned his head while rain trickled from his hair and fell to his collar. "Never."

Succumbing again to need, he touched the line of her jaw with the back of his hand. "You must know you're a beautiful woman."

A flush deepening to a blush, Beau searched for lurking mischief. Discovering none, she found the compliment even harder to accept. If she'd doubted the lethal charm before, she wouldn't now.

"And you're an Irishman who's done more than kiss the blarney stone. You must carry it in your pocket." Her voice was husky and nearly lost in the sound of the surf. "A handy talisman?" she taunted. "For one of the world's most eligible men."

"Don't." A finger slanted over her lips. A gesture infinitely gentle, infinitely uncompromising.

Unnerved by the intimacy, Beau fell silent, waiting. Her wait was not long.

"I'm sorry." His fingers flexed, curling into a loose fist. A gesture he recognized as a reflection of his effort not to touch her again. Not to kiss her.

Raking an unsteady hand through his hair, he backed away. Beyond the scent of her tantalizing fragrance, but never beyond desire. "I'm sorry," he said again. "Sorry you hate the silly title. Sorry I disrupted your schedule and your life." *Sorry hate and death have come to your island paradise. Sorry that when you look at me it's in ridicule. Sorry I can't be honest with you.*

"God help me! I'm sorry, for everything." His expression

had grown bleak, remembering the tragedy that had brought him, fearing the tragedy that might be. "But I'm here. I'll be here awhile. In that time, I hope we'll be friends. So let's not begin this way.

"Don't judge me by this." He tapped the copy of *Prominence Magazine* in her hand. "I didn't seek it out, and I like it no better than you. But it's a fact of my life. Of both our lives, since it brought me here. But keep in mind that facts and figures, glorified, glamorized, or stark reality, can never be the whole man.

"Read the article. I won't deny that what's there is based on fact. Loosely, but grounded in truth. Ask what you like, I'll answer as completely as I can. Before you make up your mind about me, judge me, Kieran O'Hara—the man before you, the man you see. Not the world's most anything.

"As I'll judge you, Beau Anna Cahill." His look eased. His smile was rueful, the dimple absent. "End of lecture. My first and last."

Touched, Beau knew she'd rarely encountered such passionate honesty. "You meant every word of that."

"Yes."

Keeping the magazine rolled in her palm, she held it between them. "You truly hate being singled out. Tell me why."

"Because it takes what I am and turns it into something I'm not," Kieran responded succinctly.

"That's it? As simple as that?"

"As simple as that." Watching a frown gather, he could almost feel her psychologist's mind processing and interpreting. "So? What do you think, Dr. Cahill?"

She stared up at him, the damnable magazine still clutched in her hand. "You do realize that being chosen is flattering? To some, an honor?"

"Of sorts." His answer was grudging.

"There are even those for whom it will be a boon."

"I won't deny that."

"Would you condemn them?"

Kieran didn't answer immediately. Beau didn't hurry him.

"How can I? There was an interval in my life when I would have enjoyed it. Even had fun with it. But that was another time, and what was right for me then, isn't right now."

"A matter of maturity?" she ventured.

"A matter of priorities."

"I see."

Kieran smiled at the telling comment. He could imagine Beau Anna dressed for the office rendering clinical judgments. "What do you see, doc?"

Until now, her thoughts had been muddled. Her emotions in chaotic turmoil. He'd caught her off guard, and at a disadvantage. From that moment, she hadn't known what she felt about this splendid man who stepped into her life virtually out of nowhere.

From the moment she'd looked up at him over the scruffy shoes he offered, all she'd understood was that she couldn't just dismiss him. Couldn't simply go on with her life as if he never existed. By his mere presence he wouldn't be ignored. With the power of his natural charisma, he couldn't be dismissed.

"I see a man who's honest with himself." In that realization, mental chaos quieted. Emotional turmoil eased as she let herself admit she liked Kieran O'Hara. She had from the first. All that had changed was that now she could face the truth. "If you deal with others as with yourself, you could be one of the most honest men I've known."

Kieran felt a twinge of guilt at the trust he heard. He hadn't lied to her. He wouldn't. Except by omission, out of need, as commanded. With a sense of dread, he anticipated the time she would learn of his deception. Lies by omission, excused by duty, might lay on his conscience like a ponderous burden, but he'd been given a role to play, a part in a macabre reality. For her sake he must play it to perfection.

"I'm a fugitive from a silly magazine article," he heard himself saying. "Never a saint."

"You sound like Rick."

"Your brother." Her playboy half brother, with glaring holes in his dossier. A man who might be guilty of murder.

"Never a saint." The disclaimer excused a multitude of sins for a beloved brother only hours younger than she, and as handsome as Kieran. "That's why I like you."

"Because I'm not a saint?"

"Among other things."

"What things?"

"You're a good sport."

"And…"

"You like the beach in the rain." She held out a hand, catching raindrops in her palm. "It is rain now, have you noticed? You're drenched, and your luggage will be when the brunt of the storm arrives. We picked a marvelous place for this conversation."

"I suspect that's because you're one helluva psychologist. Matching need to time and place."

"Oh no!" Beau demurred. "Psychology had nothing to do with it. First, I doubt you would ever need my services. Second, I wouldn't dream of accepting the challenge of treating you."

"No?"

"No!" Her response was emphatic, but she was enjoying the encounter.

"I would be a challenge?"

"Major! And I don't need it. But I have one for you."

"Name it."

Lifting her face to rain that fell lightly, she considered the sky before she answered. "A race."

She was drenched, her sodden clothes clung provocatively, but she didn't seem to mind. Her mood was bright and Kieran found her enchanting.

"The two of us against the storm?" he surmised as a spike of lightning zagged across the horizon, with a growl of thunder warning time was running out. "I'll be a gentleman and spot you ten paces."

"Twelve." She was sprinting across the shore, with the last tossed back like a gauntlet.

A grin flashed over Kieran's face.

The gauntlet was taken.

The weatherworn cottage appeared rambling and unplanned, and in the murky light of the storm, quite shabby. But as Beau led him through spacious rooms to a wide hall and utility closet Kieran realized his error.

In minutes, a generator hummed. With lamps illuminating every corner, Beau investigated a linen closet as spacious as the rest of the miscalled cottage.

"This should help." The towel she handed him was thick, and delightfully fragrant with the scent of lavender. "The cottage is spartan in decor, but never in these. A contradictory condition you'll find reflected often in Heron's Walk."

"Heron's Walk?" Kieran questioned as he scrubbed the towel over his chin. Catching himself, aware that he'd nearly made another error, he covered as best he could. "Funny, I don't think I remember hearing Norrie call the place by name."

Dragging her own towel over riotous locks, Beau explained, "That's probably because you didn't. Heron's Walk is the name given to the cottage years ago. Norrie calls it The Hideout. When he comes, he is hiding out. From the stress of work and the clutter of his life." Draping the towel across her shoulders, she wound her arms through it in shawl fashion. "It makes sense that he would offer you time here, considering your need to be invisible for a while."

Kieran said nothing, hoping she would continue, filling in the blanks of Norris Candler's quirks and foibles that no dossier could supply.

"Spending his summers at the cottage was the greatest influence in his choice of careers. The island has been instrumental in shaping all our lives. Rick's, mine, Tabby's." The nuance of a smile touched her lips when she spoke of the old woman. "Beyond Tabby, its effect is most evident in Norrie."

"Restoring old buildings, modernizing them, while keeping their antiquity intact. Preserving history," Kieran supplied, glad for the opportunity to contribute documented facts. Though couched in truth, they were more lies by pretense. When the time came for truth, would Beau Anna despise him?

Visions of contempt in those changeable, expressive eyes sent shards of regret through him. Regret for what had been done to her peaceful life. Regret for himself he hadn't yet explored.

Hearing her speak, giving the charade he must play his complete attendance, he caught the essence of a comment. "Moon Dancers Island was the genesis of his love for antiquity?"

Beau agreed, and Kieran saw that in the humid air that seeped into the cottage, her hair still coiled wetly about her throat. As she shook it back, his concentration turned again to her conversation. "Restoring Heron's Walk was his first project. Proof for his father that he had the vision and skill to blend the new with the old, without destroying the character of the structure."

Kieran knew from the concise history he'd studied that a series of buildings had stood on this sandy ground for centuries. Each belonging to some member of the Candler family. Each lost or destroyed by some force of nature or man. Storm, fire, the erosion of time and tide.

The most recent predecessor had been washed into the sea by the first surge of a hurricane. Though the present Heron's Walk was seventy years old and had been rebuilt on the exact site of the others, in the changing of land mass and sea currents, it stood on more solid ground. With accretion the sea moved back, and vegetation encroached until the tin roofed, clapboard house and its lawns and gardens were almost engulfed in sea grape and myrtle. Only the front and part of one side, with their sprawling porches and verandas, opened to an unsurpassed view of the sea.

Certainly not an undesirable retreat for one who loved the sea as Kieran.

In a moment of quiet, Beau listened as the bluster of the wind died and the storm stalled. Crossing to the window, she pulled aside a shutter to peer into a young day darkened to night. Rain fell steadily, with no sign of ending. The pathway back to the village and Cahill's Bluff would be ankle deep in runoff the sandy soil couldn't absorb. Parts would be treacherous with hidden debris. Conditions that enticed young alligators from the rookeries for a change of diet.

Every seasoned islander knew this wasn't the time to stroll any path. The longer it rained, the deeper the water rose, the farther the 'gators wandered. If the wind didn't wake, the storm would stagnate, and she would be stranded with Norrie's guest.

Her head leaned against the pane, she watched his reflection as he roamed the room. The day was not progressing as she intended. Though she'd spent many rainy afternoons at Heron's Walk, it was never with a man like Kieran O'Hara.

Once the spartan room had instilled a sense of uncluttered and spacious comfort. Now he filled every inch of it with his presence. The still air seethed with the power of his masculinity.

A sigh whispered from her like a secret breath. Trained to attend every subtlety and nuance, Kieran sensed as much as heard it. Leaving his inspection of a crudely carved lighthouse, he regarded her closely.

There was a tension that he was instinctively certain was alien. Concern about the murders? Dismay for having to deal with an unexpected tenant for Heron's Walk? Or the fatigue of a woman who was all things to all people at all times?

"Tired?"

Beau shifted away from the window. "I beg your pardon?"

"I asked if you were tired, Beau Anna."

She shook her head. "Of course not."

Kieran moved closer, his shadow falling over her. "You were a thousand miles away."

"Not really." Beau had to tilt her head to look up at him. Half in darkness, half in light, her features were spellbinding. Another step brought him to her. The scent of her mingled with the rain recalled her laughing challenge and the race across the sand. An exuberance far removed from her mood. He was tempted to coax that laughter back, but there were telltale lines of fatigue on her face, and the strain of sleepless nights marking the tender flesh beneath her eyes. She was more tired than she would admit, and he'd teased her enough for one day. "If you weren't a thousand miles away," he asked gently, "then where?"

"Here." Her answer came quickly, as she struggled not to turn away from his solemn look. Away from his tender expression.

He could have left it at that, settling for that cryptic explanation. But he didn't. With a lifted brow and a tilt of his head, he asked for more.

"I was thinking of Norrie." Her voice was husky, as if she'd spoken more than she was accustomed. Or less. With an unexpected honesty, she added, "And how the cottage changes with the people who inhabit it."

"Some homes are like that," Kieran agreed. "Though the shoreline is quite different, the cottage is not unlike the home where I spent the happiest days of my childhood. A house that made everyone feel welcome." In an afterthought, he added, "My mother calls it people friendly."

"People friendly?" As the day grew darker and colder, Beau began to shiver. Hoping he wouldn't notice, she drew the towel tighter about her. "Where is there such a house?"

"One is here on Moon Dancers Island. Another is tucked in a cove on the Chesapeake. My family has a place there with a history of its own. My mother inherited it long ago and made it into a home for us. She would like Heron's Walk."

The incomparable Mavis O'Hara, a woman as comfortable in a tent as a castle, would more than like it. She would explore every inch, pat every surface, nod and think, then pronounce it funny and enchanting, and fall madly in love with it. In the process, she would take Beau Anna Cahill under her motherly wing. Kieran found himself wishing his mother was here now, instead of on a ranch in Montana teaching underprivileged children to ride.

"The Chesapeake." Beau slipped past him, going to the kitchen that opened off the great room. Taking bottled water from the emergency stock, she offered him the choice of tea or coffee. With his nodded selection, without an interruption in their conversation, the ritual of making tea began. "It was there you learned to predict the weather by instinct?"

"For the most part." He watched as she moved efficiently, familiar with the arrangement of the cottage. Kieran wondered how much time she'd spent here as a child. Then as an adult. Norris Candler was older, but not so much that they wouldn't be friends. Or more. Determined not to allow himself to speculate in areas that had nothing to do with his purpose, he kept to the point of her interest. "The Chesapeake is a great classroom, but along the way and through the years there have been a number of other places."

"Then you traveled quite a bit as a child?" As if she'd done it thousands of times before, stretching on tiptoe, with a long skewer she hooked the handles of two bright blue mugs and took them from the top shelf of a cabinet.

"My dad is a modern day wanderer. If he'd been born in another era, he would have sailed a prairie schooner across the desert in the wake of Lewis and Clark. Even accompanied or preceded them."

An aged and peeling cabinet door opened, exposing a microwave. A modern convenience, cleverly hidden to preserve the heralded antiquity. Beau set a pitcher of water inside and programmed the time. "Would your mother have resented it if he'd been an explorer and a pioneer?"

"She would hate leaving her home, but she knew he was

an adventurer when they married, and she would have gone with him.''

"Wifely duty?"

Kieran's burst of laughter startled her. "Mavis O'Hara doesn't recognize 'wifely duties.' She would've gone because she loves him. Just as he would have stayed, if she weren't an adventurer as well. She's always glad to be home after each venture. But just as glad to leave when Dad grows restless again.''

"So you traveled the world, and learned." The tea was brewing, the tray with its bright mugs waited.

Seeing her shiver, Kieran crossed to the fireplace. After a cursory inspection, he searched out a box of matches. When he had finished, the light of a cheery blaze danced in the iron grate. Taking his towel from his shoulder, he spread it before the fire. Then he propped an arm on the mantel and a foot on the hearth. "We traveled most of our childhood."

"Where did you go to school?"

"Wherever we were. For as long as we were there."

"You make it sound like one great adventure. Your parents must be wonderful." There was a wistfulness in her. Not for the adventure. Her own life on the island had been that. Nor for the strong sense of family. From the day Rick had declared his independence from his mother, she and her father and he had the strongest of bonds. Yet there were times when she wondered what their lives would have been if her own mother had lived.

Kieran wondered where her thoughts had suddenly taken her. "Life is an adventure, and will always be." He smiled fondly. "With parents like mine, it could be nothing else."

The tea had steeped and was ready. When she finished arranging the tray, Kieran was there to take it from her. "Come," he insisted. "Sit by the fire and dry out."

Beau needed no second invitation. The continued drop in temperatures and being soaked had chilled her to the marrow. "June," she commented, with droll irony. "And we need Norrie's amazing gas fire."

"An expected happenstance with fast forming storms like this. But the convenience of gas logs is most unexpected." Kieran set the tray with its steaming pot on the table before the sofa. Two mugs were filled and Beau's was in her hand before he knelt before her.

"No!" She tried to jerk away as his fingers closed around her ankle. By a miracle or great juggling, she didn't spill the scalding brew.

"Nothing to be alarmed about," Kieran soothed in a soft croon. "Just taking off your shoes, not making a pass." He grinned the dimpled grin. "I'd be lying, though, if I said the thought hadn't occurred to me. A beautiful, unexpected woman, a day of mists and rain, a cozy fire. The music of the sea. A perfect setting for seduction."

"You'd be a fool to try." The heat of anger marked her cheeks, chasing away the blue tinged pallor of her chill.

"I know." He grinned and sighed, resuming the task he'd set for himself. "That's why I'm settling for this."

"I'm perfectly capable of removing my own shoes. If I want them removed."

"And I'm perfectly aware of that. But it's too late to object." He was stroking her foot and ankle, taking great care to avoid the wound left by the splinter.

"My shoes are off, you can let me go, now."

"No."

Settling on the floor, wrapping the towel warmed by the fire around her feet, he leaned back against the sofa. Taking up his own cup, he sipped, held her feet close to his body, and stared into the fire.

"This is ridiculous, Kieran O'Hara."

"Ahh, the lady calls my name." He was only teasing, but he wondered how it would be, hearing her call his name in a voice husky with desire. Putting the brakes on inappropriate thoughts, he held her swaddled feet tighter. "Relax, and drink your tea. Nothing's going to happen, Beau Anna."

She felt a fool, but struggling would only make matters

worse. Salvaging what she could of her drenched dignity, she settled back, pretending none of this was really happening.

The rain fell in thrumming rhythm on a tin roof. The churning sea whispered a steady chorus as the tea warmed her. The dance of blue tipped flames hypnotized, while his caressing fingers coaxed fatigue from its secret place, drawing her into a restful sense of calm.

Beau Anna didn't know when she began to drift. Nor when he rose to take the mug from her hand. It would be hours before she woke to find him watching her as she slept.

"Hello, sleepyhead."

Beau sat up abruptly, spilling the afghan that he'd spread over her onto the floor. "How long did I sleep?"

"Long enough, I hope."

She didn't question the cryptic remark. She didn't want to know what it meant. She concentrated instead on the room, finding that evening sunlight washed Norrie's favored blues and yellows in a brilliant glow. "The rain stopped."

"Some time ago."

"You should have roused me."

"Why?"

"Because..." He was standing by the window. Taking a cup from its broad sill he turned away from it. With the light at his back he was only an enigmatic shape. Though she knew his level gaze still watched her calmly, breaking eye contact made it easier to collect her thoughts. "Because this whole fiasco has hardly been a proper welcome for you."

"I like the way you welcome me, Beau Anna Cahill. Every second of it."

Something in his voice touched a chord, threatening the composure she'd managed. "I have to go."

"We both do," he reminded. "We were to meet Tabby at six, but I don't think she'll mind that we're late."

A clock by the mantel showed it was half past the appointed hour already. "Oh dear."

"If you'd like to freshen up, I'll leave you to it."

As he moved to the door, Beau saw he'd changed. His shirt and trousers were crisp and neat. The duffel he'd carried slung over one shoulder had been as amazingly wrinkle resistant as it was waterproof. He was again the world's most everything.

When she didn't answer, he smiled. "Don't rush. A few more minutes shouldn't matter, and Norrie's Island Buggy should make quick work of the trip. The sound of the engine should ward off any roving 'gators in the bargain."

"Yeah. Sure," she muttered, but there was no one to hear. Kieran, as good as his word, had left her alone.

Leaping from the sofa she hurried to the bath. Confronting her image in the mirror, for the first time in years she wondered what the patients of her bygone Charleston practice would think of the once very prim and proper Beau Anna Cahill, doctor of clinical psychology. "At the moment, *Doctor* Cahill, you look exactly like what you are," she addressed her reflected image grimly. "An idiot who just woke up in a strange man's bed.

"All right." As she splashed water on her face, she growled at the small gremlin that insisted on complete honesty. "His sofa, not his bed."

Scrounging a brush from the guest supplies, she dragged it through her hair, wincing as it tugged at snarls. "Not an auspicious beginning. What with murderers and fools running amuck."

"Talking to yourself, doc?"

He lounged against the door, the laughter in his blue eyes replacing concern.

"I didn't before." Smoothing wrinkles from her clothing, she turned to face him. "But I guess I do now."

"Trouble has a way of doing that."

"I suppose it does." As she preceded him from the cottage, she wondered if he weren't exactly that.

Trouble. With a capital T.

Four

That Norrie Candler's golf cart combined whimsy with his strong practical side was no surprise to Kieran. But he hadn't been quite prepared for the Island Buggy. The gaily decorated concoction he'd discovered tucked in its own shed at the back of the house.

The buggy was an oversized golf cart, decorated by a Mad Hatter with a penchant for Rodgers and Hammerstein. Once again a fondness for blues and yellows was apparent. Along with a smattering of green and purple, and a trace of what Mavis O'Hara would call raspberry. The cart was a modern day version of "The Surrey With the Fringe on Top," Kieran assumed, for the fun of it.

He stroked a gleaming yellow door in amused admiration. "In full sun, we'd need dark glasses."

Weaving her way through the narrow alleyway that flanked a small walled garden, Beau tried not to do anything as undignified as trip over the uneven cobblestones in her haste to avoid his touch. No matter that she'd negotiated this passage thousands of times, as a gentleman of ingrained habits, it would have been chivalrous reflex that he take her arm.

Determined not to think why she avoided another of the old-fashioned courtesies that were obviously natural to him, she launched into an explanation of the Island Buggy. "Norrie made this for the children. Actually, some of its features were intended for himself. But this?" With a sweep of her hand she gestured toward the canvas top that could only be described as electric navy, then to the multihued fringe with tiny silver bells sprinkled along it. "This is to entertain the little ones. They love it when he's here. Everywhere he goes, he collects a child, or two, or six. I've seen a dozen clinging to it.''

''I suspect he has as much fun as the children.'' Kieran leaned on the wall, folding his hands together. Taking care that his arm didn't brush hers in close quarters. She avoided his touch subtly, but not subtly enough that he didn't notice.

''He claims when he's here, he's Peter Pan. One who succeeded in never growing up.'' Beau was without tension for the first time since she woke. ''It isn't true, of course. He always brings a briefcase crammed with work. But it makes a good story. One day, though, when he's truly had enough of the frenzy, he'll become Peter in earnest.''

Kieran glanced over the garden, its casual symmetry apparent beneath its current neglect absentia. Another of his mother's colorful terms, describing her own garden after a long trek.

Heron's Walk was the flawless harmony of man and nature, comfort and restraint. Weathered walls and weathered wood merged with the land, a part, rather than an intrusion. Rare qualities Kieran found gratifying. ''From the look of the house, the repairs, the concessions to the needs of the modern man he's concealed so skillfully, I think you're right.''

There was love here, and something deeper. He saw it in every blending of antiquity with the new. In the house, in the wild, tangled garden, and the surrounding ground. ''Every man needs a sanctuary. Some of us search for it all our lives,'' Kieran mused philosophical, giving a name to the elusive and treasured mood of Heron's Walk. ''Norrie's had his all along. Here, by the shore.''

''The edge of forever, where sea meets sky.'' Beau grew pensive as she turned in profile to look out over the low wall. In keeping with the character of the land, the garden was a palette of sea island foliage. Sago and Canary palms grew in clusters, woven around a massive live oak adrift with moss. Oleander bloomed by blue plumbago, while unkempt mandevilla trailed from trellises embedded in the walls. Ivy grew rampant over the ground. With weeds and stray wildflowers poking through gentle chaos to add their own dash of color. Singularly and together, they were a perfect reflection of the house, the sea, the island.

Memories stirred. Good and hurtful. Beau's heart clenched in regret. "Dancers Island was a wonderful place to be a child."

He watched as the shadow that flickered over her face was resolutely rejected. If there were tears, a stranger such as he would never see them.

Her body stiffened. Her jaw tightened as sorrow roughened her voice. "It must be again."

"It will be." Kieran's pledge was barely a sound as she coped with grief for something cherished and lost.

She nodded absently, as if the quiet intrusion of his voice was no more than a reminder of his presence.

"Beau Anna." His fingertips brushed over her wrist, measuring the steady throb of her heart, lingering until she abandoned her study of the garden and turned to him. Drawing his hand away, he held her gaze, willing her to believe. "It will."

Eyes, darkened by doubt, regarded him steadily.

He had no platitudes, no bold assurances. Only his word, given from the depths of honor. "I promise."

Kieran drew a breath perfumed by the sea as it mingled with the fragrance of lavender and her own scent. Lavender, Beau, and the sea, it seemed right for her. One familiar and delicate, one fascinating, one filled with mystery. The fragrance of paradox. Of Beau Anna, who was her father's daughter. And as Beaumont Cahill had been, the bedrock of the island community. Its mentor, its strength. Yet, for all her skills, all her resilience, there was an innocence a monster had sullied, but couldn't destroy.

But he would try. Again and again, until he succeeds.

The conviction came out of nowhere. A foreboding with no more substance than a hunch. Yet with such swift power it literally swept the beat from his heart and the air from his lungs, sealing him in a transient void of nothing but premonition.

Shaken, Kieran shrugged away the fugue. He wasn't psychic. But he was a man who lived on the fringe of constant danger. A man whose life depended on instinct. He'd never doubted the gut-wrenching intuition. He didn't now.

The sickening presage warned that the monster who stalked the island was more than a random killer. A monster, yes. But one with a plan. He wanted something. But what?

Was it Beau?

Were these primal instincts right? Was it this small, brave woman the creature ultimately intended to destroy?

Never!

Kieran's conviction was as intense as his foreboding.

Never Beau Anna.

His vow echoed in his mind as she stood by his side, the gray gaze never leaving his face. Dear God! He wanted to touch her again, to cradle the smooth curve of her cheek in his palm, and bury his fingertips in the rippling mass of her hair. He wanted to hold her, and tell her that he'd come to keep her island safe, that he would protect her and her island folk.

"Beau." The words were ready to spill from his lips, but he knew he couldn't. Not yet.

She waited. The thick ruffle of her lashes offered no shielding veil. The line of her mouth was solemn as her gaze moved over his face with a look of… What?

Was it hope? Doubt? What banked emotions lay like sleeping dreams in the still waters of this woman's soul? What quality made him want to play the knight gallant, leaping on his charger, lance in hand, to chase the dragon from her paradise?

No assignment was simply a job with Kieran. But from the moment he'd seen her moving among creamy sails with a dancer's finesse, he'd found himself enchanted as much as intrigued. In that moment the objectivity with which he approached each assignment was forgotten. But not the resolve.

"No matter how long it takes, no matter what it takes, Moon Dancers Island will be safe again, Beau Anna."

"How?" Her question was without surprise. She didn't stop to consider why. "What can you do that hasn't been done?"

"I don't know," Kieran admitted with his usual candor. "But I'm going to try. And I won't stop until I find a way."

The same level gaze regarded him soberly. "Why?"

"I'm going to be here for a while." He lifted a shoulder in pretended detachment. "So, why not?"

"To amuse yourself during your exile, you're going to dabble in a murder investigation?" Beau questioned more in concern than doubt.

"I won't dabble, and it won't be amusing." A quick and pointed answer.

"You don't think the local investigators will object when a stranger takes it upon himself to muck around in this?"

"I don't muck around and I won't interfere," he assured her, hopefully before she could voice more misgivings.

"You realize this makes no sense."

Beau was finding his responses less persuasive than he'd hoped. Kieran braced for more.

As he expected, she continued to probe. "You've come to the island for a rest and a change, why would you involve yourself in something so sordid?"

"Many reasons."

"Name them."

Kieran didn't expect she would let him out of the muddle he'd made of this, but he had to try. "My reasons shouldn't matter. They aren't important."

"Dancers Island belongs to my brother, and to me." She challenged his evasion. "As part of Cahill's Grant it has belonged to our family for centuries. Rick isn't in residence much, but it's my home. Its people are my people. What happens on the island, and to them, will always matter to me. When it comes to murder, it matters to Rick.''

"Dancers Island?'' He liked the sound of it. A fond, shortened version, expressing her emotional attachment.

Beau refused to be distracted even as she responded. ''We've had many names, and, perhaps, in the next hundred years will have many more. But that doesn't change what I feel about it, nor how much I care.''

He was outmatched. She was a tiger when it came to protecting her own. He wondered if she would be the same with a lover, or a child, and knew before the thought was completed that she would. She was many things to many people. And to him...a tomboy who clambered among the rigging of a brigantine, the lady of the island, a gifted clinical psychologist. In any persona, a benevolent caretaker and a single-minded adversary.

Kieran wasn't sure what he expected from this woman. But the last thing he wanted or needed was adversity. ''Two women have been murdered,'' he began with great patience. ''Two very young women, hardly more than children, themselves.''

Recalling the ghastly police photographs included in Simon's dossiers, he strove to keep the anger from his voice. ''The first was found on a lonely stretch of beach where the children go to search for a particular shell. The last was discovered by lovers in a rendezvous at twilight. Now the children rarely play on the beach, and only fools seek out the dark, lonely shore.

''If Norrie were here, how many children would he collect with the Island Buggy?'' His words were terse as he recalled the numbers she had said. ''Two? Six? A dozen?''

Beau shook her head. A breeze crept about the house, rippling through the fringe of the Island Buggy, dancing to the music of tinkling bells. It was usually a happy sound, calling the children to it. Now it was only lonely.

''I don't know,'' she demurred as the breeze died and the bells were mute. Their silence screamed at her, insisting she be truthful. Looping a finger about an errant curl, she clasped it briefly in a tight grip at her nape as she admitted the truth. "None."

"Why?" He used her word again, deliberately.

As if she didn't hear, she spoke of the children, as their lives had been. "They used to run and play along the streets. Scuffing their feet in the dust. Playing stickball. Racing bikes. The older girls and boys fished from the pier, or sailed, or swam in the inlet. There's an old tire tied to a tree...." With a lift of her shoulders her comment drifted to nothing.

"But no one swings there anymore," Kieran finished for her. "Now their parents keep them close. Too close. The summer freedom they'd looked forward to, and yearned for has been stolen by a madman."

Taking her hand from her hair, letting the curls fall free, she flexed cramping fingers. "I miss them. Their laughter, their pranks. The games they played on the beach."

"I know."

"Do you?"

"Summer is made for kids." His summers on the Chesapeake with his wonderfully eccentric parents, and his brothers and sisters, had been magic. The tribe of five, Keegan had fondly called his children. And they had been that, a tribe, a close band. Devlin, Kieran, Tynan, Valentina and Patience, three boys, two girls, who made their bond stronger by becoming blood brothers and sisters. Kieran still bore the scar from the overzealous slice across his palm.

He traveled the world. But he always came home to his family and the Chesapeake. There, by the shore, he'd played and swum and sailed. And learned to love the sea. It was there, the fateful summer Patience capsized and was caught in the submerged sail of her small boat, that he discovered little was impossible, if he tried hard enough.

If he tried hard enough now, he would find this cruel creature who held the island hostage. He wouldn't stop until he did.

"You wonder why I want to help? A stolen summer is a

part of it. I'd like to give it back, especially to the children. While I'm in the village, or on the beach, I'd like to hear them laugh and sing, and watch them play.

"I wield a mean fishing rod. My particular area of expertise is catching old boots and turtles." One side of his mouth lifted, the dimple danced. "I might even be tempted to try the tire."

"After you catch the killer?"

"Of course."

"Of course? You consider it that simple?" Beau was staring at him, seeing a quality she hadn't recognized. Discovering a man unlike any she'd known. "Who are you?" With eyes narrowed, she asked thoughtfully, "What are you?"

"I thought you knew. I'm Kieran O'Hara." He swept an imaginary hat from his dark head, and executed an impossibly elegant bow. "Corporate investigator extraordinaire, at your service, my lady."

He should have looked ridiculous standing by Norrie's gaudy toy, acting the courtier. But he was simply amusing, yet with a glint of steel in his heartbreaker grin. Beneath the old-fashioned courtesies and the devil's own charm, there was a man of reckoning. Musing aloud, she ventured her own definition. "Corporate Raider, huh?"

"Not the same at all," he corrected with the shake of an admonishing finger. "Repeat after me, corporate investigator."

"All right, investigator."

"That's better. Has a nicer ring to it, don't you think?"

"I think I'd like to know what a corporate investigator investigates." Once again, Beau wouldn't be sidestepped. "How would that qualify you to catch a murderer?"

"I investigate whatever I'm called to investigate. Though I'm not part of law enforcement, my skills and methods are much the same." Much the same, but better. Simon's stringent training reinforced his own abilities, insuring that he was among the best in his field. Corporate crime ran the gamut. Murder was not excluded.

"Have you apprehended a murderer in the course of an investigation?" Beau waited and watched attentively.

"Yes." As recently as his last assignment. He bore the scar left by a burning rafter as remembrance of a company executive who tried to burn his illegal aliens alive, rather than be found out. Ironically, the hiring of illegals was not the reason for his investigation. In the midst of a toxic fire, that fine point hadn't seemed to matter. "I have apprehended a murderer before."

"You say that as if there has been more than one."

Quick! Oh she was quick. And astute. Qualities that must have served her well in the practice of psychology. "Yes."

"Yes, what?"

"Yes, there has been more than one, though I don't make it a practice of catching murderers."

"Except when they occur during the course of one of your corporate investigations."

With a conceding bow, he acknowledged that she was right again.

Plucking a flower from a riotous mandevilla, she stroked her cheek. With its rich pink fading to delicate cream at its fluted edges, Kieran found it a far better adornment of her skin than precious jewels.

She watched him over the blossom, then moved it away. "You work for a corporation? Yourself?"

"Myself. I'm freelance." That much was true. When, on the strength of an association with Patience, Valentina, and Tynan O'Hara, the wily Simon had seen the advantage of recruiting yet one more of Keegan O'Hara's tribe of five, he was a corporate investigator, he was self-employed, and he did freelance. When he accepted the invitation, becoming a member of The Black Watch, it was decided the existing business was the perfect cover. Affording Kieran access that other professions would not.

The recent project was a prime example. He'd gone in, ferreted out the culprit, and exited in a much unwanted flash of glory. But not before he'd uncovered evidence that would lead to the destruction of a ring of smugglers, who dealt in human lives. Yet no one would be the wiser, for no one would make the connection between Kieran's small, one man operation and a powerful government agency.

"So, you're a corporate investigator who catches murderers only when they stumble into his investigation." Beau knew he would cut a dashing figure in his work, and he had the look of a man who would do any task set him to the best of his skills. But there was something that suggested to her he was more than he admitted.

"That's it." Kieran relaxed, but only a little. "What you see is what you get. One man's fancy, et cetera, et cetera."

Beau smiled at that. "Are you through?"

"With the clichés?" Kieran had the grace to look abashed. "Yeah, guess I am."

The flower moved across her chin, touching the corner of her mouth. Her expression was speculative, her lashes were lowered, as she focused more carefully upon him. "Why don't you dispense with the folderol and tell me who you really are?"

"As I said, Kieran O'Hara, ma'am, at your…"

"I know, at my service." She stopped him with a skeptical look. "I'll accept that part. Let's skip to the crucial part. *What* are you, Kieran O'Hara?"

"Playing psychologist, doc? Reading between the lines?"

"Between the signals." After a pause, she added, "Maybe I am dusting off my old skills of observation."

It didn't appear to Kieran that there was very much dust on any part of the lady. She had the power of intuition that would be invaluable in her profession. In any profession. Simon, for one, would turn handsprings—dignified handsprings—for someone with her credentials. "You must have been something, doc. One of the best."

Ignoring the praise, she turned the point around. "So are you."

He knew where she was going with this, but he had to ask, "How so?"

"Evasion. You're a master at it." She tried to be stern, but a tremor in her cheek tugged at the corner of her mouth.

He touched her temple, the smooth flesh that barely covered a delicately pulsing vein. Before he even considered what he was doing, his knuckle was tracing the line of her cheekbone and down to her lips. "But you aren't going to let me get away with it."

Beau knew that she should move away. The most minute turn of her head would break the contact. But it was Kieran who moved instead. His hand rested on her shoulder as he smiled down at her. "Well, are you, doc?"

He was setting her up. As Rick had so delighted in doing through their childhood. The resemblance in the personalities was uncanny. Her brother and a virtual stranger, yet so much alike. Except for the streak of stern determination that she'd glimpsed in Kieran. But Rick was younger, and there were beginning flashes of that same quality in him. So that could be the same one day. Even with that core of steel, they were men with whom to have fun. To enjoy. But the wise woman would never let herself become serious about any man of their cut.

Yes, Kieran was setting her up. But for now, she chose to engage in his mischief. She wouldn't disappoint him. "Tease me all you like. Evade and distract." As she played her role, the weight of his hand on her shoulder was a constant reminder of his gentleness. "I insist that I know what you are."

"Why, darlin', I thought we'd settled that."

She'd been called pet names all her life. Girl, sweetie, sugar, gal. But she'd never worn a women's liberation heart on her sleeve, and never found the names disturbing. They were expressions of affection, she understood them as such. But none ever set her heart rushing as his drawling endearment.

"Indulge me." She was startled to hear her voice was hoarse. With an unobtrusive clearing of her throat, she continued her part of the game. "Refresh my memory."

"Certainly, darlin'." The endearment was drawled a little

slower, a little softer the second time. His hand lifted from her shoulder. A trailing fingertip passed between her lips and the mandevilla, on its passage to the fragile underside of her chin. Tilting her face, he let his gaze settle on her mouth.

For a wild instant, Beau thought he would kiss her. And she found herself wondering how his mouth would feel against her own. In the next moment, she was certain she was mad. With bravado, she said, "I'm waiting."

"For sure you are, sugar." He dipped his head then, brushing her lips with his. Ever so slightly, ever so softly. When he lifted his mouth away, mischief still sparkling in his eyes, his finger still at her chin, he murmured gently, as if whispering words of love. "What am I? Why one of the world's most eligible bachelors. Indeed, sweetheart, that's what I am."

Beau burst into laughter. Moving away from him, she leaned on the wall. With her back pressed against the aged stucco, and her elbows resting on the bricks that capped it, she laughed. Each time she looked away and back again, she laughed harder.

Low, deep, and healing, her laughter flowed over Kieran. A sound that made him want to laugh himself. "Well, now, I wish I'd said something to that effect a tad earlier."

"Don't wish it." Beau told him between gasps. "You know darned well it wouldn't have worked nearly so well, if you hadn't laid your trap so smartly."

"I suppose not." Kieran was solemn again, remembering the lies, and why he was here. "But it was worth the effort."

Laughter truly was a source of healing. Before he was through, before he left the island, she would laugh as easily and naturally as she had before a monster came to the shores of Moon Dancers Island.

Unaware of the sudden, sober shift of his thoughts, Beau glanced at her watch and was startled at the time. "We're so late. Poor Tabby will be tired of waiting."

Taking that as his cue, Kieran opened the passenger door of the cart. "Shall we go, my lady, Dr. Cahill?"

Beau Anna laughed again. This time an easy, spontaneous note that made him hope the mood created by the circumstance of their meeting and the memory of the murders could be put aside. He hoped it meant the wariness with which she regarded him was easing, not just forgotten in a surge of hilarity.

Becoming an integral part of the island society would be easier if someone the people trusted served as his patron. And what better patronage than the chatelaine of the island?

"Stick with Beau," she suggested, with the laughter lingering in her voice. "I haven't been Dr. Cahill in a long time."

"You trained and practiced in Charleston?"

She slanted a curious look at him as she took her seat in the cart. "How did you know?"

"Norrie." He tossed the name out offhandedly. But it was another mistake. Perhaps it was that she was more acutely observant than most. In any case he would have to be more careful with her. The next time he might not have such a convenient cover to explain it away.

"Norrie must have spoken about us a great deal."

"His favorite subject."

"He has always been fascinated with the island history. As part of the founding family we qualify for his attention."

Kieran turned the key, the engine ignited with a sound that fell somewhere between a growl and a roar. When he'd checked the condition of the cart while she slept, he'd been surprised at the power of its engine. It wasn't hard to surmise which part of the Island Buggy was for the pleasure of its owner.

"You don't really think Norrie's discussion of you or your brother is simply an extension of his interest in your history, do you?"

"Of course not." Beau turned her head from side to side. Her hair had dried in curling rivulets that she'd brushed into smooth waves. In the superhumid air that lingered after the rain, waves were becoming ringlets. Threading her fingers through the heavy mass of it, she pushed it from her face, destroying what remaining order survived. The result was an enticing halo framing her tanned face. In tattered cutoffs and faded shirt, she looked like a sleepy eyed beachcomber just risen from a lover's blanket tucked among the dunes, rather than his borrowed sofa.

Kieran couldn't let himself consider what it would be like to share an evening and a blanket on the beach with Beau Anna Cahill. Not yet.

There was still too much he wanted to know. Questions the all-inclusive dossier couldn't answer.

From its impersonal pages he knew bare, sequential facts. That she'd led a relatively sheltered, but uninhibited, life. Until college at seventeen, she rarely left the island. Then it was the usual collegiate curriculum, the masters program, a doctorate, a brief practice in clinical psychology, and back again to the island. First to care for her father, grievously injured in a freak accident. Then to assume his duties.

There was little on Roderick Beaumont Cahill's death in Simon's report. Just a sketchy description of the man, and a comment on the tragedy of his loss. And nothing of its effect on Beau.

Though the accident occurred years ago, Kieran questioned a connection with the newest tragedies. Making a mental note of the details he should check, he was hardly aware that Beau was chatting blithely on.

"Norris Candler may be a walking encyclopedia, but he's a friend." When he didn't act as if he heard her, she leaned forward, breaking his line of vision. "Mr. O'Hara?" Nothing. Touching his arm on impulse, she murmured, "Kieran?"

Drawing himself from his thoughts, his introspective gaze almost sleepy, he turned his hand to enfold hers. "Sorry."

"This time you were a thousand miles away."

"Not really." Her hand lay lightly in his, her fingers long, the nails clipped short. When he traced the line of her palm there were calluses at its edge. Moving his thumb idly over their roughened skin, he chose a safe topic. "I was thinking of the beach. We could take that route to the Tea House. Maybe swing by the brig, check for storm damage on the way.''

Sliding her hand from his, she clenched it tightly in her lap. She was certainly unpredictable today. Avoiding his touch one minute, seeking it the next. Smothering an exasperated groan, she addressed his comment, suggesting an alternate route. ''Inland is faster, and Tabby will be waiting.''

''The brig?''

''In its protected harbor, it weathered the storm better than any other craft moored in island waters. In any case, Skip and Israel will see to it.''

''Your brother's friends?''

''And mine.''

He listened closely for nuances in her tone that might suggest that one of the men was more than a friend. There was nothing. Nevertheless, he made yet another mental note. This one involved meeting Skip Hayes and, especially, Israel Johnson, whom Tabby called the smart one.

''Ready to roll?''

''Wait.'' She held up a staying hand. ''I left the copy of *Prominence*.''

''You don't need the damn thing.'' Kieran tried to dissuade with cajolery. ''Why settle for a bunch of pictures when you have me in the flesh, sweetheart?''

''Maybe I prefer the objectivity and immortality of pictures.'' She climbed from the cart.

''The what?''

''You heard me.'' Her sneakers scuffed over cobblestones. ''Objectivity and immortality!''

''What, the dickens, does that mean?''

At the doorway she turned to face him, her smile beatific. ''You figure it out, *sweetheart*.''

Kieran blinked, and as the door slammed behind her, he began to laugh. She'd set him up. With a finesse that rivaled Patience and Valentina at their finest. And he hadn't seen it coming.

"The lady of the island, is one to watch," he commented to the trees, to the garden, to the flowers.

Beau Anna dashed from the house and down the courtyard alley, the magazine held prominently in her hand. Settling in the seat, her thigh brushing his, she turned innocent eyes toward him. "Well? Shall we?"

"Sure," Kieran drawled. "Why not."

She was still smiling when, with a jingle and roar, the cart rolled to a halt in the unpaved parking lot of the Tea House.

Tabby waited for them on a small balcony overlooking the sea. A bottle of merlot, a platter of tiny sandwiches, and a bouquet of island wildflowers decorated the table.

Hearing their footsteps she rose from her chair. She'd changed her costume, but Kieran knew only because the colors in this flowing garment were different.

"Good evening, Beau Anna." Recognizing the familiar footsteps, the old woman nodded in Beau's direction.

"Good evening, Tabby. I'm sorry we're late. The storm…"

Tabby waved away her excuses and gestured her to a chair before addressing Kieran. "Mr. O'Hara." A small bow, almost a genuflect, accompanied her greeting. "Good evening and be welcome at last. We folk here on the island have been waiting for you."

Taking a stunned Kieran by the hand, she led him to the table. She poured the wine, and served the sandwiches, before folding her hands at her breasts and fixing him with her blinded stare.

"We've been waiting," she said again. "For a very long time."

Five

"Waiting for me. For a very long time." Kieran coiled the telephone cord around his wrist, dragging it with him he paced to the deck.

"Those were Tabby's exact words," he continued in a voice that matched the hush surrounding him. The sea and sky had been peaceful the whole day, with neither harboring violence. The bare and sandy shore was as trackless as in first light, with never more than the tumble of shells caught in the current, or the scuttling track of crabs marking it.

The raucous, strutting gulls were quiet as they hunkered sleepily in the sand. Strafing pelicans moved in oblivion. No plummeting dives, no current, no ruffled feathers. No sound.

Even the lone blue heron that arrived each dawn and lingered through the day, stood motionless. The namesake of Kieran's sanctuary, an elegant silhouette, blazoned against the fire of sunset.

But in that cool, fiery light there should be children. If not along Norrie Candler's isolated stretch of beach, then further past it on the neighboring strand. Near enough that the sound of their laughter and the clatter of their toys should carry to him on a breeze.

Bright sails should dip and dash amid benign swells of a placid sea, as the eldest of the young ones made their way home from a day of racing. Tails of kites should be fluttering ribbons of color, spelling out one last secret message across the canvas of the ever changing sky.

Secret messages. Did the smallest of the island children play that game? Even as he listened to Simon's concerns, he compared his own childhood by the Chesapeake. The long, lazy days with Devlin and Tynan, Valentina and Patience. Safeguarded by an innocent time, in an innocent place, with only the elements and their own folly to threaten.

It should be the same for these children. For every child.

Moving to a better vantage, he looked seaward, then inland toward the village made apparent by masts of vessels anchored for the night in its cove. He listened while Simon, the gruff, continued his cautioning harangue of an imperfect world that grew more imperfect each day.

And those who suffered most were the children.

Though his young mind had been too innocent to understand its far-reaching consequences, in the travels of his family, Kieran had seen the repercussions of cruelty and evil. It was this that had compelled him to accept Simon's invitation to join The Watch.

This that made his heart ache for the empty shore.

Another silence intruded, prompting a reply to Simon. "I don't know what Tabby meant. Perhaps she senses that I can help, or that it's my purpose for coming to the island. But there's no reason she should suspect anything of The Watch."

A draft set palmetto fronds clattering and moss weaving. In a great flap of powerful wings, the heron lifted from shore, circled once, then landed, assuming the same watchful stance.

The broken calm resumed.

"I believe she's psychic. But within a limited degree," Kieran affirmed, when once he'd questioned. "I've seen no incidence of her powers, but the islanders believe and the woman is incapable of chicanery. Though I think her gift stems in some way from her religious beliefs, she bothers with none of that sort of trappings. Tabitha is simply Tabitha. No nonsense. No frills."

Kieran chuckled, remembering brightly colored costumes. "Unless you call dressing like an exotic bird a frill. Come to think of it, she's the size of an exotic bird."

The tide was ebbing. Its nearly silent whisper grown quieter in the end of a perfect day. A time for exploring gypsy tidal pools and their treasures. If one dared.

The monster of Moon Dancers Island only struck under the cover of darkness. But none dared trust that it wouldn't change, that he might decide the multihues of morning, midday, or sunset blended well with blood.

The thought sent a shiver down Kieran's neck as he remembered Beau Anna working alone on the brig. Alone, unprotected, full daylight and seclusion. A perfect opportunity for the savage fiend to change his pattern, to better admire his grisly handiwork.

If this depraved creature were after her as he feared...

The disturbing realization severed attendance to Simon's discourse. As he struggled to put the terrifying notion aside and recapture the thread of their exchange, Kieran's body was drenched in sweating cold. Cold the lingering, but diminished, heat of the day couldn't staunch.

He couldn't think. He couldn't connect. Kieran the unflappable, could only will from his mind the image of Beau Anna violently mutilated. Her body desecrated as in the coroner's photographs of the first victims.

The first victims.

Simon had used the term in his briefing. He used it now.

Holding back a shudder, Kieran managed to answer. "Tabby has no incipient or transcendental knowledge of the murders. I wish she did. As she's first to admit, her powers are limited and selective. Her explanation is that she sees only what is 'given' to her. She has no idea if these young girls were the first nor if they will be the last.

"I'm sure she's genuine, despite her limitations. I've met her for tea the last two days." Once with Beau Anna. Once alone. "She speaks freely of her gift, or lack of it in some cases." Some things the old woman kept to herself. Why she'd waited for Kieran, for instance.

"Her idea of tea, by the way, coincides with yours," Kieran tossed in for no purpose. "A bottle of merlot."

Simon chuckled then, as men and women do when tensions become unbearable. Then he waited for Kieran to continue.

"I didn't see Tabby today, since it isn't one of her scheduled times to tell fortunes at the Tea House. Instead, I'm planning to drop by the tavern, to make what contacts I can. Alice, the first girl who was murdered, worked there as a waitress." He was going over ground Simon already knew. But the call had dragged on. Far longer than was Simon's custom. For some reason he was reluctant to break contact with Kieran, and the events of the island.

"I'm gambling someone among the regulars might remember something in the course of conversing with a new resident." Kieran glanced at his watch. "The tavern opens in half an hour. I'm told the chef serves a sensational dinner. Thought I'd catch the first seating."

The fearless leader of The Black Watch, who feared for nothing so much as the welfare of his agents, ignored the opportunity to bring the call to a halt. Putting aside his eagerness to get to the village, Kieran waited. Simon was rarely evasive. It was even more rare that he would procrastinate.

Something worried the older man. Something he could approach only obliquely. The line reverberated with a hollow hush as Kieran waited for Simon to fill the void. When the stalwart director of The Black Watch spoke, it was to ask a question Kieran hadn't expected.

He responded in his surprise. "There's been no opportunity to meet the younger Cahill." Younger by only a few hours, Kieran knew. And legitimate, as Beau Anna hadn't been. A fact that mattered to no one he'd met on the island. Beau, least of all.

But was it the case with Rick?

He had no time to explore this concept, as Simon launched into a barrage of questions. As if broaching the subject broke the dam.

"Simon, I only know what I've been told." He finally said in answer to the queries. "If I believed his advance publicity, I would expect him to forgo the launch and simply walk the water. When he finally decides to make an appearance on the island, that is.

"The man's a saint, a delightful devil, a heartbreaking rogue, and a sweetheart all rolled into one. Depending on who's speaking. If there's one soul on the island who doesn't adore him, Tabby doesn't know who it is. Neither do I.

"For reasons of my own, I'm not sure I look forward to meeting this paragon." Kieran's expression grew grim. Rick Cahill roamed when there was danger on the island. Danger to his sister. Could he be civil to this thoughtless man?

The clock in the great room struck the hour. As he heard it and knew Kieran must go, Simon finally ended the call. After he returned the receiver to its cradle, Kieran questioned the purpose of the call. Why, for once, was Simon less than direct?

"What disturbs you about this, Simon?"

With no hope of arriving at an answer, returning to the house, he concentrated on the task he'd set for the evening. A check in the mirror proved the perfect grooming he'd chosen was still intact. Not that he was given to slovenliness, but today was a bit too perfect. An intended projection of the image that purportedly sent him scurrying to Norrie's retreat.

Feeling like a peacock for posturing before the mirror, he snagged the key for the Island Buggy from its holder, and dashed for the door. Today, neither the gaudy cart with its delightful bells, nor the bright blooms of the garden could lift his spirit.

With dread for the days to come lying like a block of ice in his belly, Kieran engaged the engine. When the roar settled to a purr, he steered the pertly tinkling Island Buggy over cobblestones and onto a worn path. Rutted and washed by a second rain, the way was anything but smooth. Soon the bells stopped tinkling, and jangled instead. With neither doing anything to lift his gloom. Yet, out of sheer O'Hara tenacity, and in Kieran fashion, by the time he'd negotiated the last bump and slither over the decimated track, he'd begun to see the humor of his journey in Norrie Candler's chariot.

* * *

That the tavern was anything but typical was obvious. One needn't know its history to recognize its unique character. The building had undergone many renovations and been many things—a tobacco barn, the plantation store, a warehouse, then, falling into disuse, a derelict. Until the son of a displaced villager returned to the island and commandeered it for his home. When the charitable Cahills lodged no objection, and the new owner turned to a disreputable, but profitable trade, it became the rambling structure of today.

It was fitting to Kieran that the home of a rumrunner should house a tavern on the ground floor, with living quarters on the second. And equally so, that the current tavern keeper was a direct descendant of the first.

But Israel Johnson was more than a tavern keeper. More than a lifelong resident of the island. And more than a childhood friend to Beau Anna and Rick Cahill. One of the murdered girls had worked for him, serving drinks in the tavern. The other had been a frequent customer.

As liquor and good food loosened the tongue, people grew careless. In this case, Kieran was hoping Johnson possessed the tavern keeper's penchant for gossip, coupled with the gift of listening. As he approached the tavern door he recognized Norrie's touch in blending new with the old.

The walls of a courtyard were constructed of tabby, a colonial building medium of seawater, oyster shells, sand and lime. Over the years, he'd seen it in many colors. This, he suspected, owed its pink hue to the shells and sand available, rather than to paint, or the glow of the setting sun. The plants were those one would have found growing in the days of the great plantations. Together they created an ambience that enticed the thirsty and hungry to the tavern doors.

Johnson was a discerning and enterprising man. Kieran recognized and admired his purpose. He was, indeed, intrigued and enticed. But as he crossed the threshold, there was much more on his mind than food or drink.

The lights were dim in the cavernous dining room, and the

windows open, letting in an occasional breeze and the ruddy glow of sunset. As he paused, allowing his eyes the time to adjust, he listened and absorbed. There was music and the hum of conversation, broken by the clinking of glassware. The scents of alcohol, food and perfume blended into a tantalizing bouquet.

Feeling the weight of curious stares, he stepped to the bar. Before he was settled, the occupant of the neighboring stool shifted to stare at him. With a pleasant nod, Kieran said, "Good evening."

Cynical eyes looked from the folds and sags of a massive countenance with shelves of woolly brows. "Good evening? Good? Humph!" The old codger swung back to his mug, an arthritic finger stroking its lip. His voice was surprisingly strong. And except for the occasional slurring, distinctly proper. "Tell me what's good about it."

"I can think of a number of things."

"A number! A number? You can, can you?"

"Certainly." Kieran endured the grim stare.

"Well." Heavy shoulders hunched, weighting down a slender frame. A fringe of curling white hair, visible beneath a captain's hat, straggled over an ascot tucked into the collar of a worn, but impeccable blazer. "Suppose I could too. S'pose I could. If I'd taken our girl for a walk on a rainy beach."

"He didn't take me, Times Two. I took him." Beau stood inches away, one hand on a worn sleeve, a tray in the other.

Rearing away from the bar, Times Two fixed his faded glare on Beau. "You took him! You? Well, I'll be."

"What you'll be is drunk, if you don't go easier on the root beer, Captain." Beau set the tray on the bar, and grinned at Kieran.

"Aw, you know I'm only pretending, little Beau. 'Sall I got since the damn docs took the real stuff away." Sliding an age spotted hand through the handle of the mug, he palmed it and drained it. The face he made conjured wrinkles within wrinkles. "Gawd! I hate this stuff."

"Then why drink it?"

"Well, hell, Beau. You know. You surely know."

"Because you refuse to order anything less than beer. Of some sort."

"Damn straight! Damn straight." He'd begun to weave on the stool, and Beau grasped his shoulder to brace him. "Won't fall. No sir, won't."

Kieran heard a touch of New England in the rambling speech. Times Two was a long way from home.

"Are you sure?" Beau was asking. "You mustn't go home with a black eye."

Her gaze met Kieran's over the faded cap. From her manner he knew this was a ritual between friends.

"Am I sure? Sure as anything." The massive head bobbed. "Anything."

"Have you met Mr. O'Hara, Norrie's tenant?" Beau said, changing the subject.

"Yep. Yep." Times Two fumbled in a pocket for an empty pipe. Clamping it between his teeth, he puffed away.

"A good smoke?" Kieran ventured into the routine.

"It's fading, son." The pipe was laid lovingly on the bar. "The taste is fading."

The bartender who was definitely not Johnson, stopped before Kieran. When he signaled that he'd have the same as Times Two, she hurried away.

"You drink this filthy stuff?" Eyebrows like lambs' tails lifted toward the bill of the cap.

"Thought I'd give it a try." Kieran reached for the frosty mug as it was set before him. "My dad says root beer is the drink of a real man."

"Pshaw! He didn't! He didn't?"

"Well, no." Kieran grinned. "But it sounded good."

"Indeed. Indeed." Times Two leaned close. "Let me tell you a story. Story! Ha! A farce. The farce of the golden years."

This was not serving his purpose, but Kieran was enjoying

the old geezer. He suspected Times Two had been a hell of a man. "I like a good story, even when it's a farce."

Times Two leaned close, his breath redolent with root beer. "Don't buy the guff about the golden years. They're awful. But the damned doctors are determined to prolong it. They take away your brew, your pipe. Tell you, you mustn't eat salt, or sugar. They stuff you with low fat junk better suited for candle wax. For what?" The silvery white head bobbed, nearly dislodging his hat. "For what?"

"To make you live longer, Times Two," Beau put in gently.

"Living? This?" The strong voice quavered from his outburst. "What good does it profit a man to live forever when he can't drink, can't smoke, can't eat. Hell, when even his pecker won't…"

"Oops!" Beau slid her palm over the old man's mouth. "Let's not get into that."

Times Two wagged his brows. When she took her hand away, he asked querulously, "Because it would upset Miz Emily? Upset her sweet sensibilities?"

"I think it would," Beau agreed.

"She's delicate. Delicate."

Beau agreed, "Very."

Times Two looked at Kieran. "Do you know Miz Emily? Do you?"

"Sorry," Kieran responded with his usual courtesy. "That hasn't been my pleasure."

"A pleasure it is." The silver head bobbed again. "We must have you to dinner, Miz Emily and I. We must." Taking Beau's hand he brought it to his lips. "You as well, sweet Beau Anna. You as well."

"Thank you, but I think we should check with Miss Emily first." Keeping her hand in his, she helped him from the stool. "It's seven o'clock, Times Two."

"So it is. I must run. Indeed."

Kieran stood. They were the same height, but Times Two

was frail beneath the width of his shoulders. "Meeting you has been my pleasure, sir."

"It has?" For once there was no repetition as the faded gaze fixed on Kieran's face.

"Yes, sir. I hope we meet again."

"I'm here every day. Six to seven. Six to seven."

"Then so will I be, on occasion."

"I shall look forward to it." He took a tottering step before he gained his balance. Beau and Kieran reached for his arm to steady him. Beau was faster, with Kieran's hand closing over hers. The warmth of his touch lingered on her skin, long after he had released her. Long after Times Two doffed his hat, bowed, and shambled from the tavern.

As they watched him out of sight, Beau was first to speak. "That was nice."

In the muted light her eyes glowed softly. Kieran had come to anticipate that fascinating, dreamy second, then the sharpening focus of her regard. "He's quite a fellow. Very nice beneath the cantankerous exterior."

"I meant you. Not everyone is so kind to him."

"They're cruel?"

"No! No!" She laughed, thinking how much like Times Two she sounded. "Just not patient."

"How old is he?" Kieran gestured her to the seat Times Two vacated and took his own again.

"None of us knows. We aren't sure who they are. For years, they've just been Times Two and Miss Emily." Realizing the root beer sat before him, she summoned the bartender. "What can Jillian bring you?"

"Scotch, rocks." He gave the abbreviated request and focused again on Beau. "No one knows who they are?"

"Not even they know. Though, we think Emily is her name. When he was taken from the sea a mile off our shore, they were the only words he said. He didn't stop until Rick and Skip found her. We don't know how long they were in the water, or how either managed to hang on to their scraps of flotsam."

"Piracy?" The practice neither common, nor unheard of.
"We assume so."

"How did it happen that they remained on the island?"

"They were both ill for some time. Emily's hip was so badly shattered she still doesn't walk well. Once they recuperated, my dad brought them here."

"No family?"

"The authorities tried. We tried. Their pictures ran for weeks in nearly every newspaper along the eastern seaboard. No one came forward."

Kieran sipped his drink. "So you let them stay here."

"It was that or send them to a home. I don't think either would have survived it."

"How long have Captain Times Two and Miss Emily lived on the island?"

"Fifteen years."

"Your dad must have been quite the samaritan."

"He was." Only the tightening of her folded hands betrayed her grief for her father. "If he could help, he would. Always."

"As you do?" At the question in her expression, he responded, "You're here." A glancing look traveled over her, noting the pretty scrap masquerading as an apron, and a pocket bulging with change. Tips, left by the weekend visitors. Undoubtedly to be distributed among the regular staff. "You're dressed for work."

He wondered if there was anything Beau Anna wouldn't try. Repairing the sails had been a challenge, but she'd managed. He guessed that she was the primary caregiver for the Captain and Miss Emily. As self-sufficient as Tabby appeared, because she lived alone there would be times when she would require aid.

"Dinah, one of the summer waitresses, has a killer toothache and a swollen jaw. She's lying down in her room. Being shorthanded is a disaster, when the tavern is at its busiest.

"What you see tonight, isn't customary. The weekend trade always picks up a few weeks before the Moon Dancers

Carnival. We all pitch in when we're needed.'' She was reciting, ticking off reasons to convince him what she did was no great sacrifice. "Since Jillian's fairly new, this was too much for her alone. Along with that, the kitchen is short staffed. Israel had to step in there.

"When he yelled for help, I had the time. So here I am, doing what he usually does. The bar, the tables, some hostessing, a lot of glad-handing among the mainlanders. A little of everything.'' She lifted her shoulders in a dismissing gesture. "No big deal.''

"When do you rest?''

"During the dancers' season? When I can.'' She ignored his stern expression. "I get as much as I need.''

Kieran let it go. Though he knew he would continue to worry about her. Beau Anna had a way of getting under a man's skin, making him care. Each time he was with her, he wanted to scoop her up and tuck her close, keeping her safe from the smallest hurt.

Though the hurt that threatened was far from small, being the independent she was, she would reject protection. His most of all.

Putting aside, but not forgetting, his concern, he considered asking more about the carnival. But there would be time later. For now, he wanted to meet some of the locals.

"I should go.'' She slid from the bar stool. "Barry Johns looks ready for seconds.''

Catching her wrist, Kieran detained her. "Before you go, I'd like to meet Israel.''

"Of course.'' She scanned the bar and the dining room. "That's funny, I saw him a few minutes ago. It's odd that he wouldn't be here. Israel is a stickler for prompt service. He wouldn't leave. There he is, by the kitchen door. I should have realized he'd have to cycle through there more often tonight.''

"What with being shorthanded and all.''

"And all,'' she agreed decisively.

"Since he's so busy I can wait.''

"No need." Beau took his hand from her wrist and held it as casually as an old friend. "He'll make time for a chum of Norrie's.

"Israel." Calling his name, she strolled past clusters of tables, taking Kieran with her. There would be chances, later, for more introductions. But for now, Kieran had expressed an interest in Israel. She hadn't stopped to think why. But this newcomer with nothing to gain from his thoughtfulness, had been patient with Times Two. That was enough for Beau Anna to offer courtesy in return.

"Israel." She stopped before the tall, dark skinned blonde. "I'd like you to meet Kieran O'Hara, Norrie's summer tenant. Kieran," as she released his hand, she looked up at him with incredible warmth in her gaze, "Israel Johnson, the island tavern keeper, and a good friend."

Johnson's greeting was brief, his handshake firm, his smile personable. His blond hair was stylishly cut, but left long enough to be drawn and clubbed at the nape. His greeting was relaxed and nonchalant. "One of Norrie's city buddies, huh?" He laughed, his teeth as perfect as matched pearls. "You have my sympathy."

"For Norrie," Kieran drawled with an easy mischief in his voice. "Or the city."

"The city, whichever it is." Dressed in casual clothes that exuded an elegance simply in the way he wore them, Israel Johnson could have modeled for any couturier in the world. Or easily be selected as another of *Prominence Magazine*'s most eligibles.

Better than I, Kieran thought as he answered. "Could be any city, since both of us travel. Like you, I prefer the shore."

"Israel! Have you cut yourself?" Beau interrupted. Catching his fingers, she brought his hand closer for inspection.

"Not me." Israel laughed again. Something he seemed to do a great deal. "See?" Licking his thumb, he ran the pad of it over the streak of blood that marked the back of his hand. "Cookie stabbed himself, instead of a cabbage. Zapped it with one of those razor sharp knives he wields. I was checking on him just now.''

"Will he need stitches?'' Beau asked as the blonde took his hand away and tucked it in the pocket of his trousers.

"Not this time. His palm's going to be sore as hell by tomorrow." Israel groaned. "I may be cooking for a while. In fact, I should be pitching in now." The pearl white smile flashed at Kieran. "We'll talk more. Soon. And you?" He dropped a kiss on the top of Beau's head. "Sister-girl, you're working today, remember?''

"Is he always like this?" Kieran asked as Israel left and he subdued the rush of anger the kiss provoked. This was an investigation, he couldn't allow personal likes or dislikes to color his judgment.

"Usually worse. Now, would you like a table?" Laying a hand on his arm, she realized she'd gone from avoiding his touch, to initiating it. "You did come for dinner, didn't you?''

"At Tabitha's recommendation.''

"Oh?" Beau led him to a table that overlooked a second, small garden. The back gate garden, replete with sculptures and flowers, and a twisted and gnarled pecan tree with an old rope swing hanging from a massive branch. "Then you've seen Tabby lately.''

"For tea yesterday.'' Taking his seat and the menu she offered, he asked, "Will you join me?" At her look of surprise, the dimple appeared. "You do take time to eat, don't you?''

"Of course. But not until the last launch leaves and the mainland folk are away.''

"I'll wait." Sliding back his chair, he rose to his feet again. "Tabby promises that the only thing that makes one of Cookie's dinners better, is sharing it with an interesting and compatible companion.''

"Do I fit the bill?''

"Do I?" he countered.

He was so close, she could smell the hint of lavender that

guests of Heron's Walk always brought away with them. A pleasing accent for his own masculine scent of soap and sea air. As seductive as his voice, and his smile. If she weren't careful, saying no to this handsome intruder could become impossible. But she was careful. And she'd begin as she meant to continue.

"Of course, you do," she admitted, intending it to be the first of a gracious refusal. "But…"

"Then I'll wait." Threading a finger through fallen curls, he tucked them behind her ear. Letting his palm drift over and down the slender column of her throat, it came to rest briefly on the taut muscles of her shoulder. "You'll find me in the garden, when you're ready."

Confounded at her own game, she watched as he walked away. Not so very tall, but tall enough. Slender and broad shouldered, but not overwhelming. Rugged, masculine, attractive, with the mark of life on his face. A man of the world. And though she'd scoffed, a bachelor, most charming, most eligible. And sexy.

Spinning away from the sight of him, yet taking his image in her memory, she rejected the direction of her thoughts. "I won't do this. I'll simply explain."

Sighing, she cut her foolish monologue short. What would she explain? To whom? And why? Kieran O'Hara offered friendship. What harm was there in sharing a meal?

"Nothing," she muttered, hurrying to answer a mainlander's imperious summons.

Determined she wouldn't think of dinner, nor of the man who walked the tavern gardens, Beau immersed herself in her work. She was grateful for the influx of curious tourists attracted to the island in the weeks before the Moon Dancers Carnival. But, unlike local patrons, she found them demanding and insistent. Thankfully allowing her no time to think or regret.

Darkness had fallen and she was placating a particularly obnoxious tourist when a disturbance erupted in the back gate garden.

"Murder! Murder! Most foul."

Recognizing the distinctive voice of Times Two, even in its hysteria, Beau rushed to the porch. Stopping at the top of the stair, she stared into shadows broken by tiny lights that marked the pathways.

Times Two was sprawled on the stones, his head on Kieran's thigh. Blood like a darker shadow pooled around his head.

Kieran's face, when he looked at her, was ghostly pale, with lines and clefts so handsome in the sun, drawn in caricature by falling moonlight. His lips moved, the sound from them drawn from a great, echoing abyss.

"I'm sorry, my love." He caught a grating breath. His hand convulsed, crumpling a captain's cap. He looked away, staring into the distance, delaying what couldn't be delayed.

"What is it," she whispered, rooted where she stood.

He nodded, accepting the inevitable. "I'm afraid there's been another murder."

Six

"Poor Times Two." Beau Anna shivered. "For this awful thing to happen to him."

Breaking off her thought, she walked in a stifled hush along the trodden pathway. Kieran said nothing, leaving it to Beau to continue as she must. When she shivered again, he neither drew her to him nor volunteered his finely tailored blazer.

The night was hot and humid, the air shimmered in its sultry fever. As she walked through it, the cold that racked her mind and body was of another plane. There was anguish in every breath and word. Yet, he knew the compassion he would offer willingly, would be rebuffed.

So, he walked by her side, listening. Hands tucked in his pockets, quelling an unwelcomed need to comfort, he waited.

"I don't understand this," she confided in a strangled undertone. "Why do this to Times Two?"

Stopping in the middle of the rutted path, she grasped his arm. "Is there anything we could have done?"

"To protect Times Two? Or Dinah?" Slipping her cold hand from his arm, he folded it in both of his and drew her close at last. In silvered beams as cold as her hand, moonlight broke free of low lying clouds, flooding the path. "There was nothing."

Sensing her rejection, with their joined hands he tilted her face. "Don't second guess. Don't play 'what-if.' Berating yourself for not being omniscient is a fool's errand. Tabby will do enough for all of us, because she wasn't 'given' this to see."

"This isn't Tabby's fault! What she sees, or knows, is beyond her power." In normal times, the elderly women was philosophical about the illogical limitations of her gift. But murder and human suffering were hardly normal. In this there would be no absolution.

"Poor Tabby," she mused brokenly. "She shouldn't worry, but she will."

"Exactly! If the resident seeress had no forewarning, how could you?" Having made his point, with her hand still clasped in his, they walked the meandering track to Cahill's Bluff.

Night creatures serenading the sparsely wooded path fell mute with the passage of these troubled interlopers. In secret they waited with the patience of aeons. Taking up their interrupted songs of darkness only after the cadence of matched footsteps faded.

In the windless air, sparse tatters of low lying fog descended, weaving among the trees like gossamer drifts of moss. Coiling, clinging, it thickened, enveloping this seaside world in patches and ribbons of mystery.

Drawing down a gray veil, it sought low ground. Providing a muffling blanket for footsteps that followed. Hiding eyes that watched. Eyes colder than the white glow of the moon. Crueler than any familiar with the tall slender figure would believe.

As she moved through the haze, Beau's voice was vibrant with sudden hope. "Kieran. Do you suppose Times Two saw something?"

"We'll know more when the doctor's sedative has worn off." Stroking a thumb over the pulsing flesh of her wrist, Kieran cautioned, "Don't get your hopes up, sweetheart. This killer's too cunning to be discovered so easily. He'll make a mistake, but it won't be something as moronic as allowing an old man to stumble over him."

Beau stopped, taking her hand from his to clutch the railing of the footbridge they were crossing. This had always been a favorite spot. A place to play imaginary games as a child, and simply to imagine as a dreamy teen. After her father's death, with the responsibilities of the island and its people falling to her, it became a place of respite. A place to listen and absorb, and regain a sense of serene good humor.

But now, the chuckling brook seemed to laugh at her, not with her, as it mocked her questions. Undaunted, she asked another. "Do you think one of us was intended to find Dinah?"

"I'm convinced of it."

"Not Times Two."

"Never."

He was so emphatic, she peered up at him, wishing the mists she usually found fascinating, weren't so obscuring. "Why are you this certain?"

Kieran shifted subtly. Listening, without appearing to listen, to an absence of sound. Watching, without appearing to watch, the part of their path where the rekindled cacophony halted again in a disturbing rush.

With divided attention he addressed her concern. "Who among the islanders knows the captain's schedule?"

"Everyone." Beau's bewilderment was apparent. "From the oldest to the youngest."

Nothing moved beyond the bridge. Neither bird, nor animal, nor man. Kieran relaxed, only a little. Perhaps the concerted silence was a meaningless coincidence. Perhaps in response to a falling leaf, or a shifting stone. Perhaps not. He kept his secret vigil.

"Everyday, without fail," he murmured. "From six, sharp, to seven, Times Two treats himself to root beer and conversation at the tavern."

A wisp of fog drifted, caressed, moved away. For a stolen moment she saw him clearly. A thoughtful face. The face of a man to whom laughter came easily. Yet, for no reason she could explain, beneath the laughter she'd begun to sense a watchful reserve. An ambience of something undefinable. Danger, per chance? Potential violence?

Danger. Violence. The words themselves should strike fear

in her heart. Instead, standing alone with him in the darkness, with the gathering mists enveloping them in a private world, she felt only fear for her heart.

But that was ridiculous. As much as she loved her brother, she'd determined long ago, that she would never be vulnerable to one of his dashing, charming sort. Kieran O'Hara was dashing and charming enough for two. But she would never let herself be at risk.

Putting wandering, troubling thoughts to rest, she addressed his oblique question. "Times Two never changes his routine."

"Until today."

Two words, spoken softly, startling her. "Until today," she repeated hoarsely. "When he forgot his pipe."

Kieran nodded, and fickle moonlight set his dark hair ablaze with glittering droplets left by fog. "The pipe he never smokes."

"But is never without. Times Two was coming back for his pipe! Something he'd never needed to do before. If Dinah's body was left for someone to find, it wasn't Times Two. But who?"

Kieran let her puzzle out the riddle on her own, wondering if the conclusion she reached would match his. Would agreement make it so? He would like to think not, but intuition and wisdom warned that even a single opinion, his opinion, was right.

"Dinah was lying on the pathway Times Two always takes home. But not until he passed that way the second time on his way back to the tavern." Head down she stared at the little of the creek she could see. In her mind its mocking babble chanted a name.

"It was me!" she cried. "I walk that same path home. I was supposed to find her. Whoever this creature is, for whatever reason he's driven to kill, he left Dinah there for me to see. He wants me to know the terrible things he can do." She was shaking more than before. "Why?"

When he took her in his arms, she didn't resist. When he

held her close, she clung to him. Her fingers curled tightly about the lapels of his blazer, rough woven silk crushed in her palms. In a moment of blind terror, the elegant cloth was her link to reality. This man she'd just met, yet knew so well, was the rock she needed. His strength was her strength, his courage her courage. With no meted price.

"Why?" She asked again from the security of his arms. "I hardly knew Dinah. What reason would he have for wanting me to see and to feel…"

Her halting speech stopped as she lifted a pale face to Kieran.

"To feel!

"Is that it? Does he want me to feel what Dinah felt? Does he want me to know the horror she have must known as she died. Defiled, alone. Afraid."

There was hysteria in her repetitions as she grasped at straws. But, Kieran feared, the right straws.

"I don't know, sweetheart," he lied as he stroked the length of her hair with his palm, brushing his lips over her throbbing temple. In for one lie, in for a dozen. How much hotter could the flames of a liar's hell be?

"I don't know," he whispered again, with no less remorse and no more truth. Holding her, Kieran stared over the path they'd taken. In exaggerated contrast to the lazy burbling of the creek, the still, quiet night endured.

Too still, too quiet.

Too long.

Preying birds or animals would have moved on. The rare concerted coincidence would never last so long. Certain now that he understood, he cursed himself for rejecting the Island Buggy. For finding its whimsy obscene when a young woman lay dead.

The monster who walked like a man was out there.

Kieran didn't know who, but he knew what. He knew why.

With the heel of his hand resting at her cheek and his fingers threading through her hair, he shielded her from prying eyes. From the eyes of a killer come to gloat and to feed on her horror and grief.

The cruel promise in Dinah Marks's death and discovery had gone awry and remained unrealized. Beau Anna hadn't found her as was intended. For now, her mind was too filled with concern for Times Two and Miss Emily to grasp the full import of the daring theatrics.

Kieran had. Kieran knew. He understood.

But you won't have her, he vowed, to himself and to the watching monster. You'll never do to Beau what you've done to Dinah and the young women before her. So gloat. Feed on her fear. Thrive on her grief. "This is all you'll have."

Stirring at the sound of his voice, Beau stepped from his embrace, a questioning look on her ashen face.

"It was nothing, Beau," Kieran answered quickly, hoping to slide by with pat answers. "Thinking out loud."

"About Dinah?"

"Yes." For once, not quite a lie.

With the back of a shaking hand, in a habit he'd come to recognize, Beau smoothed back her hair. "I'm sorry I fell apart. You must think I'm a weakling."

"There's nothing to be sorry for, and you're as far from a weakling as anyone I know." Letting his voice rise a decibel, hoping the excuse for a human still waited and listened in the shadows, he spoke in a low snarl. "Only something inhuman wouldn't be sickened by this."

"But I should deal with it and not involve you." She was struggling for composure, regaining it inch by agonizing inch.

"I volunteered, I'm already involved. I'm going to stay involved. You're not in this alone, Beau. First there was Tabby, and now there's me. No matter what comes of this, we'll deal with it. The three of us."

As she absorbed his words, she watched him, judging him. Exquisitely aware of every nuance, hearing the minute inflections in his speech. In his seething rage, she'd discovered startling changes.

But were they changes? Should she be surprised that where there had been laughter, now there was fury? Was it startling that when she'd expected a dilettante, the man who came to Moon Dancers Island was a man of substance?

It seemed right that it was he who dealt with Times Two, then with Dinah. In the beginning, she hadn't realized how taxing and dreadful that responsibility had been. But she remembered the anguish on his face, as he moved from seeing to medical help for Times Two, to Dinah. Taking charge. Taking care. Touching nothing. Seeing that nothing was disturbed.

Then, most telling of all, loath to leave her alone as she'd been in the last awful moments of life, he'd waited with Dinah.

When the deputy arrived from the mainland, the report he'd given was concise, to the point. He was an investigator, preserving evidence was the nature of his work. Accompanying death was not. Now Beau saw the toll the night had taken. "Why would you do this?"

"Why would I not?"

Beau held his gaze. "I don't know."

"I think you do. I think you've known from the first. As I have." He smiled. Only a twist of his lips that left his eyes untouched. "But we'll leave that for another time."

The humming of night creatures surrounded them, as he took her arm. "You're exhausted. It's time I took you home."

Beau went with him. Her thoughts were too full of hurt and tragedy to resist. In the deepest recesses of her mind, there was Kieran, kind and caring, irresistibly charming. And—even as she drew strength and courage from him—a threat to a heart she meant to hold inviolate.

The way from the village was not long and soon the path began to climb. The slight rise from which the Cahill home took its name was unique among the barrier islands. Yet hardly a true bluff. Even so, it set the expanse of land apart.

Creating an arresting scene as the old Southern manor, walls of brick and pink tabby rose grandly out of the dissipating fog.

Kieran had caught glimpses of it as he moved around the village. But nothing prepared him for Cahill's Bluff in shrouded moonlight. Charles Cahill had chosen wisely and built strongly. The hundreds of storms that had surely assaulted the island through the centuries, had done little but prove the manor's strength while washing it with a patina of antiquity.

"Good lord," Kieran exclaimed in low voiced appreciation. "It's no wonder you came home."

"When I was seventeen, I could hardly wait to leave," she admitted. "It wasn't long before I could hardly wait to return."

"Do you miss it?"

In control and calmer, with her mind and memories blessedly numb, Beau walked without speaking. When the path gave way to a shell covered drive, the sound and rhythm of their footsteps altered. "I don't miss Charleston, if that's what you mean. But if I should, it's no great feat to go in for a day, or an evening, or perhaps a weekend."

"What about your practice?" As he waited for her answer, he listened again to the night. But he knew there would be nothing amiss. The watcher had seen his fill, gloated his fill, and, engorged with human suffering, had left them.

They were alone before they left the bridge, long before they began the climb to Cahill's Bluff. "Do you miss using the skills you were years learning and perfecting?"

"Sometimes I do," Beau admitted. "I enjoyed the study, then the work. Best of all, I liked the children my practice centered around. And the sense that I was helping." Pausing, considering, she interjected, "But I have that here. So it isn't as if I left everything."

"Child psychologist, first mate, waitress, bartender, nursemaid, island chatelaine." His half smile was only a flash of white in his shadowed face. "Is there no end to your talents?"

Would lover be one? he wondered. Considering her familiarity with Heron's Walk, and the kiss the startlingly handsome Israel Johnson dropped on her head, it was possible. But, on a second thought that came swiftly, he knew it was unlikely Beau had a lover.

Kieran hadn't a clue why he was so convinced of it.

In a side glance, he watched as she skirted a small pothole with the skill of long practice. The slight of foot and hip was a guileless and intriguing move. Gracefully provocative without intention, as she considered his question.

"What other talents? You really want to know?" She laughed, and it was as if the horror of the evening hadn't happened. A lovely illusion.

"Yes." He discovered that his voice had grown husky as he thought of Beau with a lover. "I want to know."

He wanted to know everything. The simple things, the small pleasures that made her happy. The hurts and disappointments that made her sad. How she looked when she woke in the morning, and when she fell asleep at night. He wanted to know what she dreamed of, and wished for. He wanted to hear her laugh, without the shadow of waiting horror haunting it.

"A lot of what I do, I've learned out of necessity. I'm no artisan. Just a jack-of-all-trades who believes that for every problem there's a solution. If I try hard enough."

It was extraordinary, hearing his own philosophy reiterated in nearly his own words. But it shouldn't have been, considering how she felt about the island, and her people.

Matching the length of his step more carefully to hers, he walked closer. So close their arms brushed. "So tell me, Jack, what did you do today before you waited tables at the tavern?"

"Miss Emily broke her glasses."

"So you repaired them."

"All they required was the replacing of a small screw."

"But...?" He watched as she sidestepped another pothole, with equal agility. "I assume there's a qualification in this story."

"There's always a qualification when it involves Miss Emily. You should have seen how hard it was to find the little devil."

"She had no spares?" In the course of the evening, Kieran was learning that Times Two and Miss Emily were beloved friends and beloved nuisances.

"Nary a one." Beau spoke with exasperated amusement.

"Of course it couldn't be as simple as finding a single screw."

"Finding anything is never simple when Miss Emily's concerned."

As they moved higher the mist lay in layers, growing thinner at one turn, disappearing at another, only to thicken and deepen again around the next. Her silky blouse clung to her, weighted by collected moisture, but she didn't notice. "Miss Emily crochets. The house abounds with bags of tangled yarns of every color and description. She couldn't quite remember which afghan she was working on when her glasses broke."

"So you searched through the yarn."

"Eleven bags of it," Beau replied drolly.

"Sounds like fun."

"The kittens thought so."

She laughed, and in the sound of her laughter, Kieran heard again her patient affection for the disorganized Miss Emily and cantankerous Times Two. "How long did it take you to untangle them?"

"There are only three, thank heaven. Still I barely finished in time to report for duty at the tavern."

"A full day."

One that ended in tragedy.

With that unspoken reminder lying between them, the comfortable small talk ended. For a time they walked in utter silence, the crackle of shells under their feet all that marked their passage. Nearer the house, a cobblestone drive supplanted the rough path. Palmetto and longleaf pine gave way to dual lines of live oaks standing like sentinels along the way. Where there was sand and scrub, there were clusters of bushes, and beds of flowers, surrounded by lawns.

Passing beneath the oaks was like passing through a tunnel. Only moonbeams falling through clusters of leaves to lie like scattered tiles over the dark land, dispelled the illusion. The steps of the veranda loomed suddenly in their path. At the base of the stairway, Kieran took her arm.

This time she didn't stiffen or resist. As in sync as longtime dance partners, they climbed the dimly lighted stairs.

"I'd almost forgotten." Beau stopped at the top of the last step, facing him in the glow of a single lantern.

For one dreaded instant, Kieran worried that she was suffering the stings of conscience. That the short moment of forgetfulness would end in guilt and grief for Times Two and Dinah. But the smile that barely tilted the corners of her mouth eased that dread.

As his heart lifted, it would have been so easy to take her in his arms. To hold her, simply hold her. But, in the end, it wouldn't be enough, and it was too soon for more. Sliding his hand from her elbow and down her forearm, he clasped her fingers briefly.

Drawing in a breath filled with the intoxicating essence of the island and its mistress and something more, he asked, "What had you almost forgotten, sweet Beau?"

"What it's like to have someone watch over me." Her smile trembled, then steadied. "Someone who wants nothing, except to give comfort with small courtesies."

"What I've done, anyone would do. Especially for you."

Their bodies were almost touching, but with shadows stronger than the small light cloaking his face, she could only imagine the fine details of the planes and angles that had grown so familiar. He would be solemn now, as his keen gaze probed the murky darkness of the veranda. As he returned that same keen gaze to her, there would be small lines creasing his temples as his eyes narrowed in contemplation of what she'd said. With no smile flitting over his mouth, the dimple would be in hiding.

He was a vigilant, careful man. But there was a thoughtful gallantry leavening the wickedly delightful teasing. She'd seen it in Rick most of their lives, and watched women, young and old, fall under his spell. Until Kieran, she'd never understood this powerful and mesmerizing charisma.

If she stepped into his arms, he would hold her, and make her forget the ugliness that stalked an island that once was paradise. But what of tomorrow, when the real world encroached? How would she deal with the indiscretions of the night?

"No." One explosive word, rejecting her own needs. Succumbing to her private fears that the price of indiscretion would be too great, she repeated it. "No."

"No, there's no one who would watch over you? Or no, there's no one you would allow that privilege?"

Kieran's question, more observation than query, took her by surprise.

Into the fall of silence the scrape of a match over a balustrade sounded only a millisecond before it burst into fire.

As she was whirling in surprise, a steadying hand was on her shoulder. Before the unannounced visitor bent to the flame, Kieran was speaking, more to assure her, than in greeting. "Good evening, Mr. Johnson."

Israel touched the tip of his cigarette to the match, inhaled, then exhaled with a show of nonchalance. "I expected you would know I was here."

"I've known since we climbed the first step."

"What gave me away? Sixth sense? The prickling of the short hairs on the back of your neck?" Israel chuckled, but for Beau, his laughter rang false. Now that she knew he was there in the recesses of the veranda, she could make him out easily.

"Nothing so sophisticated." There was no responding edge in Kieran's reply.

"Oh?" Israel flicked away an ash as he lounged against the banister. His lanky body was completely relaxed. Completely at odds with his tone. "What was the telltale clue?"

"Your aftershave. It doesn't blend with the flowers or Beau's perfume. Or your mouthwash." There was no challenge in the reply, even in this verbal fencing.

Dismayed, not sure what was happening, Beau kept silent.

"I damn well hope I don't smell like a garden or a woman," Israel declared, the laughter in his voice real and unforced. "I spent a fortune on the stuff last time I was in the city."

"If you wanted subtle, take it back," Kieran drawled in an excellent imitation of Charlestonian intonations. "If it's a statement you want to make, your money was well spent."

"Too loud, huh?" Israel flicked the cigarette on the lawn.

"Too distinctive."

"I suppose so, if you recognized me by that alone."

"And the mouthwash," Kieran reminded.

"Yeah, sure, the mouthwash." Drawing a package from the breast pocket of his jacket, Israel shook out another cigarette. Match in hand, as if just struck by the thought, he muttered, "I could have been a stranger. Or the murderer."

Kieran's hand rested on Beau's shoulder, its position or pressure unchanging. Yet she found it a source of security.

"I knew you were no stranger, Johnson. If I'd believed you were intending murder, you wouldn't be alive."

Beau took his hand from her shoulder, feeling the loss even as she turned. "Kieran! What are you saying?"

It was Israel who answered in a drawl, but his choice was patois. "Don't be mad, sister-girl. What he's saying is that anybody who tries to do you harm will have to go through him." Moving from the murky shade of the veranda, the match lost, but the forgotten cigarette still dangling between his fingers, he draped an arm over her shoulder, and kissed the top of her head. "I appreciate that Mr. O'Hara feels that way."

"It sounded like a threat."

"Nah! Just a little man to man thing. One tough guy facing down another. You've seen Rick and Skip and me do it often enough when we're edgy about something, or just plain disagreeing. Tempers flare, but it don't mean spit." Israel hugged her and ruffled her hair. "But what if it was a threat? Anybody could be a suspect, right about now. Won't hurt for Mr. O'Hara to suppose and be extra cautious."

A little of the pretended drawl fell away as the blond man looked sharply over Beau's head. "That was supposition, wasn't it, Mr. O'Hara?"

"Purely."

The succinct response rankled with Beau, but Israel seemed satisfied. Releasing her, he backed away. "Since I came on a fool's errand, I'll leave you folks to the rest of your evening."

"Israel!" Beau called as he strode to the side steps of the veranda.

"Yes, ma'am, sister-girl?" Pausing, he made a bow that began eloquently then turned clumsy. "You wanted something?"

She took a step toward him, then realized what she'd been too distracted to notice. The mouthwash Kieran spoke of was bourbon. Israel had been drinking. Israel who never drank was only another drink away from falling down drunk. "Why did you come? How did you come?"

"By horse, of course." He laughed, inordinately pleased with his rhyme.

"Why?" Beau was aware that Kieran listened as intently as she. "What reason brought you here tonight?"

"Reasons. The word is plural, sister-girl." Two fingers wagged in the half light. "Two."

Holding in her impatience, Beau waited.

"I came to check on you. But Mr. O'Hara, here, had seen to that pleasant little chore quite nicely. Though why he would choose to bring you through the path with a murderer on the prowl..." Israel broke off abruptly. "Never mind, water over the sea."

"We came by the path because it's the shortest way, the way I wanted to come. And we're here, quite safely."

"That's what I said. Water over the sea."

"You sound like Times Two."

"Do I, sister-girl?"

"What was the other reason you came?" She spoke as if he were a dense child.

"To see about Rick, of course."

"Rick isn't here." The back of her hand pushing her hair away from her face was a barometer of her irritation quotient. "He won't be for several more days."

"Wasn't supposed to be, but he is."

"Who told you that?"

"Someone in the bar."

"Who?"

"Don't remember." Israel reared back. "What is this, twenty questions? Since when can't a man check on his friend to warn him? Never mind." He wheeled around giving them his back. "I see I wasted my time."

"Rick isn't here, Israel," Beau called after him.

Israel didn't slow or turn. Nor stagger as he took the path to the stables. Neither Beau nor Kieran moved until the staccato beat of hooves pounded across the backyard, and down a bridle path leading to the village.

"What was that about?" Kieran stood at her back. Not touching her. But never far away.

"I'm not sure about his attitude toward you. But the part about Rick goes back to the deaths of the other two girls." In the dark light her face was cast in shades of worry and regret. "In each case, Rick was away. Yet, someone circulated the rumor that he'd come, secretly, before the girl's death."

"Creating suspicion. Pointing the finger with gossip. Yet no one seems to know which denizen of the island professed seeing him."

"Typical small-town rumors. Just as typically, no one knows its origin, yet everyone hears it." But this rumor concerned her brother, and now three young women were dead. There was nothing typical about it. "I don't know what to make of any of it."

"Nor do I," Kieran admitted.

When she shivered, though he knew it was still not from the dampness, he drew her back against him. His arms crossed over hers, as he held her. "We'll find the reason. I promise."

Resting the back of her head on his chest, she looked down on the village. Lights were burning in most of the houses, but the tavern and shops were battened down for the night. No one had the taste for commerce or personal gain. In the wake of tragedy, it was better to spend the time with family and cherished friends.

Israel was a lifelong friend, yet he'd acted so strangely. "I don't know what came over Israel tonight."

"Don't you, Beau Anna?" Kieran's arms loosened slightly as he turned her to face him. He saw then that she hadn't any inkling what prompted Johnson's belligerence. "Part of it's that he's jealous."

"Of us?" What was she saying, there was no us. Kieran was fast becoming a trusted friend, but he would never be more. Even if she should want more, even if she was tempted in weak moments, she wouldn't allow it. She'd seen too many young girls and women fall in love with Rick when he hadn't intended it. When he'd only been teasing, or kind, or simply being himself.

He never meant to hurt anyone, yet, wherever he went, he left a string of broken hearts. She'd told herself in a constant litany that Kieran was the same.

In his own way, so was Israel. But he'd never turned his charm on her. "Israel and I grew up together. He thinks of me as a sister. He even calls me sister-girl. He always has. You're mistaken, his problem isn't jealousy."

"It's late. Too late to argue. If you'll be all right, I'll leave you to get some rest."

"I'll be fine and I won't be alone. The housekeeper will

be waiting up for me. Opal's run Cahill's Bluff like a staff sergeant for nearly fifty years. In that time she's never gone to bed before all in residence are home. That isn't about to change.''

"Then I'll say good-night.''

He looked at her so long she wondered again if he might kiss her. Yet, when he reached out to her, it was to turn her and march her to the door. Reaching past her, he turned the knob and pushed it open.

"Go.'' His voice was softly rasping. "Lock the door behind you.'' His fingers flexed around the bones of her shoulders. "We'll talk tomorrow.''

When she stepped through, before she could turn, the door had closed and Kieran's footsteps crossed the veranda and faded away.

Lingering by the door, she thought of Kieran and Israel and jealousy.

"Never.'' As she obeyed Opal's called edict that she must go to bed, she whispered again, "Never.''

Seven

The tavern was closed for the second day.

"It looks like a mausoleum." Israel's face was hard and angry.

"Shouldn't be much longer now." Abandoning his contemplation of the marsh bordering the Tea House, Skip Hayes contemplated his third best friend instead.

"The lucky thing for you, Israel, is that Jericho Rivers is in charge of the investigation."

"Our erstwhile quarterback, home from the big leagues, busted knee and all."

"Back and making a damn good lawman." Keeping a speculative look on Israel for a curious beat too long, Skip shifted his attention to the tavern. Investigators who had probed every inch of the building and gardens, were nowhere in evidence. "As good at sheriffing as football."

"We made him look good. You and I. If Rick had gone to the mainland high school before college, it would have been all over for Rivers."

Ignoring the caustic remark, Skip continued, "Maybe, but he made us look great. Did all right in the pros without us. It was his bad luck his knee blew, and our good luck he's back. You should appreciate that he's a meticulous investigator."

"How do you figure that?" Determined to wallow in his bad mood, Israel refused to credit anyone.

"Look." Skip gestured expansively. "Nothing's been disturbed. His men combed every inch, and the damn place looks like it was just spit shined."

"So he's neat."

The sarcasm made no dent in Skip's judgment. "He's careful and thorough."

"Yeah, yeah, I know," Israel groused. "But what are they looking for?"

"Clues, dummy. Dinah lived above the tavern. Maybe she knew this guy. Maybe there's something in her room, or her station in the dining room that could tell who he is."

"You keep saying he." Israel's hands flexed into fists. "What makes you so sure?"

Wondering why his friend was being deliberately obtuse, Skip sighed in exasperation. "I'm not sure. But Dinah was all over Rick last time he was here, and you, daily. So I don't think she was the type to slip out for a tryst with a woman."

Israel ignored the mild derision. "You think he lured her out to meet him?"

"Considering the medical examiner's report says she didn't have a swollen jaw, and likely not a toothache? Also, considering that at the tavern's busiest time, with the biggest tips, she skipped out? Yeah, that's what I think."

"Considering."

"Yeah, considering." Rocking back his chair, Skip held Israel in a coal black stare. "Man, you're in a bastard of a mood. Anybody's fair game, from Jericho right down to me."

"I know." Israel had the grace to look ashamed.

"Can't be the hangover."

"Thankfully my head has returned to normal size."

"What I can't figure is why our tavern keeper, whose stock-in-trade is that he doesn't drink, decided to tie one on."

"Try murder. It's not exactly good for business."

"Maybe not. But the other two didn't drive you to drink, and one worked at the tavern too. So why Dinah?"

"Cumulative effect. Or maybe I don't like Jericho and his posse poking in my personal things. I live over the tavern, too, you know."

"Lord love a gator, Israel! A woman is dead. *Another*

woman." Skip's tilted chair banged down. "Jericho's doing his job."

Israel glanced at his watch for the third time in as many minutes.

"What's with the watch? You're gonna wear it out looking at it."

Israel's shoulders moved sharply against the stylish cut of his tailored shirt. "What's keeping Beau?"

"Probably one of the hundred and one things she does before lunch each day." Skip rocked again, his heavy frame threatening the spindly chair. "She said twelve, so it will be twelve. You can set the clock by Beau. And call the police when she's late."

"If you haven't noticed, the police are already here."

"It isn't twelve yet," Skip reminded. "But, with the mood you're in, she'd do better to have lunch with someone else."

"Like pretty boy? What's his name?"

The chair tipped down. "His name's O'Hara, and he's an all right kinda guy."

Dragging a package of cigarettes closer, Israel looked up sullenly. "Thought you took a charter to Bermuda. When did you meet him?"

"This morning, down by the wharf. As we brought the *Island Lady* in."

"What was he doing there?"

"Just sorta nosing around. Getting a feel for the island."

"Was Beau with him?"

"Good grief, Israel! Since when are you so concerned with Beau and who she's seeing?"

"That's what I'd like to know." Breathless from rushing to their appointment, Beau threw an arm around the shoulders of each as she kissed stubbled cheeks. Taking the seat both stood, competing to draw out for her, she stared at first one, then the other. Then especially incredulously, at Israel. "Gentlemen?"

Folding her hands in a prayerful steeple, she regarded them over her fingers. "You're treating me like gentlemen? Instead of island brothers who spent their lives acting as if I were the fourth wheel on a three wheeled bicycle?''

Neither man had the usual response. But, if Skip's ebony skin could show it, Beau was certain there would be a flush of embarrassment. "Oh, forget it." With a wave, she sent them to their seats. "Sit down."

Once seated, Israel reached for the cigarette packet, remembered Beau wouldn't approve, then drew his hand away.

Skip grinned behind his hand. No one intimidated Israel, except Beau. For all his macho savoir faire, she'd been an inadvertent expert at it since childhood.

"How was the charter, Skip?" Beau was genuinely interested. Though he'd always been one of the gang, Skip's family had less than most. As a result, he was most driven to succeed.

"So good I could be looking at adding to the fleet." He grinned at this. The fleet of Island Charters consisted of one sloop, *The Island Lady*.

"You've worked hard for this. I'm proud of you."

Skip's grin softened to a smile. She'd been his chief rooting section since he and Israel were nine, and she and Rick were seven. "It's been a long, hard time coming."

No one knew that better than Beau. She'd spent some long, hard hours with him, ferreting out a problem with a stubborn engine. Or dealing with the hundreds of other obstacles that plagued him. Skip rarely complained. His way was to do, not talk.

Israel was the opposite. He stood back while the rest tackled a problem or a game. But he was always there, in the end. When Tabby called him the smart one, she didn't always say it as a compliment.

But Israel was good at what he did. As a boy, he was a strong leader, the one who instigated adventures, and planned projects. As overseer, he saw to it his plans were put into action. As an adult, applying those same talents, he became the consummate host, meeting people well. Captivating his customers completely. Until Rick was around.

In his drunken scene at Cahill's Bluff, Israel had painted his friends and himself with the same brush. A sweeping generality and wrong. Skip, the good-natured peacemaker, never competed on a petty level. His energies were focused on success. First in games, then sports, now the shoestring charter.

"When will you look for another craft?" she asked.

"Soon. But before that I need a captain and crew." He slanted a grin at Israel. "I offered the job to Izzy. Thought he might take a break from the tavern and work for peanuts. He turned me down."

"What did you expect?" Israel demanded, a modicum of gruff good nature returning. "I've been the Tom Sawyer in this group. The con-er, not the con-ee, thanks to my superior brain power. Why would I change now?"

"Why, indeed." Beau's thoughts returned to the evening when Israel was less in control and less like himself than she'd ever seen him.

"Joking aside," Skip continued around the jousting. "The business will be solvent. Another coupla trips like the Bermuda cruise, it could boom."

"Your dad would be proud. The first Hayes of Moon Dancers Island to own his own fleet of charters." Turning her attention to Israel, Beau studied him carefully. A muscle in his jaw tensed before she spoke. "You look better than the last time I saw you."

"Be glad you didn't see me the next day." His clenched teeth eased into a smile. "Not pretty."

"A hangover?"

"The mother of them all."

"Serves you right."

"Guess it does." Israel's hand snaked out to clutch at the cigarette pack. Like a worry stone, he spun it end over end, tapping it on the table. "I think I owe you an apology. But I'm not quite sure for what."

"You *think* you owe me?" Her tone scolded, questioning his choice of words.

"Okay. I know I do." The pack was still. Israel crushed it in his palm. "O'Hara too. If you see him, tell him."

"I think not."

"Why?" Israel scowled, unaccustomed to resistance.

"Because any apology you feel you need to make to him should come from you. The opportunity will present itself any minute. He's joining us for lunch."

"Joining us." The packet crumpled completely. "Why?"

"For lunch, Israel. Even mainlanders have to eat." Beau picked up his glass and sipped the juice he'd scarcely touched. "You've had a problem with Kieran from the time you met him."

"In the tavern," Israel admitted. "But the problem wasn't O'Hara. I was short staffed. What with Cookie stabbing his hand and the dining room filled to capacity, I was distracted."

"Were you distracted at The Bluff?"

Israel touched the rim of his glass, stroking a fingertip where her lips had touched. "I wish distracted was the word. My head wouldn't have ached so from distraction. My secret's out. I don't drink, because I can't. I found out in college that after a few sips I'm out of it."

"So you drank a sip to block out the memory of what happened to Dinah. Then, you leapt on your horse and rushed to rescue me from..." Beau lifted her palms in annoyance. "From what?"

"I'm not sure I was rescuing you from anything. I just didn't think you should be walking about in the dark after a murder."

"How else would I get home?" There were no automobiles on the island. Most islanders walked or rode horseback. Those who couldn't walk or ride puttered about in golf carts. There were a few small ATVs, and Jobe, the enterprising bootlegger, rode a tractor. Beau preferred walking or riding horseback. "If there had been trouble I would rather be afoot than in a cart."

"Afoot with a strange man. For all you know, he could be the killer."

"Israel!" Beau grew more irritated with his determination to be negative. "What's with you? You've never acted this way. Not even when the first girl was murdered."

"Rick isn't here, so someone has to look after you."

Skip laughed at that. "Someone to take care of Beau, because Rick isn't here? Are you sober yet? Rick's never here. And Beau's the one who looks after all of us. Including you. Who did you call when you came up shorthanded? Who did I call when the last engine problem stumped me? Who finally repaired the sail on the brig?

"The answer is the same to all of the above." The ice in Skip's lemonade chattered as he spun the glass in small circles. Looking up, his eyes narrowing, he muttered, "If I didn't know better, Izzy, I'd think you were jealous."

There it was again. But Beau knew nothing could be further from the truth. "Whatever your reason for the other night, if you feel you owe Kieran an apology, make it. If not, don't."

There would be no apology, because Israel wasn't truly feeling particularly apologetic. But there was no time to ponder this strange behavior of Israel Johnson.

"Beau." Kieran's shadow fell over her. As she tilted her face toward him, the familiar unfocused look flitted over her eyes and a frown creased her forehead. The first eased in the millisecond required for her eyes to adjust. The frown was slower to fade. Something was troubling her. "Have I come at a bad time?"

"Of course not. You were invited, after all."

"Then I hope you won't mind that I brought a second guest." With a half turn, he indicated a man who stood a few feet apart.

"Jericho!" Beau exclaimed.

Jericho Rivers was lean, hard, a goliath. Part French, part Scot, with strong traces of American Indian attested by his coloring, and all gentle stoic. He wore an air of utter calm, and never seemed to hurry, even when he did. As he closed the space between them, his gray gaze was steady, passing with penetrating scrutiny over Israel and Skip. His nod to old friends and teammates was curt. The broad brim of his standard issue Stetson shaded his face for a considering moment, even as he swept it from his head.

When he turned to Beau, the smile that should have been completely at odds with his hard features, was genuine. A wide, gold band flashed on the third finger of his right hand as he folded her hand in his. His voice was deep, as with a nuance of affection, he murmured, "Hello, little girl."

Skip grinned at the endearment recalling a camaraderie of the past. Israel scowled. As he took a seat by Beau, neither attitude escaped Kieran.

Lunch, he decided, should prove interesting.

"So?" Kieran pushed his cup away. "What do you think?"

He'd listened and observed through the stilted meal. Now that they were alone, he wanted Beau's perspective.

"About Jericho's meeting, or Israel's manners?" She was more than weary of a day only half over.

"Skip's no problem." Assessing her mood, and abandoning his original purpose, Kieran addressed an easier issue. "Making waves doesn't appear to be his style."

"He's never difficult. And, of the four of us, he's had it hardest."

"Skip's life was different from yours and Rick's, or Israel's?" Not an idle question. There was one single clue somewhere, the first thread of the whole cloth that would lead to the killer. Perhaps it would be something tangible. Perhaps, only a word. In Kieran fashion, he would hear every word, study every path.

"Tell me how." His subtle demand softened into query. "Economics? His station in the island hierarchy?"

Beau smiled wanly. "It was never anything like that. None of that matters on the island. The Cahills were planters. The

Johnsons, innkeepers. The Hayes, shrimpers. All valuable within the island community. But Skip's father was special. Mine swore Dugan Hayes was the best shrimper on the east coast.

"Even with phenomenal skills shrimping was a hard life. Too hard for Skip's mother. One day, while Dugan was away and Skip was playing with the rest of us, Amanda took their baby daughter and left the island."

"Dugan tried to find her?"

"Of course. So did my father. But she literally disappeared. After a time, realizing they were alone and always would be, father and son did the best they could. With moral support and a little help from friends, they prospered and moved forward. At that point, little had changed for Skip. Then, when he was eleven, there was a freak accident. Dugan was injured and paralyzed from the waist down."

"An accident aboard ship?" Working the nets was far more dangerous than many understood. After a life with a family that loved the sea, Kieran understood it well.

Beau looked out over the marsh, at the wharf with flocks of gulls wheeling and strafing, hoping to cadge an easy meal from a newly docked shrimper. The day Dugan was carried from his boat to the wharf was burned indelibly in her mind. Israel, Skip, Rick and she were playing at the water's edge, and she could remember, as clearly as then, how still Dugan had been. How like a broken doll he was with his dark skin turned pasty gray. "A winch went haywire. His foot caught in the rope. The lever smashed across his spine severing it."

"An injury that could have been fatal."

"It nearly was. He was in hospitals and rehab for a long time. When all was done that could be, he concentrated on building the strengths he had left. Then he returned to shrimping, going out everyday. No matter the weather, no matter how bad he felt.

"Skip became his legs, helping on the boat while the rest of us were still playing pirates and Indians. When it came time to go away to high school, so that he would, Dugan left the boat and the life he loved to set up shop as a mechanic.''

''Skip couldn't stay and study on the island?'' Kieran knew the answer, but he wanted to hear the story with Beau's sentiments.

''He could have. There was a small school here, and private study provided by my father.''

''But he didn't stay.'' A statement, not a question.

''Neither did Israel, though he chose the mainland school because he was feeling restless and caged in by island life. Skip would have stayed for his dad's sake if he'd been allowed. But Dugan had different plans and ambitions. He wanted college and a safer life for Skip. The only way was a scholarship in sports or academics. Something best achieved through the public school system.''

''So, Skip and Israel went away to the mainland.'' Kieran let the observation hang, encouraging Beau to continue. As he waited, he watched the sun tangle in her hair, proving that black was never truly only black, but a matter of degree and shades.

She seemed distracted by her memories. After a time, Kieran asked, ''What happened to Dugan? He must have been terribly lonely.''

''I'm sure he was, but not completely. He never lacked for business or company. Much to my stepmother's distaste, Rick and I became his shadow. Pirates and Indians was replaced by playing mechanic. We mucked in grease and oil and engine parts for hours on end. How they worked fascinated me more than Rick. Dugan was patient and welcomed my curiosity. It didn't matter that I was a girl. Best of all, none of Fionna's protests swayed him.''

Fionna, a name woven into the fabric of Beau Anna's life. But, Kieran had come to realize, an entity without substance.

Yet, with a single act of desertion, Fionna Elliot Cahill, Beaumont's wife of convention, had shaped all their lives. Tabby had shown him the photos of Beau and Rick, and described the startling physical resemblance between the arrogant and pretentious wife and Anna Bonnet. Thus it was that half bother and sister born only hours apart, were often mistaken for fraternal twins.

From that same elderly fount of information, he knew that though she'd come in the aftermath of a killing hurricane, though she played the forgiving lady of grace, bearing gifts of food and clothing and precious supplies for rebuilding, Fionna returned to Moon Dancers Island out of jealous greed. Ensconced by rights of Beaumont's legitimate son, for the next six years she used the boy as a weapon in her campaign to have Beau disowned and sent away. Her rage and spite increased when Beaumont turned a deaf ear to her haranguing, having Beau Anna declared a legitimate heir, sharing an equal part of Cahill's Grant.

It was Rick who finally defied her. Becoming from that day, the son to Beaumont he'd longed to be. Beau, who had loved him from the distance Fionna decreed, loved her half brother all the more.

As he'd listened to Tabby, Kieran waited for some hint of darker purpose or jealousy creeping into the brother–sister relationship. There was never any. Though he knew from his own brothers and sisters such complete and selfless loyalty was possible, he recognized its singularity. And reserved judgment until the day the wayfarer came home.

On that day he would see for himself what sort of man Rick Cahill had become. He would know if a threat to Beau lay beneath the much beloved wit and charm of her brother.

He would know, Kieran swore. He must.

"Kieran?" His name was like a siren's song drawing him from his thoughts.

"Sorry." Rousing from his concerns, he returned to the subject of Dugan Hayes. "In your curiosity you became his student. In his patience he became your teacher."

"That's exactly how it was when he saw the fascination was real. Together we discovered I had an ear for the aberrant sound in a failing engine, and the gift of diagnosis. The relationship was good for all of us. Even Rick, though the engines never fascinated him as they did me.''

"How was it good?"

Beau looked at him in surprise. "We missed Skip and Israel. In finding a common interest, we closed the void their absence left.''

"I assumed they would only be away from the island for the five school days, then return for the weekend. That wouldn't be so long.''

"That's how it was in the beginning. But those days seemed like forever, and the weekends were minutes.'' Beau folded her hands on the table, a gold bracelet Kieran hadn't seen glinted in the sun.

A gift from an admirer he didn't know?

Something stirred inside him. Something he wasn't ready to acknowledge. A peculiar circumstance for Kieran the imperturbable. Yet, if he were honest with himself, a lot had perturbed him since he'd come to the island. Most of it centered on this fascinating woman.

"As they grew more acclimated to the mainland, the schedule changed. With neither coming home more than once a month,'' Beau explained. "The school curriculum was demanding, there were extracurricular activities, sports, girls, parties. In Skip's case, a weekend job. We felt cut off from them all over again.''

"In this sojourn on the mainland, did either find what he wanted?''

"Both did. Israel got a taste of the world and learned that he wanted to have it both ways, dividing his time on the island with long visits to the mainland. Skip got his scholarships for college.''

"Scholarships.'' Kieran waved away a hovering waiter. Without missing a beat, he queried, "Meaning more than one?''

"Meaning one of each, for academics and for football.'' The bracelet glittered as she moved her glass absently. "Never one to let Skip outdo him, Israel, who was a good student in high school, became better in college. He even played football as a walk-on. That's when they met Jericho. For the remainder of their college years, he spent as many weekends on the island as the mainland. We were five, rather than four.''

Beau pushed the glass away. ''When I was seventeen, almost eighteen, I had a flaming crush on him. Jericho Rivers was everything I thought a man should be. But he never noticed me.''

Among the photographs Tabby had displayed over glasses of merlot, were a number of Beau and Rick when they were seventeen and radiantly stretching their wings. Kieran doubted Jericho Rivers, or any young red-blooded stud had ever been so blind.

''Speaking of Jericho, it's almost time.'' Casting a glance at the sun, he knew they were only minutes away from the appointment Jericho requested. More than an hour had passed since he, Skip, and Israel had departed, each claiming some matter needing attention. In this hour of quiet conversation, Kieran counted not a minute wasted. In his quest against the impossible, he believed there was something to be learned from every contact and conversation.

Today he'd learned much about Skip Hayes, and nothing of Israel Johnson. He found it curious that all of Israel's relationships and communication were with his young friends. Yet he had a family, one strongly connected to the history of the island. It was common knowledge that he was a direct descendant of the enterprising young man who had claimed the derelict building that ultimately became the historic tavern. Yet the Johnsons who came after the canny rum-runner, and before Israel, were shadowy figures. Unremarkable men and women, without substance.

The Johnsons, a family cloaked in mystery? Island misfits? Or simply, truly unremarkable? Questions, added to the mental list running like a tab in Kieran's head, to be addressed another day.

Jericho waited.

"Shall we?" As he offered his hand, he found himself anticipating the touch of hers. In his palm her fingers were cold from the icy glass. When he tucked them at the bend of his elbow and left his to rest over them, her face filled with pleasure in the simple courtesy.

She was surrounded by people who relied upon her, who trusted her to fulfill their needs. Yet beyond Tabby and the housekeeper, none understood that the strongest among them needed someone to watch over her.

The islanders loved her. Many of them gone to ground, and anonymous. Some of them he knew—Tabby, Times Two, Miss Emily, Skip.

The faceless Norrie Candler.

The somber, watchful Jericho.

But for someone that love was a lie.

Kieran's eyes were cold as his gaze swept the deserted street. Nothing stirred but a dust devil whirling over the unpaved surface. There was no sound, but the creak of a john boat tied by the Tea House dock. Even the raucous gulls had fallen silent. In the glittering hush, weathered buildings hunkered in the sandy soil. With splashes of brightly painted shutters and doors worn like festive jewels, the village could have been a pastoral still life of a lazy afternoon by the sea.

But, Kieran sensed an aura of malaise as palpable as the beat of his heart. Where there had been alarm, now there was unchecked terror.

Murder on the beach in the secrecy of isolation was fearsome, yet peculiarly removed. Now the killer had brought his lurid violence into the village. Though there was no diminishing the lonely, hidden deaths of Carol and Alice, Dinah's body sprawled in the crook of a common pathway, rather than secreted in that sandy darkness, violated the sanctuary of both the village and the mind.

Islanders were not strangers to death. They lived with it all the days of their lives. The wrath of the sea, the hurricane, the tsunami, wild creatures, the vagaries of fate, all of them had killed. It was the rare islander who had not lost family, friend, or lover to one.

Death was neither easy nor tolerable by any emissary. But none was so horrific as senseless, needless death meted by the hand of man. None sucked the life from the village itself, none desecrated, as his cruelty.

A village that should be thriving and alive lay deserted and mute as sunlight poured down in beams of gold. As their brilliance sought out every shadow in every crevice, even rich velvet puddles of shade lying beneath ancient oaks bleached to murky gray.

Heat lay like an invisible banner over chimney caps and rooftops, and distant thunder rumbled in a clear sky. As with the threat of storm, there was a sense of waiting, of foreboding and dread.

While Kieran led Beau from the veranda to walk along the boardwalk and by the wharf, she was quiet. Too quiet. The same quiet as the frightened village.

When they stepped from sunlight to the shadows of a channel of oaks, Kieran stopped her. "You're worried," he said as she looked up. "Don't be. Jericho won't ask more of you than you can give."

"I'm not a profiler. I can't look at a clue and tell him the murderer is left-handed and his mother made him what he is by forcing him to use his right." Breaking off, she frowned. "Forgive me, this isn't the time to be facetious."

"Or frightened?"

Her eyes burned like feverish pools that even shadow couldn't ease. She looked away, afraid of what he might see. "I'm a child psychologist. One who hasn't practiced in years. I don't know what Jericho wants from me. What if there's something I should know, something I should see and understand…and someone dies because I…"

"Shhh." Framing her face in his palms, he turned her gaze to his. "Jericho isn't asking you to be clairvoyant. He wants your insight, your knowledge of the island and its people.

Forget the psychology, forget profiling. For what it's worth he has access to the best in the world.''

"For what it's worth?"

"We've talked, your sheriff and I. Neither of us believe the murderer will fit any profile." Neither did Simon and the wealth of experts he'd called in. "Just listen to what Jericho has to say."

He stroked the length of her hair, his hands wandering over her shoulders to her throat. Lacing his fingers at her nape, with his thumbs at her chin he tilted her head a bit further. "Will you do this, Beau Anna? For Jericho? With me?"

Tensing at the last, she muttered, "No." Yet even to her own ears there was no spirit in the denial. As he held her, soothing the taut muscles at her nape, she wondered where dedication had gone. Where was the resolve that she wouldn't fall beneath his charm? Where the strength she needed to deny him?

"Why?"

His single word of question for her single word of denial. One that left her needing to think, and reevaluate her faltering convictions. She would have stepped back, if he allowed it. But had he really stopped her? If she truly wanted to move from his touch, would he keep her?

No.

Yet she was still within his reach. His hands still caressed her throat. What that said of her, sent her reeling, with every tenet that formed her relationships with men lying in ashes.

"Beau?"

Her name, a gentle question, she couldn't refuse. "I can't."

"Because you're afraid?"

"Yes." Truth was easiest.

"Of me."

She wanted to deceive, but her lips would form neither sound, nor syllables of the lie. "Not of you," she confessed raggedly. Her eyes were dark, unfathomable, never leaving his face. "Of myself and…"

"And?"

A steady look held his, the longing she couldn't speak, eloquent in their smoky depths.

"Beau." His voice was nearly lost to him. "I've promised I won't hurt you."

"Don't," she whispered, quieting covenants she didn't need. "I know."

She did. She had. Always.

Tentatively she touched his face, her fingertips learning the strong, hard planes. Her silver contemplation believing, trusting, needing the kindness, the tenderness of Kieran O'Hara.

As foolish, rigid rules guarding her heart shattered, with her own promise of never forgotten, she stepped into his arms. Sighing as she came to a place of rest and peace, she bowed her head to his shoulder.

"Sweet heaven," Kieran managed in a strangled voice.

He'd wanted this. Since he saw her clambering over the rigging of the brigantine, he'd wanted her. As her body curled into his with the tension of days and weeks easing from her, consuming desire raged white-hot. Desire that would be answered, but must wait for another day. Another time.

Contenting himself with that, he held her, comforting her. With her yielding body saying more than any words, he bent to take a kiss.

One kiss.

In it the promise of heaven.

Eight

In quaking splendor, the sun lifted from the sea. Flooded in the merciful forgiveness of first light, morning promised a perfect day.

The air was fragrant with the scent of flowers. Birds chattered among tree and shrub. Ribbons of moss glittered in slanting sunlight like sturdy cobwebs. And beyond the bluff, the sandy shore sprawled toward sea and sky, melding into an endless horizon.

"The edge of forever."

"What's that?" Allowing no time for Beau to reply, as Opal set a breakfast tray on a table by the open door she demanded, "What do you mean, sitting at your dressing table, moping, talking to yourself?"

Beau reached for her brush. Drawing it through her hair, she turned a half-focused stare to the mirror. Remembering the housekeeper waited for an answer, she paused, the brush at her shoulder. "Just thinking aloud, Opal."

"Humph." With a huffing breath sending a hennaed shock of hair from her forehead, Opal prepared for lecture number one of the day. "Thinking! You do too much of it. You need to forget the folderol of the island and have yourself a holiday."

"Murder isn't folderol, Opal. How can I take a holiday..."

"Never said it was."

"...when I'm needed here," Beau finished as if the housekeeper hadn't interrupted. Which was the only way to get in a word when the older woman launched into a lecture.

"This island won't sink into the sea if you aren't here.

Besides, if I know Jericho Rivers, which I have since he was a babe of twenty, he has things in hand.''

"Anyone under fifty is a babe to you, Opal. When I met with Jericho last week, he had nothing to have under control.''

"You met with Jericho?'' Opal advanced to stand at Beau's back. "He isn't trying to involve you in this, is he? Lord knows, you have enough on your plate. What's more, you'll have more to do when the carnival begins.''

"If there is a carnival.'' The brush tangled in snarled curls. Beau winced as she tugged it through.

"Let me do that.'' Opal took the brush to begin a ritual of Beau's childhood. "Haven't done this in a time.''

"Not since I was thirteen.''

"The very day you turned thirteen,'' Opal interjected. "The day you decided to be Miss Independent.''

"You had spoiled me.''

"Can't spoil someone who don't take to it.'' The brush glided, turning an unruly cloud to midnight silk. "You always had to do for everyone, but let no one do for you. Miss Independent, holding yourself apart. Never letting anyone close, 'cept your daddy and Rick, and Tabby.''

Beau caught her hand. "And you. You and Tabby were my mother's substitute.''

Clasping the hand that held hers, Opal blustered, "Someone had to see the lady Fionna's neglect didn't turn you into a wild creature.''

Beau laughed, remembering how she and Rick ranged the island, dressed as little castaways. Each a black haired copy of the other, daring the devil, trusting in their own security. Spending happy days exploring, loving the land that was theirs.

"Not completely wild,'' she qualified for this elderly Scots woman, who was as much an institution on Cahill's Bluff as Tabby.

"Carefree,'' Opal grumbled, and the brush began again the hypnotic strokes. "You were carefree.''

In that statement Beau heard the pride neither Opal nor Tabby succeeded in hiding when a slip of a girl with only boys for friends could best them in all but strength. Rick was proud of her competence. Skip, completely unthreatened. Israel never liked to be bested by anyone. When Jericho entered their circle, with his more mature perspective, he was amused by the friendly rivalry. Above all, kind and tolerant.

"Not an easy task for you or Tabby, standing guard, seeing to it that an unwanted child was happy."

"Unwanted." The brush clattered to the table. "You were never unwanted. Your dad loved you enough for your mother and himself." Thin lips drew down. "Which only set some folk harder against you."

"Some? No," Beau corrected. "One. Fionna."

"'Twas enough, with her constant nattering at your dad to put you aside in sole favor of Rick. Trying to turn Rick against his own father, when he refused. The day Beaumont made you a legal Cahill, this house nearly went missing a roof."

"In a way, I can understand her hatred. Having to tolerate the child of her husband's lover."

"Anna was his only love," Opal's tone softened as remembered anger faded.

"Which made the situation worse. My father loved another woman. I'm proof Fionna lived with every day."

"Don't be so magnanimous defending the grand Fionna that you forget she left her husband the day after their wedding. Your papa thought to give her some time. Then, when he went to her weeks later, asking her to return, did she tell him about the baby she was carrying? Nosiree! She let him come home thinking he would spend the rest of his life alone." Opal's face was stern. "Tabby and I had some rough days. Then Anna came, defying her father and every tenet of her world."

"For a while he was happy," Beau added to the story. "Anna made him happy."

"Longer than a while." Opal ran a gnarled hand down the

shiny mane she'd put into rare order. She'd missed this morning ritual. "Anna left him the lasting gift of her love."

"He did love me." Gray eyes bright with unshed tears met Opal's gaze in the mirror.

Surreptitiously scrubbing a hand over her face, Opal crossed to the table. Picking up the tray, she paused, caught in nostalgia. "My goodness, yes, he loved you. More than anyone."

"Except Rick."

Opal hesitated, but only to remember Rick, sturdy and winsome as a child, growing strong and handsome as a man. "Except your brother."

"Poor Rick," Beau murmured. For the first six years of his life, he'd been kept from her. As if she were unclean. But she never resented the boy she saw as her mirror image. Instead she'd pitied the energetic child kept prisoner by hate. She missed him in her life, and longed to have him be truly her brother. "Hate does strange things. Fionna loved him, yet she made his life as miserable as she tried to make mine."

"Until the Cahill asserted itself in the boy, and he realized what was being done." Taking a plate from its warmer, Opal set it on the table. "The day he chose to become a full-fledged Cahill, defying his mother, refusing to be her weapon and her prisoner, was a grand day for all of us."

"The best for me." Abandoning the past, Beau watched Opal as she prepared the table. A twinge of guilt stirred, for the days she'd risen before dawn, denying the aged housekeeper this small pleasure. "I hope you brought enough for yourself. I can't remember how long it's been since we shared breakfast."

Opal set a second place. "Been a while. Too long a while."

Drawing her dressing gown closer, Beau stood. "Then I'm glad I indulged in a lazy morning."

"Humph!" Opal grunted in loving derision. "Never indulged yourself in your life. Never had a lazy day since you took your daddy's mantle. Would be more like this morning is the product of a sleepless night. I heard you prowling."

"I disturbed you." Beau was instantly contrite.

"Didn't disturb me." Napkins and silver joined crystal on the table. "When a body's as old as Methuselah, sleep ain't so necessary."

A crystal vase bearing a cluster of summer wildflowers was set with precise care in the center of the table, signaling the conversation wouldn't be pursued.

With the light of sunrise streaming through the open door, and the songs of birds as music, Beau joined Opal for a meal prepared by loving hands.

Glancing at a mantel clock, Beau slid back her chair. "That was wonderful, Opal. Gotta run."

"Not so fast, young lady." There was a stern note in the old voice.

"Sorry. Forgot my manners." With a bow in Opal's direction she added, "The manners you so meticulously pounded into my head." With laughter only in her eyes, Beau said in her most genteel voice, "If I may be excused, I must run."

"That's better." Opal's concern didn't ease as Beau hoped.

"But not better enough?"

"Your manners aren't the issue." Gnarled fingers patted the folds of a napkin. A troubled gaze lifted to Beau's. "You haven't explained what Jericho wants from you?"

That particular question, among other things, had contributed to Beau's sleepless nights. "I don't know. I'm not sure Jericho knows. As a psychologist, I'm no help to him. Understanding the criminal mind is hardly my field of expertise. At any rate, when it comes to profilers, he has access to the best in the world."

"So?"

"So." Beau pushed her chair into place. "I think he wants my input on our people."

"He wouldn't be planning something foolish like put you in danger."

"Jericho wouldn't do that. You know better, Opal."

"'Course I do. But what he considers danger and what I consider danger could be different. The same goes for you."

"Since I was six?"

"At least." Opal pursed her mouth, setting wrinkle upon wrinkle. "Always had to keep up with the boys, do them one better when you could." An edge of real worry crept into her voice. "Don't try to do one better in this."

"Wouldn't think of it. This isn't a game, lives are at risk. It scares me that I could do the wrong thing." Beau's gaze was drawn to the village lying quietly in the distance.

"The island has been the responsibility of the Cahills far more than a century. I'm a Cahill. One of the last. Frightened or not, I have to do what I can."

"There you go, taking the weight of the world on your shoulders."

"Not the world." Beau crossed to a closet. Throwing open a door, she pulled out a pair of jeans cut off below the knees. Next came a knit shirt, several sizes too large. One of Rick's discards. Looking at it, she frowned. "My fashion statement, not that anyone will notice."

Startled by her own cynicism, she didn't hear Opal until she repeated her comment a second time.

"Who needs help today?" The housekeeper was always grousing that many of the islanders who called on Beau saved the money that should have been spent on the salary of a hired hand. "Use you, they do. And will as long as you let them."

"I'm not being used so long as I do what I do willingly." Stepping behind a screen she called out, "It is willingly, Opal."

"Willingly, huh? Everything?"

"Of course."

The dressing gown was tossed over the screen. A night-gown of silk and lace followed as Opal asked slyly, "Even what Jericho has asked. Will you do that willingly? Catching a killer can be dangerous work. If this brute suspects you're after him, he might decide to get you first.''

The rustle of clothing ceased. The shape visible through the translucent *papier* stood immobile.

Opal waited.

''I'm frightened,'' Beau admitted. ''But not for myself. The women he's singled out have been so young.''

''I don't think you should view yourself as aged, or immune.''

Beau still hadn't moved. Her voice was tight with tension. ''If the killer wanted me, he could have taken me as unaware as anyone. I could have been first. Or second. That could have been me on the path, not Dinah.''

''So you think since you weren't first or second or third, you're safe?'' Opal folded her hands tightly in her lap. Possibilities she'd considered before loomed too real when spoken aloud. ''Do you think it's impossible that you could be number four?''

Beau was still for a long time. Then the shadow thrown against the screen moved jerkily, a puppet at the mercy of a bungling puppeteer. From a nether region beyond the sienna *papier,* she drew a tiny garment and slipped it over her head.

A camisole with lace as delicate as an evening mist. Opal knew it would smell of white flowers. Lilies, roses, gardenias she dried herself, then scattered through closets and chifforobes.

''I know it could be any of us, Opal.'' The strain remained in Beau's voice.

''Then you will be careful?''

''I promise.''

''Where will you go today?''

''Skip is dropping a new motor in the *Island Lady.* I promised to help.''

''Borrowing your ear?'' Opal took up the tray. She would leave the flowers Beau loved.

''So to speak.''

"Where will you go?" Glasses clinked against china as the old woman walked to the door.

The figure behind the screen slipped the oversize shirt over her head. "We won't go farther than the point, in case there's trouble."

"Then dinner at seven sharp shouldn't be a problem?"

"Can't see why not?" With the buzz of a zipper the truncated jeans settled on narrow hips. Opal had never been particular about serving dinner to the minute. Beau wondered why she would be now. Stepping from the screen, fully dressed except for shoes, Beau commented, "Seven's fine. But why sharply?"

"Because I don't want our guest to be kept waiting."

"Our guests?" Beau was searching for shoes she'd misplaced again.

"Guest," Opal emphasized. "One."

The housekeeper was more family than employee. It bothered no one that she often invited one or the other of the islanders to the Cahill table. Times Two and Miss Emily were frequent guests. So were Skip and Israel. Tabby came at least once a week. Sometimes Beau joined them. Sometimes she was away attending a stubborn problem.

"Will it matter if we hit a snag and I miss dinner?"

"Of course it matters." Opal's gaze moved over the young woman she would always consider her own special person. "I forget how much like your mother you are."

Beau laughed and lifted her arms, letting the shirt drape like angel's wings. "I doubt my mother wore castoffs."

"Oh but she did. When she was small, she liked nothing better than running about in one of your dad's old shirts she'd confiscated. The best part, she always declared, was that they smelled and felt like him."

"She was in love with him that long ago?"

"First she loved him. Worshiped him, more like. Then she fell in love."

"It's a beautiful story, like a fairy tale." Beau had whiled away many sultry afternoons, listening to Opal or Tabby tell of her mother and father.

"If your daddy could see you now..." Opal broke off, her gaze suspiciously watery, her nose as red as her hair. Clearing her throat, she glowered at Beau as if she were six and had been naughty. "What time are you to meet Skip?"

Reading Opal's signal that the subject was closed, Beau dutifully followed her lead. "Less than half an hour."

The shoes were discovered hiding under the bed. Beau slipped her feet past untied laces. "I should be out of here in five minutes to be on time."

"See that you're on time tonight. Soufflé for dinner!"

"Your seafood soufflé?" Beau grinned. A rare sight in the weeks since the murders began. "Who is this guest anyway?"

"The new young man staying at Norrie's place. The one whose pictures are in the magazine you keep in the nightstand. I met him at the open air market the other day."

Beau stopped tying her shoe. "You invited Kieran to dinner?"

"At seven. Unless you want rubber soufflé."

"You could start without me," an unsteady voice suggested.

"Could! But won't." Black eyes flashed at Beau and she was a little girl all over again. "Seven, Miss Cahill."

Sighing, she agreed, "Seven."

"Wear your prettiest dress." The door banged shut.

Beau stared at the paneled facade. "Dinner," she muttered. "Tonight."

She hadn't seen Kieran since the day they'd met with Jericho. The day he'd kissed her.

"I haven't been avoiding him." Her fingers were clumsy. The knot refused to stay. "I just haven't made an effort to see him." Standing, she bent before the mirror. Destroying Opal's handiwork, she dragged her hair from her face and banded it with a dare that it escape.

"Seven." She lectured the slant-eyed woman who glared

back at her. "Seven sharp, if I can decide which is my prettiest dress."

The clock in the hall was striking the same hour when she bounded down the stairs. A different seven, thank God. One not so fraught with concern. Avoiding the foyer mirror, considering it an unnecessary reminder of how little like the island chatelaine she appeared, she dashed from the house.

"I won't worry about it." Yet as she hurried to meet Skip, thoughts of the evening loomed in her mind.

Her dress was scarlet. A demure little scrap when folded among the gold tissue of the gift box that arrived the week before. But on the human body, it became a metaphor of provocative grace and sultry elegance. With each move and gesture, it reeked quietly, but unmistakably of the delights of sex and sin.

But Beau hadn't bothered to notice as she dashed home late, offering her scolding housekeeper the valid excuse of engine trouble aboard the *Island Lady*. After a quick shower, she was simply grateful that Opal had spared her the trouble of making a decision by laying out the latest creation Rick had sent her from whatever country he was currently roaming. As a rule, she deemed his choices better suited to his lady loves than to his rather staid sister. This time, Beau was quite pleased to see he'd chosen with rare restraint.

In her hurry, she slipped into a matching teddy, tossed the narrow crimson column over her head, smoothed it down her body, and tackled her hair. Still damp from the scrubbing she'd given it to remove stubborn sea spray, there was no hope for it but to pin it up. A quick twist and an ebony pin anchored it at her crown.

An impulse...something...had her pausing before the mirror, reaching for her skimpy supply of makeup. A sweep of kohl across her eyelids, a smudge beneath, a touch of glossy lip stain, and she was done.

If she'd spared time for the woman in the mirror, she would have seen a siren, a beguiling witch, with her complexion darkened and rose tinted, while shadowed eyes glittered like silver diamonds from a face framed by drying curls.

A master of makeup and coiffeur couldn't have created a more alluring creature. Nor one so unaware, as she went to greet Opal's guest waiting in the drawing room.

She saw him as she stepped from the last riser and crossed the foyer. With his back to the room, he gazed out an open French door that offered a wild panorama. A view she'd loved all her life. But tonight her attention was riveted on the man who constantly filled her thoughts.

Tonight she noticed that during his stay on the island, his hair had grown to the collar of his jacket and fell into attractive disorder. Wondering if anything about him was not attractive, she imagined how it would be to brush the black mane into order with her fingertips, and watch as it fell again into tempting disarray.

Realizing the foolishness of her fancy as he moved from the doorway, she set it firmly aside. Stepping into the room, she greeted him, quietly, "Good evening, Kieran."

Her voice, husky and tentative, summoned him from his study of an astonishing collection of leather-bound books. That they had been well read over the years was evident. As he faced her, Kieran wondered which were her favorites.

"Beau Anna." His bow was only a nuance of the gallantry she'd come to expect. "It was kind of you to invite me to dinner."

It was on the tip of her tongue to tell him the invitation was Opal's, but a good look at him tied her tongue.

Kieran had dressed for dinner. If the dark jacket and trousers paired with a silver paisley vest didn't truly constitute formal wear, it did one better. The word casual elegance had always flown over her head, leaving her wondering what it could possibly be. Now she knew.

His shirt was pale gray, with a black stud at the collar. His time on the island had darkened his skin and burnished his hair with a hint of light. His eyes were impossibly blue, and the look in them swept the strength from her knees.

"Opal and I are glad that you could come." She managed the welcome with the aplomb taught her. Now she looked back gratefully on what had been repetitious drudgery.

Minutes ago, the socially correct welcome would have been a lie. Now she had no idea what it was. To silence the chaos of her thoughts, she crossed to the bar. "Would you care for a drink?"

"Not tonight." A gaze like blue fire moved languidly over her. A smile more wicked than amused curled his lips. "I suspect I'll need all my wits before the evening is done."

"Ahh, you expect debate?" Taking up a decanter, she poured a glass of a pale rosé. "Not to worry. My father had a strict rule that conversation at dinner was to be pleasant, neither business nor quarrels were allowed past the dining room doors. Rick and I continue his policy."

Kieran wondered if this warned him from discussion of the murders. If so, there was no need. Murder and mayhem were the furthest elements from his mind. Tonight he wanted to concentrate on the fascinating and seductive woman who stood before him, poised as if she would flee at the first wrong move.

"Your father was a wise man." For a beginning, he chose safe ground.

"The wisest I've known."

"How many have you known, Beau Anna?" His question startled her no more than it did Kieran. He hadn't intended slipping from safe ground so immediately. But seeing her dressed as she was, set him wondering, questioning things he hadn't before. Ever the realist, he knew the tightening emotion he'd never felt before could only be described as possessive.

He was envious of the men Beau Anna might have known. The man for whom the dress that gleamed subtly like a ruby might have been chosen. Before the thought was completed he recognized his mistake. He was as certain as he was of anything, that the dress had not been chosen by Beau. But by a man who loved her.

Envy seethed, becoming jealousy.

The ugly emotion brought him up short. Kieran had never in his life cared enough for a woman to feel so strongly, or need so much.

"How many men have I known?" Beau lifted her glass and sipped the wine. "Not very many, and only a few very well. Which is apparent." She laughed softly. "How many women meet one of the world's most eligible bachelors while dressed as a scruffy beach bum?"

One of the world's most eligible bachelors. The term hadn't been used between them in some time. And with time, as she intended tonight, had no sting.

Kieran smiled in return. New concerns filed away, if not put to rest by her easy comment, he crossed the room to her. "Indeed, how many?"

His fingers itched to wind through the fallen curls and draw her to him, making her forget the few. Instead, he slipped his hands into his pockets, as a reminder to keep to his best behavior. She might look like a lady of the world tonight, but, in her own words, nothing was further from the truth.

"I promised you the island chatelaine, weeks ago." Beau tilted her glass in a small salute, and meeting his gaze, found herself riveted by the intensity she encountered. For a second she floundered, with the regal dignity of a chatelaine, but floundered nevertheless until she regained the thread of conversation. "Here she is. Though a bit late."

Chatelaine? Kieran agreed. But tonight, so much more. "Let's take a page from your father's book and pretend that time doesn't matter any more than business, or dissension."

Or murder. The word seemed to hang between them, as Kieran cursed himself for the misstep. Something he seemed to be most adept at when it came to Beau Anna.

The tinkle of a silver bell was a welcome intrusion. Opal waited by the door, her white apron crisply starched and a tasteful contrast with her dark, formal dress. "Mr. O'Hara, if you would escort Beau Anna, dinner is served."

"Thank you, Opal." Turning, his smile rakish, he executed the same small bow.

"My lady," he murmured waiting for Beau to take his arm.

Dinner was a culinary masterpiece. Opal had outdone herself. Once Beau recovered from her surprise that she and Kieran would be dining alone, conversation flowed smoothly.

Beau listened in obvious fascination as he spoke of his family and their travels. Though she admitted that growing up on the island with Rick and Skip and Israel was like having three brothers, she turned wistful at the idea of a sister.

"Patience is the youngest," she mused, fitting the pieces together. "She practices veterinary medicine in Arizona, and is married to Matthew Winter Sky. Patience O'Hara Winter Sky," she repeated. "What a lovely name."

"Matthew's mother was French, his father an Apache. As is his name," Kieran explained.

"Valentina is second youngest, and married a Creole. Rafe Courtenay?"

"Right."

"Since you each have some special gift or skill, what is hers?"

"Val rides a horse as few can, and no one is a better sharpshooter. She won an Olympic gold medal for it. At the moment, she does neither while she waits for the birth of their first child." Kieran sidestepped an honest answer. If he were allowed to tell Beau the truth, how could he make her understand that a woman could be as beautiful and gentle as his sister, and a sanctioned assassin for The Black Watch.

Pleased that she accepted his explanation, he answered questions about his brothers. First addressing Tynan, a rancher in Montana. Then Devlin, who flew planes like Valentina rode horses.

Beau had the lonely child's fascination with lively, sprawling families. As he indulged her over coffee and dessert, he watched her, wondering if she had the vaguest idea what she was doing to him. Had she bothered to notice that the little red number defied its modest cut by clinging where it should, and as it should, while leaving the rest to an aroused imagination? Did she understand, though the dress was an invitation, the aloof look still lurking in her steady gray gaze was an even greater challenge few men could resist? Least of all, Kieran O'Hara.

"You were lonely for a long time," he observed into a brief silence.

"For the first six years of my life. Rick and I were two lonely children locked away from each other in this great, reverberating house."

"Reverberating?"

Beau smiled, ruefully. "That's what I remember best about the early days. My own voice echoing through the emptiness of my life, coming back to me, reminding me I was alone."

"But your father spent a great deal of time with you."

"As much as he could. Though there were times…" She left it for Kieran to recognize there were adult responsibilities precluding the presence of a child.

Kieran understood quite well. But in similar times, he'd had two brothers and two sisters to fill the void. His gaze strayed to the portrait behind Beau. For most of the dinner, he'd found himself glancing from the real woman of flesh and blood, to the woman captured in oils on canvas. Except for some small indefinable element—perhaps an air of petulance, or even conceit—the painting could have been of Beau.

"I suppose the loneliness made the loss of your mother even more poignant."

"It did," Beau agreed, pleased that he understood. Following the direction of his gaze, she smiled sadly. "The painting is of Fionna, not my mother. Though I'm told with a pleasant expression and a touch of abandon, it could easily be Anna Bonnet."

"Or you."

"I could never be as beautiful, but I suppose you're right. The portrait explains how Rick and I look so much alike."

"Why do you keep it there, when the woman caused so much pain?"

"To keep peace. Fionna is prone to dropping in unannounced. Then when she has everything thoroughly unsettled, departing again."

Kieran lifted his coffee cup from the table, started to drink, then changed his mind. "Where is she now?"

"The south of France, I imagine. Or wherever the wanderlust has taken her."

"Like mother, like son?"

"Perhaps in that." Beau made the admission reluctantly, qualifying immediately. "But only that. Fionna puts us from her mind between visits. Rick doesn't. He constantly sends little mementos. And some not so little. He sent this dress from his current location." A move of her hand drew his attention unnecessarily to the crimson raiment. "The bracelet came the week before, from the country before."

Kieran felt a weight lift from his chest. He spared only an instant wondering why he should be so pleased the dress and bracelet came from a brother who saw her as beautiful, not a would-be suitor. "What purpose does his travel serve?"

"None." Beau made no excuses for her brother. "He wanders."

Kieran doubted it was that simple. But he said no more.

From talk of travel, the conversation ranged to the villagers he'd made it a point to meet.

"Goodness!" Beau exclaimed. "You get around. Most people could spend months on the island and never meet the people you have."

"I came for a change of pace, not to become a recluse. Speaking of pace, I should go. I have an early morning planned for me."

"Planned for you?" Beau couldn't believe anyone planned Kieran's time. Unless he wished it.

"Tabby decided I should be useful and repair the fence around Hattie Whitehall's garden."

Beau stared at him. "Hattie never lets anyone near her, or her property."

"Looks like she's had a change of heart." Sliding back his chair, he rose. As Beau came to her feet, he took her hand, tucking it in the curve of his arm. "Hattie's an interesting lady, almost as well versed in the island history as Norrie and Tabby."

"Hattie never talks to anyone except Rick."

"And now to me," Kieran added cheerfully. At the door, he stopped, sobering. "You look lovely tonight. Lovely, but tired. Skip asked too much of you today."

Drawing both her hands to his lips, he kissed them, then took her in his arms. He thought for a moment that she would resist, then his heart leapt as she leaned against him. He felt the utter fatigue he knew she would deny, and anger stirred. His voice was harsher than he intended, when he whispered, "Rest, and practice saying no."

Yet, when he raised her face to his, his lips were tender as they brushed across each heavy eyelid, then sought her mouth. The kiss was brief, gentle. Another promise of much more. A promise that lingered long after he admonished her to bolt the door, and wished her pleasant dreams.

As she listened to his fading footsteps, then to the silence of a house too empty, too big, and too lonely, Beau knew her dreams would be of Kieran.

Nine

Dreams of any kind weren't to be.

Within minutes of retiring Beau knew she wouldn't sleep. Rather than wear herself out fighting the restlessness, she left her bed. Slipping a comfortable negligee over a flimsy gown, she returned to the drawing room. The room that once had been central to the family. Where its greatest treasures lay.

Sitting on the sofa, she opened a book that chronicled the history of the Cahill Family. From the first page, a familiar and favorite line leapt out at her.

Cahill, once O'Cathail, derived from the Old Irish catuualos, meaning strong in battle.

"Strong in battle." The phrase always made her smile, for it was that quality and a thirst for adventure that brought Alexander Cahill to the new world. The quality that caused him to be granted the land adjacent to, and encompassing, an island off the coast of Carolina. Alexander, the warrior, had little patience with becoming one of the landed gentry, and no taste for the isolation of an island.

But in time there were others who understood and appreciated Cahill's Grant. The first was Charles, who, in 1807, turned this gift of the crown into a thriving sea island plantation. The last was Roderick Beaumont Cahill, her father. A man whose life was so entwined with the island that he felt the need to preserve its heritage. And thus, for his children he had written this loving and accurate account.

For some it was ancient history. For others, the rambling of an idealist. To the rest, it was simply the past and "dry as dust." But Beau never tired of reading it, and each time was as exciting as the first.

But tonight even this favored story couldn't hold her attention. Closing the book, she stared blindly, her mind filled with Kieran. Who was everything she thought. A tease, a flirt, a gallant. Yet much more.

She felt safe in his arms. Safer than she'd ever felt. His kiss was tender. Asking little, taking only what she gave.

In a short time, he had become a trusted friend. Yet she had avoided him for the past week, and was unhappy when Opal had invited him to dinner.

"Why?" she wondered. Why did she waver where Kieran was concerned? It had never been the case with Skip, or Israel. Or Jericho, despite her short-lived crush. They were good and trusted friends. She was completely at ease with them and looked forward to the company of each. What was different with Kieran?

A small sound interrupted her thoughts. A nuance, yet it seemed wrong, as if the natural order of things was disturbed. With something moving as it shouldn't.

Beau waited, her breath ceasing.

There was nothing more out of the ordinary. The old house creaked as old houses would in the night. A tree limb, stirred by a breeze too slight to notice, tapped against a windowpane. A hinge creaked, a gate banged as in a sudden gusting.

"The garden gate." Opal must have failed to fasten the fragile latch securely. Recognizing the familiar sound, assessing the problem, Beau breathed again in relief. She would see to it tomorrow. Perhaps install a new latch.

"Some psychologist," she grumbled as she laid the book aside. Questioning how she could ever have understood the minds of her small patients, when she didn't understand herself, she crossed to the bar. Taking up a delicate goblet, she splashed in a measure of Benedictine, her father's favorite after dinner drink.

"A bit long after dinner," she admitted wryly. Lifting gob-

let and liqueur to the shaded light, she admired the rich color.
"Yes, Dad, the monks did say it best."

Her glass still raised in honor of the man who had given
her life and loved her completely, she repeated a favorite
toast Beaumont Cahill had taken directly from the Benedictine bottle. "*Deo Optimo Maximo*. To God, most good, most
great.

"Please." The single word was her own prayer for many
things. Most of all, for the poor creature who was driven to
kill. "No more."

The glass was halfway to her lips when she stopped, listening, waiting.

The house still creaked, the limb still tapped the windowpane. But the garden gate was silent.

"What?" The word was a stilted movement of her lips
more than spoken. Her grip threatened the fragile glass, as
she willed the disturbance to repeat itself, so she might find
its place among the subtle cacophony of the night, and forget
it.

Had it been the nearly silent call of a night heron? The
slither of a snake across the veranda? The scratch of clothing
against tabby walls?

The last had her shivering. More than the thought of a
snake, two snakes, a dozen, coiling and writhing. Waiting
outside the door.

"Stop!" Her command, though quietly spoken was thunderous. She was playing the imaginative child. There is nothing. "Nothing...."

The rap on the door startled her into silence. Swinging
about, she watched from the distance of the drawing room
as the ancient bolt rattled.

It was past midnight. Who would call at such an hour?
Why?

Suddenly fearful that something terrible was wrong, she
set down the goblet and hurried to the door. Concerned for
Tabby, or Times Two and Miss Emily, she forgot her wari-

ness. Until, caught in the reflection of lamplight, a grotesque countenance loomed in the oval of leaded glass.

Staring into the distorted face, her mind reeling, she searched about for a weapon. "What is there?"

The bow and arrows and the guns her father used for hunting had been put away. The dueling pistols in the display case were useless. Alex Cahill's rapier was mounted far above her reach, and her own handgun was locked in a drawer by her bed.

"What?" she whispered, her gaze ranging the foyer.

The bolt rattled. A fist hit the glass. Beau whirled, seeking makeshift protection for both herself and Opal. Her father's cane! The one that concealed a whip thin rapier. Drawing it from the umbrella stand, she advanced a cautious step.

"Beau!" a muffled voiced called. "Open the damned door." A foot kicked the wooden base. "Open it now."

The distorted face was no less grotesque in the planes and angle of the patterned glass, but the halo of gold and the voice were familiar. "Israel?"

It took only that moment of recognition for misconstrued features to become recognizable. Sliding back the lock, she threw the door open. "Israel. Great blue herons! What are you doing here this time of night? What's wrong?"

Israel brushed past her. "Is he still here?"

"Still here?" Not bothering to close the door, Beau rounded on him, her fear and relief turned to bewilderment. Thoughts of the murderer loomed in her mind. Her throat was dry and her voice cracked. "Who would be here?"

"The pretty boy."

"The pretty…" A multitude of fears coalesced into a flash of anger. "If you mean Kieran, no."

"But he was." Israel swayed. The stench of stale beer wafted to her.

"Kieran was here, but that's no concern of yours." Realizing it was the alcohol talking, not the Israel she knew, Beau struggled to bank her anger.

"When did he leave?"

"What is this? An inquisition?"

"Just seeing that you're safe." He looked about owlishly, his sharp stare belying his befuddled manner.

"Do you think I'm lying?" Perhaps it was the diminishing effect of fear that defeated her resolve to stay calm. Perhaps it was his presumption that as an old friend he could question her. "Do you think I have Kieran hidden away in some dark corner? Or maybe he's returning for an assignation?"

"Is he?" Israel's shoulders had been slumped. Now he straightened to his full height.

"Maybe." Beau laid the cane aside. Her gaze narrowed in a sign that she was more than merely angry. "Must I remind you, again, it's no concern of yours."

"I think it is." Israel took a step closer. "What with fiends and murderers running amuck on the island."

"If you're suggesting Kieran had anything to do with the murders, I would also remind you that he was nowhere near the island when the first girls were killed." No, Beau remembered, he was saving lives, not taking them. The photographs in *Prominence Magazine* were incontrovertible proof.

"He was here when Dinah died."

"He was here, but with quite a number of witnesses at the time of the murder. I was one," she added. "You were another."

"Fiends and murderers with their twisted minds know tricks innocents don't."

"*A* fiend. *A* murderer. Only one."

"Are you sure?" A scowl of derision marred Israel's face.

"You're serious." Beau never thought there could be one murderer among the island folk. The possibility of two was unthinkable. "This is ridiculous. Of course there's only one."

"You're a psychologist, surely you've heard the term copycat."

"Copycat." Beau could barely comprehend the terrible thought. "You can't mean…"

"That some sick puppy gets off on the murders and tries

a few of his own?'' Israel's smile was a caricature of true
mirth. ''Can you be so naive you don't know it's possible?''

Before Beau could respond, he slid his hands through her
hair, cradling her head in his palms. ''Are you so naive you
don't know why I worry?''

Were it not for the tragedy of their discussion, she would
have laughed, thinking this was one of Israel's practical
jokes. But when her gaze met his, she saw no humor in the
depths of his eyes. ''Israel.'' She grasped his wrist, her fingers closing over the brawny width. ''Don't.''

''Don't?'' He smiled, but only with his lips. His face remained oddly unchanged. ''Why not?''

An old, dear friend had become someone she didn't recognize. ''We grew up together, played and fought together.
Neither of us ever felt like...''

''Like lovers?'' Israel finished for her. ''Do you really believe that? Do you think any normal man could spend a lifetime around you and not want you?''

''We shouldn't be having this conversation.'' Beau tugged
harder on his hands, drawing them from her hair. But her
freedom was short-lived. Her heart sank as his fingers closed
over the curve of her shoulders. ''You've been drinking. By
your own admission, that isn't wise. This isn't wise.''

''Maybe I don't want to be wise. Maybe a drink or two
has given me the courage to do what I've wanted to do for
so long.''

Beau turned her face away from his kiss. His lips only
grazed her cheek. How different this man was from the person she'd known all her life. The man who only weeks ago
had kissed the top of her head like a brother.

''Israel! No!'' With her fists on his chest, she held him
away. A futile effort if he wished, given the disparity in their
size. She considered calling Opal. The old woman's stinging
tongue might achieve what her arguments couldn't. But this
was a scene she'd rather the housekeeper not see.

As he dragged her closer, she stiffened. ''Stop this!''

''Why?'' When she wouldn't give him her mouth, he

kissed the curve of her throat, bared by the gaping of her negligee. As he straightened from her, his look was harsh, with none of the passion he claimed. "Why should I stop? Because your mainlander lover is coming back?"

"Yes!" She seized on the lie. "Kieran is coming back."

Israel laughed. "Such a fib."

"No."

"Yes. No." The smirking tavern keeper growled in a mocking singsong. "Which is it, Beau Anna? Sweet, sweet Beau Anna."

Beau made one last effort. "That's enough. You'll regret this tomorrow as much as the hangover."

"And because your newest lover is returning."

She'd never called him her lover, but if it would discourage Israel's advances, she would give Kieran that name. "Yes. Kieran is returning once Opal is asleep, and I don't want him to find you here again."

"Liar, liar, pants on fire." Israel intoned an adage from their childhood.

"Calling my lady a liar, Johnson?"

Reacting to the deep, calm voice, Israel wheeled about. The startled abruptness of it flinging Beau away.

"Tsk-tsk." Slowly with casual ease, Kieran straightened from the doorjamb. With his jacket gone, and the vest, and with his shirt open, he looked the part of a man returning for a rendezvous. "Here I was thinking you were a gentleman."

"O'Hara." The tavern keeper's voice was rusty with strain and surprise. Surprise that turned to rage as he looked from Kieran to Beau, and back.

"In the flesh." Kieran's grin was cool, the lines of his body at ease. Only his eyes rivaled the blue ice of a glacier. Extending a hand to Beau without taking his hard stare from Israel, he murmured, "Come here, darling. Please."

Beau hesitated for only a heartbeat, before she went into Kieran's embrace. As his arms closed about her, latent fear and confusion vanished. While she stood in the sheltering circle, the look in Israel's eyes turned an old friend into a stranger. Instinctively, she moved closer to Kieran.

When he folded her closer, he cupped her head much as Israel had, but in his touch there was no dread. Beau felt only the security Kieran had come to represent. As her cheek pressed against his chest, the beat of his heart was the cadence of peace. Savoring the gentleness of the brush of his lips over her forehead, she barely held back a sigh.

"I'm sorry to be late, sweetheart." His voice was filled with contrition. Any who listened would believe he'd broken a solemn vow. "It won't happen again."

"It doesn't matter." A tilted world righted and changed. The center of it forever this kind, beguiling man. "You're here."

"Yes, my love." The pad of his thumb stroked the corner of her mouth, and followed its subtle curve. "I'm here."

Though Israel's cold gaze moved from one to the other, Kieran never looked away from this man who had become a threat to Beau's peace of mind. If not her safety.

Gradually, the younger man's demeanor altered. Shifting to a display of awkward chagrin. The painful attitude of a man bested by the greater strength of another. "It seems I made a mistake."

"Did you?" Nothing in Kieran's voice revealed his thoughts.

"I, ahh," Israel stumbled over what was beginning to sound like an apology. "I must have been a fool to presume that because I feel so strongly about Beau, she would feel the same."

"But she doesn't." Kieran's voice took on a harsh note. "Then you tried to force it."

"I thought…" Israel shrugged. "It doesn't matter now."

"That's right, Johnson, it doesn't."

"I suppose that's my cue to leave."

"You suppose better than you think." As if falling into habits of long standing, Kieran let his fingertips move in a caress over Beau's throat and shoulder and along the décolletage of her negligee as it dipped precariously over her breasts. Then as a lover just aware of his intimate impulse, and protecting what was his from the eyes of another, he gathered her clothing in close order about her.

"Yeah." Israel's disgust was patent, as his glittering gaze traced every intimate gesture Kieran committed. "Maybe I should chalk it up to the anxiety of murder and booze."

"Maybe." Kieran was unforgiving.

An unbroken silence fell like a weighted curtain, sealing Israel further from them.

"Is there something else?" Kieran's voice held a trace of impatience. A trace as unmistakable as a shout.

Israel shook his head. "What could there be?"

Again, a long silence. This time Kieran waited without speaking.

Israel fidgeted, cleared his throat. "I should go."

"Beau and I would be grateful if you did."

"Oh."

Like a scolded schoolboy Israel shuffled past them. At the last second, Beau stirred in Kieran's arms and reached out to her old friend. Hoping to make him that again, needing to regain what had been lost. "Israel."

When Kieran would have kept her, she touched his cheek with her fingertips. "It's all right, my darling, Israel would never really hurt me."

Their gazes locked and held. One corner of Kieran's mouth lifted in a smile and the dimple she knew now that she'd loved for ages danced just for her.

To Israel, she said sadly, "I'm sorry."

His smile was wobbly. "So am I. For a lot of things."

"I wish…"

"Don't, Beau. Be angry. Be disgusted or disappointed, but don't pity me. No man likes to be pitied by the woman he loves."

She closed her eyes, shutting him from her sight. Stepping away, she returned to Kieran's embrace. When his arms were around her again, there was a sense of peace that could only be called homecoming.

"You're a lucky man, O'Hara. Don't forget it," Israel admonished. Before either Kieran or Beau could respond, he spun on his heel, stalking through the open door into the night.

When she would have called him back, Kieran stopped her. "Let him go, Beau. Leave him the tatters of his pride."

She looked into the darkness. Beyond the veranda in a starless night, nothing moved. Crickets and tree frogs that should be filling the night had gone silent. There was only darkness, and nothing of Israel.

"I didn't know." As he turned her to face him, she murmured sadly, "I never had a clue that Israel considered me more than a friend."

"Maybe he didn't know himself. Until there was danger of losing you."

"Losing me?"

Gathering her hands in his he kissed the knuckles of each. "To me, sweetheart," he said in a low rumble. "By your own admission."

As quickly as it had come, amusement faded from his eyes. For the space of a long breath, he regarded her solemnly, expectantly.

Though a blush flagged her cheeks, Beau wouldn't let herself look away. "I suppose you're waiting for an explanation about what I told Israel."

"No explanations needed. You took the only option open to you." At her look of askance, he explained. "I have eyes, my love."

"And twenty-twenty hearing," she recalled from the day they met. Another day when he'd heard things she hadn't intended.

So much had happened. So much of it unreal, so much of it real. Beau hardly knew where to begin. She chose gratitude. "I should thank you, for stepping in, playing the role I created."

Kieran's eyes held a hint of amusement.

The door was still open. The night was still dark. The clock struck the small hour of another day, reminding that time had not stood still. Beau knew she should step away from the comforting strength of his body. Away from the warmth and the clean, masculine scent that intoxicated. Away from the longing he awoke in her.

In that effort, taking her hands from his, she moved back. With his fingers spanning her waist, Kieran kept her. "Stay. I want you here, close to me."

"Why?"

"For obvious reasons, I should think."

Israel, Beau realized. Even as her heart ached for something lost, it ached more for something needed. "Of course." Her face cast in somber expression, she continued the charade. "What now?"

Kieran's laugh was low. The intimate, teasing laugh of a lover. "Now, Miss Beau Anna Bonnet Cahill, my lady, it's time you kissed me."

"Because Israel might be watching?"

"Among other reasons."

When she made no move to do as he asked, he was delighted that she was uncomfortable playing the game. For Beau, love would never be a game. "You begin, dear heart, by putting your arms around my neck. Like so." Catching her wrists, he slid her hands over his chest to his shoulders. When she linked her fingers at the nape of his neck, he murmured for her ears alone, "Good girl. If you'd like to run your fingers through my hair, just for the effect, I won't mind."

"For Israel's benefit, in case he's watching."

"Of course."

As he'd bidden, Beau brushed his hair back from his face, and watched in secret pleasure when it fell again into charming disarray. "All right," she said, and was horrified at how prim she sounded. "What next?"

"This." There was still the teasing amusement in his

voice, and laughter again in his eyes as he bent to her. "Ahh, yes this, my impatient little chit.

"Impatient," Kieran muttered again, and wondered if she knew he spoke of himself. "So impatient."

Then the long wait ended. As his mouth sought hers, she was rising to meet him. Once initiated with a touch like fire, he let her take the kiss where she would, let her set the pace.

But, heaven help him! Her lips were soft, bewitching. Sweeter for their tentative touch. Maddening in their tender exploration.

Steeling himself, forcing impatience to become patience, he waited. Waited and ached for the moment her lips parted for him. And when that moment came, like a man thirsting in the desert, he took the gift she offered. The gift of innocence and trust. A gift that left him trembling as he drank deeply of her, his tongue seeking and caressing, his hands touching her. His body responding to trust and innocence as never to accomplished, practiced lust.

He'd been playing a role. One that paralleled truth. He kissed her because he wanted it. If Israel watched...

But he couldn't think of Israel when she moaned softly, a sweetly wanton sound. He could think of nothing but Beau as her fingers curled tightly in his hair, drawing him down to her, keeping his kiss until she sank from her tiptoes and leaned her forehead against the freshly washed fabric of his shirt.

The rhythm of his breathing was erratic. The sound of it harsh. With her body folded against his, as he marshaled his strength, leashing rampant desire, he held her.

As she listened to the racing beat of his heart, and felt the ragged rise and fall of his chest, Beau clung to him. With her hands wrapped in the open edge of his shirt, she accepted the strength he offered and let it blend with her own. She needed to think about what had happened between them. But even one unaccustomed to the game knew it was more than a performance given on the chance of watching eyes.

"For Israel?" Her lips brushed the tanned hollow of his throat.

Kieran's low response was a pleasant rumble. "For Israel?" With a finger beneath her chin he lifted her face. Her lips were slightly parted, delicately shaped, and bore no mark of his kiss. But to Kieran there was a difference. In his mind's eye she wore the brand that made her his. "For Israel. But most of all for me."

"Why, Kieran?" Her fisted hands crumpled cloth. Her gaze searched his for answers. Why had he come back? Why had he kissed her? Why did he watch her now as if his heart ached?

"Shhh." The same finger that had lifted her face slanted lightly over her lips. "We can discuss all the whys, the what-fors, and whatevers later. For now, we should deal with this moment, this night alone."

She was tired. In the week since he'd seen her, she had grown thinner, smaller. Despite a day in the sun, the evidence of more sleepless nights marked her skin with an ashen pallor accented by blue tinged shadows. He knew she was working too hard. Everywhere he went on the island, there was talk of her. Quiet conversations that expressed a groundswell of worry. Tabby expressed grave concern when he met her regularly at the Tea House.

Though Opal would never give Tabby credit, it was the old seeress who suggested tonight's dinner. Hoping Kieran would provide a pleasant break in the self-imposed schedule Beau set for herself.

Talk to her, laugh with her. Woo her. Do whatever is needed to give her an evening's respite. Take her mind from the murders, the old woman had demanded.

It required no effort for Opal to convince him to come to The Bluff for dinner. Even Tabby's admonition was unnecessary. Kieran would have grasped at any excuse to see Beau.

He could have tracked her down. For all its sprawling acres, the island remained a closed community. He was considering it when the housekeeper approached him. Sharing a meal, watching Beau over the dinner table, promised a far better encounter than over a screeching engine, or a heap of reeking fish.

This was better. Even with Israel, and his own dash to the rescue, it was much more than better.

"Come," he said in a quiet voice, as he pushed the door closed and folded her hand in his all in a single move. "You need to be in bed, but first, something to help you relax."

Mutely, she followed him to the sofa. Now the surge of adrenaline had faded, she was more exhausted than ever. If she'd wanted to protest, she hadn't the will or the strength.

"I see we had the same idea," Kieran observed as he settled her on the sofa and took up the goblet of Benedictine.

"I'd just poured it." Remembered tension lay on her shoulders like a stone.

"Then Israel came," Kieran finished for her, seeing how unsteady she was.

"This is ridiculous." She was exasperated with herself for allowing Kieran to see her weakness. "He meant no real harm. Now that he's gone, there's no reason for coming unglued."

"Perfectly natural, doc. A little post-traumatic stress syndrome here." Kieran had seen worse reactions with less provocation. "Let me help you."

Sitting by her, he placed the goblet in her hands. When they closed around the fragile bowl, he added his own to steady her. "Sip just a little at first. Slowly," he cautioned. "One at a time."

No one knew better than Kieran how the throat could close, blocked by fear or grief. His first taste of it had come when Patience was seven and her runabout capsized, tangling her in the submerged lines of the sail. He thought he couldn't reach her. Was even sure that he couldn't. Then, his throat filled and choking with pain, he'd decided that if the Chesapeake meant to take Patience, he would take her back. Or go with her.

There were other times after that, many, many times, when

neither food nor drink found easy passage past the remnants of violent emotion. But none as vivid as that crisp autumn day when he learned little or nothing was impossible, if he cared enough.

"Just a bit more, love," he cajoled. "Only a little left."

Obediently, she drank. With his arms securely around her, she would have done anything he asked.

"All done." He set the goblet aside and eased her back on the sofa. "Rest. Give the Benedictine time to work its magic. Don't think of tonight, or yesterday. Or the day before. Think of flowers, or a heron in flight. A strutting egret with his aigrettes at full staff. Anything, so long as it's pleasant."

"Kieran, I'm being foolish and cowardly."

"It isn't foolish or cowardly. My lady doth protest far too much." Casting about for something to ease her way, he noticed the book. "You were reading this?"

"I intended it. But I couldn't concentrate."

No wonder, Kieran thought, with mind-boggling fatigue defining every word and gesture.

In a quick perusal of the small, leather-bound treasure, he discovered it was Beaumont Cahill's account of the history of his family and its lands. From its well-thumbed condition, he knew it was among her favorite reading. "I'll read it to you. A bedtime story."

"You don't have to. Most consider it the boring history of a nowhere island."

Kieran could see she was growing drowsy. "Having to has nothing to do with this. History is never boring, and Moon Dancers Island is definitely a somewhere kind of place."

If she thought to question the convoluted nonsense, when her eyelids fluttered down it was forgotten. As he began to read, his thigh warm against her own, Beau drifted. His mesmerizing voice flowed over her, drawing her closer to the edge of peaceful sleep.

Kieran read quietly, the account of primitive Indians, who made the island a summer fishing settlement. Then of Francisco Cordillo, the Spanish-speaking Yemassee, and the Huguenots.

While he read of Blackbeard and Stede Bonnet—one a rogue, the other a gentleman, yet both pirates—it was easy to imagine a very young Beau sitting at her father's feet in rapt attention. He knew no one ever claimed the Bonnets of St. Helena Sound were even remotely related to this larger-than-life figure out of history. But in her girlish dreams, surely Beau wondered.

Next Kieran read of Alexander the warrior, then of Charles. And Beau's drowsing became light sleep. Laying the book aside, he brushed her hair from her face and let his fingers trail down her cheek.

Beau stirred, her eyes opened only a bit. "Kieran?"

"Everything's all right. Just tell me which is your bedroom."

"I can take myself to bed."

"Of course you can. But I'm here, so why don't you just tell me where."

"Top of the stairs. Last bedroom. But…"

"No argument, my lady," he said even as he scooped her from the sofa. Holding her carefully, he kissed her forehead and her cheek. Then her mouth. When she roused, her arms circling his neck, her lips brushing his throat, he was enchanted all over again.

She was light in his arms, too light. He could have raced up the stairs unhampered by his delightful burden. Instead he carried her with painstaking care, for he'd disturbed her enough for the evening.

Her room was exactly what he expected. No frills, no nonsense, classic elegance. A reflection of Beau. Allowing himself no more than a second of admiration and approval, he crossed to the bed to set her amongst the tumbled covers. Kneeling before her, bracing her with one arm, he stripped away her robe.

"Dear God!" he muttered more in prayer than curse, as

the careful control of a man on the edge came tumbling down.

She was more than lovely in a wisp of a gown he would never have suspected. Fine lace of deep, tawny cream cupped and caressed, while revealing more of her breasts than it concealed. The matching satin spilling from it was less revealing, but no less sensuous in the way it clung to her waist and the curve of her hip.

"Surprise, surprise." He growled as he found his gaze riveted by a rosy nipple made more intriguing by the web of silken threads scarcely containing it. What man in his right mind wouldn't savor the pleasure of seeing Beau in this improbable and maddening concoction, simply for the sheer pleasure of taking it off?

"But I won't," he promised, while his body screamed that he should. Turning a deaf ear to desire and need and hunger, he leaned her back against the pillows. When he straightened to gather the covers, he allowed himself one hungry look.

In the diffused light, lace and satin blended with the color of her skin and all but disappeared. And maddening she was.

Fists clenched, his breath coming in labored rhythm, and his body rebelling against his resolve, he drew the light cover to her chin. The kiss he brushed over her lips was slow and long and lingering.

And dangerous, he knew, as he barely managed to draw away. After a check assured all was in order, he turned to leave.

"Kieran." Her voice was still drowsy, a little petulant.

He smiled at that, finding it hard to visualize Beau ever being petulant.

"Why did you come back tonight?"

"I came back for you."

"But you're leaving?"

"For now."

"Will you be back?"

"Someday." The word was a vow. To it he added, "Someday, soon."

"Soon," she whispered.

Kieran waited. There was no more, and he knew she slept deeply, at last.

Ten

He closed the door, allowing no sound but the click of the latch. Laying a palm on the solid plane, his mind filled with memories of the woman who slept only a little distance beyond the barrier. His thoughts focusing on the poignant loveliness of the tawny gown, and her tantalizing scent. White flowers, Opal had told him that day in the market. Tiny blossoms gathered and dried to scatter among Beau's possessions.

How like her to wear only the fragrance that clung to her clothing. Keeping her sensual side to herself, expressing it only in exquisite and alluring lingerie.

Leaving her was the most difficult thing he'd ever done. Only the ugliness of the evening and her complete exhaustion, had given him the resolve to walk away.

"I'll be back. When all of this is done, I'll be back."

"Then I take it all is well for the night." Opal's voice came from the darkness of the hall. As she spoke she stepped from an obscuring doorway.

Kieran was greeted with a sight both macabre and comical. The old woman with hair like untidy flame and a body like a reed, carried a weapon that strongly resembled a long rifle. Whatever its make, it was long and mean, half as big as she, and twice as old. That it was well cared for was apparent. The oiled barrel gleamed like black oil, and a wooden stock shone with a richness poor light couldn't dull.

"Going to shoot someone, Opal?"

"Was," she answered shortly. "Not anymore."

"Israel?" Kieran asked in a lazy tone. "Or me?"

"Whichever of you needed it. Israel first. You second. If it came to it."

"I wouldn't harm her."

"Never thought Israel would either." Crossing her arms over the stock, she kept the barrel pointed away from him. "I don't know what's got into the boy."

The "boy" was thirty-some years old. His behavior tonight jarred with all Kieran knew of him. "Then you wouldn't expect Israel to hurt anyone?"

"Didn't say that."

"What did you say? Something's bothering you. Something about Israel."

"Don't rightly know. There is something. Just can't put my finger on it."

"Something that doesn't ring true?" It was the feeling he'd had about the tavern keeper from the first. He'd chalked it up to two males bristling as they circled a female. Though he'd never dismissed the feeling, he'd set it to the back of his mind.

But if others had the same reaction... "Opal, if you ever need to talk about what's bothering you, will you call me, or come to Heron's Walk?"

"Might. Might not. Got my duties here."

"Standing watch over Beau."

"Somebody's got to, what with Rick gallivantin' all over creation."

"When will he be home?"

"When the mood strikes."

"A free spirit?"

"The freest."

"Until he's home, you'll guard her?"

"With my life."

Kieran didn't doubt it. As old and frail as she was, he wouldn't tangle with her. Opal could be brusque, with as many sharp angles in her personality as her skinny body. But tonight and every night he would be infinitely grateful for her.

Stepping close, before she could dodge, he kissed her cheek. "Thank you. For dinner. For this."

Like a boy petting a shaggy sheepdog, he ruffled her hair, grinned, and walked down the step and to the door.

Long after he'd gone, after she'd managed to take her hand from the spot he'd kissed, Opal took her place in the chair secreted in a doorway. "Land sakes," she said. "It's no wonder our little Beau is finally in love."

There were more direct routes from Cahill's Bluff to Heron's Walk. But because he wanted to think, he chose the long way. The painful way that passed the tavern and the cul-de-sac where Times Two discovered Dinah. Wondering what intuitions he hoped to stimulate, feeling like a masochist for inflicting that terrible night on himself again, he began the journey home.

Passing beneath the cavern of oaks, he walked the incline that leveled into a trail. At the bridge over the stream, he lingered, remembering the last time, with Beau.

Tonight every cricket and tree frog on the island was in full voice. Only his step caused them to go silent. As he listened to the splash and dash of the creek, no eyes staring from the darkness raised the hair on the back of his neck.

Yet when he moved on, his thoughts still with Beau on Cahill's Bluff, it was no surprise when a lighter, shorter tread joined in time with his.

"I wondered when you would come." He adjusted the length and pace of his stride.

"Then you're psychic. You knew I would be here?"

"Hoping. I leave the knowing to you."

The remark elicited a gruff chuckle. The quavery voice turned serious. "How is she?"

"Hurt. Confused. Weary."

"The island folk ask too much of her. But she would give too much, even if they didn't ask."

In the time he'd been on the island he'd learned that much

of the taxing pace Beau followed, she set for herself. "Why does she do it?"

"It's part her nature. Part proving she's worthy of being a Cahill."

"Worthy?" Kieran snarled. "Another gift from the grande dame Fionna?"

"Among a number of others. As a psychologist, Beau realizes how foolish it is. But the subconscious conditioning of those first six years can be hard to overcome."

"What she needs is someone to watch out for her."

Tabby grunted her assent. "Only so long as the watcher is discreet. She doesn't take to being cosseted."

"Cosseted. That's an old one."

Tabby chuckled. "You mean archaic. If you haven't noticed, I'm archaic."

"Never."

Tabby laughed again. "It's no wonder our little girl might be falling in love with you."

"Is she?"

"You would know that better than I."

"I doubt that."

"The kernel, the first of love, is there and has been since the first day. Trust, the element that sets desire apart from lust, is growing. Trust of you, but more of herself and what she feels. Only time and Beau Anna can tell the rest."

"Not the head over heels sort, my lady Beau."

"She will be," Tabby insisted mildly.

"It's too soon, Tabby. She's carrying too much trouble to know her own feelings. If it happens, I want it to be..." Kieran found himself without words. "I don't know."

"I do." The old woman dodged a low hanging limb Kieran hadn't seen. In the starless, moonless darkness what little vision she had would be useless. He'd watched her moving like the fully sighted, wondering if she knew the secret to human radar.

"Is this knowing, or 'knowing,'" he mocked, not unkindly.

"Human nature. You want to be loved as you are. For what you are. Not some great deed you might have done. You want this for Beau Anna, as much as yourself."

"Love the man, not the knight in shining armor."

"No," Tabby contradicted. "Love both. In some men the two are inseparable."

"I don't have a white horse."

"Tease all you wish. Modern men can be throwbacks, as suited to the days of chivalry as the present. You're one. Rick is another. Though few know it."

Kieran would have doubted, based on what he'd seen and heard. Yet he would decide for himself what sort of man Rick Cahill had become, when the wanderer came home. Until that time, there were others. "Skip seems nice enough."

"Skip Hayes is a good man. A little too focused on his own success to qualify for knighthood."

Kieran would have laughed at this. No one was more amiable than Skip. Then he considered this day. "Blinded by ambition, he can't see how much he demands of Beau."

"Oh, he sees. But, in his mind, the result justifies the long, hard hours. Expecting help from Beau is a habit."

"For a number of people."

"There are a number who see and care."

"Jericho Rivers?"

"Knighthood." Tabby's answer was spontaneous. "He sees everything, and he cares. But not like you think."

Kieran wasn't ready to trust his assessment of Jericho's feelings for Beau. Two meetings weren't basis for judgment. "He wears a gold band on the third finger of his right hand. A wedding band?"

"The ring is Jericho's story to tell. Not mine."

It could have been a rebuke, but Kieran understood it as the old woman's respect for privacy. Beau was fortunate in her substitute mothers.

"Times Two?" He tossed the name into darkness broken by scintillating patches of scattered moonlight.

"Too busy raising hell and sowing oats to bother with honor in his youth I suspect. But age and love of Miss Emily have taught him humility. Some men have to grow into chivalry. So far, he has one foot in the kingdom of Camelot."

Kieran could see that in Times Two. He thought it might be the same for Skip.

"Israel?" He'd saved the most complicated for last.

Tabby walked in thought. Her sure step taking her ever toward the village, her flowing garment a conflagration of color in errant moonlight.

"Israel is…" she paused. A twig snapped under her foot. An owl lifted from a limb in a whirring of wings. Tabby was too intent to notice. "Difficult," she mused as much to herself as Kieran. "Yes. Israel has always been difficult."

"Difficult?" He prodded gingerly, hoping to stimulate, not interrupt her contemplation.

"He was always the leader. But only because he had to be. Without realizing, the others knew how important it was to him. Skip took the easy way, conceding at every turn, while he dreamed his own dreams. For Beau Anna and Rick, it was instinctive compassion. Over the years it became a habit, and Israel became an opportunist."

"At the brig, you called him smarter."

"Slier would be the better word. Israel had a way of seeing to it that any preliminary work was done on their games or projects. Yet he did little himself."

"But he was there for the fun."

"Always, and first."

"Then it wouldn't have been Israel who might fall trying to hang the old tire swing down by the river. He wouldn't climb the rigging to snare a loose sail."

"Never was. Never would be," the woman who knew them all best replied.

In a pensive tone, Kieran asked, "Do you think he's in love with Beau Anna?"

"No."

Tabby's unequivocal answer equated with his own. But, until he understood better, he wouldn't discuss his thoughts.

"A nice night." Tabby's observation signaled that for her, as well, the subject was closed. "The moon plays hide and seek with the clouds, but still nice."

The few lights still burning in the village were visible in sporadic stretches of the path. Each step brought a sense of regret as they neared the dark, winding point where Times Two stumbled over Dinah.

"He's fine."

Kieran made no answer.

"You were thinking of Times Two."

Though he knew she couldn't see, he nodded. "And Dinah."

"Poor girl."

"Have you seen anything, Tabby?"

Her grunt was regretful. "Nothing. I've tried, but trying is never the answer. I learned two things long ago. First, never interpret dislike as an omen. Second, accept what is given without mourning over what is denied. But this time denial has been hard."

Kieran had known other mystics in other countries. Each with different flaws. Few had learned to cope as philosophically. "It's enough that you tried. Even so, your insight tonight has helped. More than you know."

"Not more than I know," she disagreed. "Yet not enough."

At a fork in the path, one he hadn't noticed, she motioned that he should follow. Marveling again at how she negotiated the little traveled path, he walked single file behind her, then by her side when the way allowed.

The undergrowth was denser, the going slower. They'd traveled a little distance along the path when Tabby stopped and brought Kieran to a halt as well. Laying her fingers across her lips, she signaled he shouldn't speak.

It was then he realized the night was silent. In the hush the air was electric with expectation. Yet held no intuition of menace. Kieran was puzzled, but at ease, as he stood near the path where murder had been revealed, with a woman who was the modern day Methuselah.

When he would have moved on Tabby kept him with the fleeting touch of her hand. "Wait. See."

While she spoke, a cloud drifted, a patch of moonlight flooded the path. Into its spotlight stepped the biggest buck with the biggest rack he'd ever seen. The animal was magnificent, strong, muscular, agile. It wasn't until he faced them that Kieran saw the mutilated eye glaring like a dead thing through the darkness.

"Blue," Tabby said in an undertone.

Kieran expected the wild creature to flee. Instead it ducked its head in its own greeting.

The old woman said nothing more while she stood at the edge of moonlight. The ramrod posture eased. Kieran knew this was a meeting of old friends. One not common, but neither was it rare.

The antlered head lifted. Haunches quivering as if the deer would run at the least provocation, from a wealth of scars one perfect blue eye and one blinded travesty fixed on Kieran.

"Don't be afraid, Blue. Kieran is a friend come to help Beau. And keep her safe."

For what felt like an eternity, neither man nor animal moved, as one took the measure of the other. With a dip of the great head and the marvelous antlers, the buck looked away. As if that dip signaled permission a small fawn leapt in a prancing step onto the path.

Tabby advanced toward the small creature. With fear for the aged woman lurching in him, Kieran waited for the wrath of a protective sire. Instead there was only Tabby's murmur of pleasure as her gnarled hand stroked the spotted body of the quivering fawn.

"Handsome, Blue," she pronounced. "Handsome, indeed."

There was more Kieran couldn't hear. After more whispering and petting, buck and fawn trotted from the path into the underbrush. Tabby stood as they left her, her face a study in ebony, her hand outstretched in farewell.

When he joined her, she didn't look away from the way Blue had gone. "Beau found him when he was barely a day old. She brought him to me." Tabby turned her own scared eyes toward Kieran. "One of the islanders had mutilated him. A child, I think."

"Our murderer?"

"Yes."

"But you don't know who." Perception, not a question.

"I know it won't be who you think."

Kieran muttered a grim understanding. Murder was never so simple. Especially with this murderer.

"Tomorrow, Jericho will call a meeting," Tabby informed. "This is difficult for Beau Anna, and will continue so, but she's the key. I won't ask you to watch over her."

"You know I will."

"You have."

Together they walked on. Kieran's voice was first to intrude on the profound hush. "The deer." He reflected again on what he'd seen. "He came to show you his fawn."

"Sometime, somewhere, each year he finds me. Sharing his good fortune."

It should have sounded ridiculous. But it was far from that. "He understood what you said."

"Yes."

"How?" The word asked volumes. A complete answer would take hours and much thought.

Instead, Tabby observed, "Your sister, Valentina, talks to horses."

They all did, to a degree. Patience, Valentina, Tynan, Devlin and he. Though he'd told Tabby little of his family, she would know the rest. With each of their foibles as well.

Needing no answer, the old seeress continued. "It's much the same with Blue, as any creature. He's only a little wilder."

Kieran accepted the comparison, as content as Tabby in the companionable lull. Eventually his thoughts focused on murder. Intent on his concerns, he didn't notice when Tabby dropped back and moved into the underbrush.

When the path rejoined the main thoroughfare at the edge of the village, he realized he was alone. Feeling the warm, humid air swirling around him, he stared up at The Bluff. Its tabby walls and sprawling veranda were just visible above rustling palmettos.

"I'll guard her, Tabby. With my life, if need be."

Jericho had asked that they meet at The Bluff. When Kieran arrived, he knew by the low hum of voices that the sheriff and Beau were in the drawing room. Signaling to Opal, he made his own way to them. When he entered the room, darkened by the threat of an early storm, his gaze sought Beau.

"Good morning." He spared no glance for Jericho, remembering the last of his walk from Cahill's Bluff.

As he'd climbed the steps to the veranda of Heron's Walk, the hide-and-seeking moon stripped itself of clouds. Unfettered, it set the black, rippling sea ablaze with the reflected light of countless silver moons. For longer than he realized, he'd stood watching the water, breathing the lingering scent of Beau Anna. When he'd gone to bed at last, and slept at last, in the endless whisper of the sea, he heard her voice.

The voice that called him darling.

"Kieran." Leaving her place by the window, she came to him, her hands outstretched, taking both of his. "Good morning."

The sea had better look to its laurels, he decided. Even dressed in moonlight it couldn't rival the sparkle in Beau's eyes. "Good morning," he murmured again as his hands closed over hers. "I hope you slept well."

Curbing the endearments that had grown so natural to him, his gaze feasted on her, as though it had been weeks, not hours since he'd seen her.

Beau's smile was tremulous in her pleasure in the sight of

him. He'd dressed for work, in jeans, a bulky T-shirt, and boots. She wondered what chore Tabby had set for him this day. It hadn't taken long to realize the two of them were conspiring to shoulder part of what was expected of her.

Once she would have rebuffed his efforts. Now, she was glad of them. "I slept well. Better than in a long while."

"I'm glad." Inane, from the heart.

Neither spoke. Neither moved.

From his place by the open doors, Jericho watched. A smile pulled at his mouth as Kieran's thumbs move in a caress across the backs of Beau's hands. Realizing how it was with Beau Anna and the corporate investigator, perhaps better than they knew themselves, he drawled, "Might as well kiss her and be done with it, Kieran. We won't get much done until you do."

"Jericho!" Beau scolded.

Kieran laughed. "I think you're right, my friend." Drawing her back to him, folding her body against his, he whispered her name softly, adding, "My lady."

The touch of his lips was magic. And as hers parted, yielding as she'd never yielded, she found solace for all her sorrows, healing for her hurts. Desire she'd never known. And the hungering madness that knew only abandon.

Yielding that she'd mocked in the women and girls who had fallen beneath her brother's spell. Madness she'd decried. Desire that usurped all she believed.

In a world and a life telescoped to this moment, there was only Kieran. His arms guarding bands about her. His body lithe and lean and incredibly strong. His breath warm on her cheek. His mouth caressing hers.

Should he sweep her into his arms to take her to her bedroom as he had the night before, she knew she would go willingly. This time not to sleep.

If she considered Jericho, she wouldn't care what he did or didn't think. There was no shame. Only the bittersweet longing Kieran kindled and stoked.

But her fantasies were to be only that, as Kieran lifted his lips from hers. Holding her, keeping her, while he stared into her eyes, reading all that was in her heart.

His expression was tender, but no longer teasing or wicked. Everything he saw in her beguiling face, he wanted as desperately. But, because this was Beau Anna, a woman like no other, when he made love to her, it would be without shadows.

"Too soon," he whispered. When she frowned, her look puzzled, he smiled. Gathering her close, he hugged her as he would Patience or Valentina. It was the little he could allow, if he meant to keep his word. The scent of her hair filled him as his lips touched her brow. "One day."

With hope to sustain him, he put her from him.

"We've entertained Jericho enough for one morning." His voice was ragged, but he gave no other sign of the lasting turmoil of her kiss. "It's time we heard what he wants to discuss."

Beau expected to find Jericho's amused gaze watching them. But they were alone. "Jericho?"

"In the garden," Kieran said.

Beau sought out the solitary figure strolling among the plants and shrubs Tabby's grandnephews tended so carefully. Her look traced the lines of Jericho's athletic body. The broad shoulders, the lean, hard torso. Long, straight legs, one no longer as powerful as the other. "He's so alone, and he works so hard, as if it's all he has."

"No wife, no lover?"

"None any of us have known about. But not for lack of trying by every unattached female within a hundred mile radius." A frown reflected her distaste. "Some not so unattached."

"He would be quite a catch."

"Quite. He's handsome, well traveled, worldly. What he earned before he ruined his knee, was invested wisely. He's kind, considerate."

"Thrifty, brave, true," Kieran interrupted. "Once you had a crush on him."

Beau chuckled. "I was one of many. Every girl on campus was half in love with him."

Kieran touched the scarlet band at her nape. Scarlet, the color became her, whether a demure little dress designed to bewitch and beguile, or a sensible blouse tucked into jeans. "And now?" A slight pressure lifted her face. "What is Jericho to you, now?"

He knew, but he needed to hear it. To watch her lips shape the words.

"A friend." Her fingers pressed against his wrist and the race of his pulse. If there was a tremor in her grasp at the look in his eyes, her own gray gaze was steady. "A much loved friend. Only, and ever, a friend."

His palm cradled her cheek, his thumb traced the bow of her mouth. When her lips parted in a kiss, he caught an uneven breath. "When this is over…"

Leaving the promise unfinished, he drew her to his side. With his arm at her shoulder, they looked to the tall, dark man in the cloud shrouded garden. Unaware of their scrutiny, Jericho paused in his stroll. There was weariness in him as he stared down at his hands. For a long while, he was motionless, caught in a flicker of lightning and immersed in his thoughts. Then his face turned to the dull, overcast sky, and from their little distance, the anger in the heave of his chest was unmistakable.

Beau had never seen Jericho so desperately angry. All the time she'd known him, he had been the gentle stoic, the tolerant friend. Yet when he turned, perhaps warned of their study by the athlete's sixth sense, he had a smile for them. Only his fisted hands, the right with its flash of gold, betrayed his mood.

"Go on with the carnival as we always have?" Beau was surprised by Jericho's suggestion. "Can we? Do we dare?"

"There's risk," the sheriff admitted. "But the positive aspects outweigh the danger."

"Because it gives you the opportunity to bring investigators on the island." As she repeated Jericho's plan, she looked to Kieran, but could read nothing in his closed expression.

"What better opportunity than to have men and women, trained in every aspect of criminal behavior, masquerading as carnival revelers. It's a slim chance." Jericho's chiseled features were cast in a grim scowl. "But what else do we have?"

What, indeed, Kieran wondered, as he listened with renewed interest.

Beau leaned forward, toyed with a cup filled with coffee from a tray Opal prepared. Discovering she had no desire for the strong brew, she huddled in the chair that had been her father's favorite. "This is a small county. Thanks to you our police force is a step above the norm, but certainly not staffed with experts."

"There are other sources and resources. All that's needed is your agreement to go on with the carnival."

"You're serious about this." She was in a quandary, unsure which way to turn.

"Dead serious." No flicker of expression crossed Jericho's face. With the copper hue of his skin and the darkness of his hair, he was the epitome of the stolid savage. Until one saw the concerned gray gaze.

"Dead!" Beau cried. "That's what frightens me. So many people…"

"Beau." The man who had been her friend for so long, stretched out a hand to her. Clasping his fingers over hers, he tried to reassure her. "Our man doesn't kill in crowds, or when there's chance of discovery. With mainlanders on the island, there would be safety in numbers."

Reluctantly, Beau admitted his point. Casting a glance at Kieran, wishing he would do more than listen, she addressed Jericho's plan. "These experts, who are they? Where will they come from."

That was what Kieran wanted to know as he sat apart, away from the lighted lamps, with the dreary glare from the

open doors at his back. While he was a pale figure, silhou-
etted against the stronger light, he could see both Beau Anna
and Jericho clearly. Letting his attention pass over both, it
was to Rivers his hard stare returned, as he searched for answers to more than one question.

Simon admitted to an agent in place. A man familiar with
the area. Was Jericho Rivers, sheriff extraordinaire, a man of
The Black Watch, as well?

He demonstrated the skills and temperament. He was a
man possessed of qualities Simon respected and admired and
liked.

It was possible, even likely, this great, good friend of Beau
Anna's was one of Simon's own. Jericho had given no indication. But, as Simon warned, he wouldn't until the time
was right.

Wondering when that time would come, Kieran leaned
deeper into his chair, watching more. Waiting longer.

"I understand why you brought this question to me, Jericho," Beau was saying as she glanced again at the quietly
detached man who had kissed her only a little while ago.
"But the island folk must make the decision about the carnival."

"I've talked with a few of the more vocal citizens. To a
man, they favor continuing with the carnival."

"You can't say everyone is in favor, until everyone has a
say, Jericho," Beau chided.

"Then you'll put it to a vote?"

It was strange, putting to a vote a ritual that had been part
of island life for most of its history. It seemed wrong, and
she resented the need. But what other solution was there?

"I'll call for a meeting. Hopefully we can engage in an
open discussion of the matter, with anyone who wishes having a say." Agreeing to her own provision, she continued,
"I'll do it immediately."

This had been the manner of island government since the
days of Charles Cahill. For that reason, unto this day, most
of the descendants of the original islanders had never left it.

"Majority rules?" Jericho asked.

"Always."

"You understand, don't you, Beau, that no one outside this room can know the reason the carnival must continue?"

"I understand perfectly." There was steel in her voice. The voice of the island chatelaine. Its protector.

Taking no offense at her stern tone, the sheriff smiled for the first time in a long while. Taking his cup from the table, he leaned back in an attitude of relief.

But Beau hadn't finished with the subject. In a conscious parroting of his caution to her, she said, "You understand, don't you, Jericho, that the carnival only continues so long as the majority wishes it? If they vote no, no carnival."

He said nothing.

"If we continue with this, I hold you, you, Jericho," she repeated for emphasis, "personally responsible for every life. Mainlander and islander alike."

"So do I, Beau," the man who was sheriff, and perhaps an agent of The Black Watch, answered quietly.

A nuance more than a sound, drew Kieran's attention from the intense conversation to the doorway behind them. Framed there by the light of the foyer, was a tall man, with hair darker than midnight and a body harder than stone.

He lounged against the door frame, a smile curling lips he laid a forefinger across. His eyes, as they met Kieran's, were that rare silver of a storm lit sea. Cold, yet feverish. After fleeting communion, the glittering gaze passed lazily from him, to Beau.

The intruder was, by any standards, magnificently beautiful. His face barely saved from classic perfection by its rugged edges. And by the cynical look he hid behind a rogue's grin.

Fatigue scored his features, and the shaggy, too long mane had been disheveled by one too many rakes of an agitated hand through its dark wealth. It was a look Kieran had worn. Though never so handsomely.

Was this the beauty of Lucifer, the fallen archangel?

Or the gentle goodness of Michaelangelo's *David?*

Time would tell.

As if he'd sensed and waited for Kieran's reaction, tossing him a sardonic grin, Lucifer or David straightened away from the jamb. His smile changed subtly. His voice was soft, and fondly amused.

"Let 'em dance." Advancing a weaving step, he laughed. "The Moon Dancers have danced for more than a century, come heaven or hell. I don't think they'll let murder stop them."

The uninitiated would have called him intoxicated. Kieran recognized bone-deep, man killing exhaustion. The total annihilation of human resilience.

With a curious frown, he watched as Beau leapt to her feet. Before she cried out his name, Kieran knew him.

He'd known at first glance that Rick Cahill, the charming bad boy of Moon Dancers Island, had come home.

Eleven

The tavern was crowded.

As he leaned against the bar, Kieran sensed the excitement of the revelers.

Locals, with two exceptions. Himself, and the sheriff. Though, watching Jericho Rivers moving among the diners, he realized the mainlander bonded seamlessly with the islanders.

"A good lad," Times Two observed, following the direction of Kieran's interest. "Good."

In his first visit to the tavern since discovering Dinah's body, the old man stayed late to be part of the celebration. "From the day Israel and Skip brought him here, he was one of us. Till he went off to play the football. Till then."

A frown drew woolly brows together. "He looks like an islander. Can't see who though. Can't."

Kieran could. His casual study settled on a booth away from the heavily trafficked area. Four friends had sat there for most of the evening, heads inclined in conversation. They were joined now, by Jericho. As he took a seat by Israel, a hand on his shoulder welcomed him.

This was how they were as children, Kieran mused. The four of them a single unit. Then Jericho had come into their midst, and as naturally as tonight, he'd been welcome.

Kieran had recognized Israel's early spurts of ill humor. The territorial male, defensive of his leadership in the presence of a stronger male. But, beyond the exigencies of his duty, Jericho felt no need to lead. Now even the prickly tavern keeper was enjoying his company.

Observing with clandestine interest, Kieran saw the resemblance Times Two couldn't. Of the five, one was black with ebony hair and eyes. One blond, his eyes blue-black. Three were black haired, with tawny skin, their eyes sea gray. There were other features the three shared. The angle of a cheek, the jut of a chin with the suggestion of a cleft.

Beau Anna and Rick had been mistaken for twins. A likeness explained by the sharing of a father, with mothers bearing a strong resemblance.

But what of Jericho?

Wryly, Kieran wondered if the infamous Stede Bonnet had been a busy little gentleman pirate on the mainlands as well as the islands.

"Are you a historian, sir?" He addressed Times Two, who had taken out the pipe he never smoked.

"Yes. Indeed, yes."

"Then you're familiar with the legends of coastal waters."

The pipe was laid carefully on the bar. "One should know the past. Should, indeed."

"There are stories of pirates." Kieran left the thought for Times Two to take up.

"Ahh, yes. The scoundrel Teach, better known as Blackbeard. A positive scoundrel."

"Weren't they all?"

"Ahh, sir." Times Two jumped to the bait. "Don't paint even pirates with the same brush. One was a gentleman, who plied his trade for adventure. Only adventure."

"A gentleman?" Kieran scoffed.

"And honorably born. A planter from the islands, was Stede Bonnet."

Before the repetitions could begin, Kieran interjected, "He had no people here? No descendant?"

"None. None at all."

"Beau Anna's mother?"

"Major Stede Bonnet was hanged in Charleston in 1718. Many coastal families trace their lineage to that time. But none to the gentleman pirate. None."

Heading off repetition, Kieran exclaimed, "I'd forgotten, Stede's home was Barbados."

"Indeed." Times Two reached for his root beer. "Indeed."

Kieran continued his watch. Intrigued as he was by the similarities between the Cahills and Rivers, he was most interested in Beau and Israel. This was their first meeting since Johnson's infamous declaration of love.

Kieran's temper flared with memory of those rough hands on Beau. Yet, neither she nor Israel bore his grudge. His gaze narrowed, he tuned out Times Two, concentrating on Israel's baritone booming a half-heard comment about sister-girl. There was nothing half heard about Beau's answering laugh.

"History," a cold-eyed Kieran growled. "A lifetime spent together must outweigh one foolish night."

At least with Beau, from the look on her smiling face.

"I say, sir." Times Two nudged his shoulder. "Have you heard about the carnival?"

"Only that it will go on as scheduled." He was becoming quite adept at limiting the old gentleman one shot at his pontifications. "Do you agree with the vote?"

"Indeed, sir. The dances are a part of our history." The ever active brows wagged. "I worry, though, about our girl. I worry."

Everyone on the island worried about "their girl." All save one. A killer.

"Rick is here, thank God. But I hope another will appoint himself her special guardian." With suspicious innocence Times Two watched the booth as its occupants took their leave. "I do." He looked pointedly at Kieran. "I surely do."

"Someone will." Kieran clasped the frail shoulder, aware that scars from the fall in the back door garden hadn't faded from the ruddy face.

"I know, my boy. I know." When Kieran excused himself minutes later, the old man smiled.

The drums had begun.

For two days their rhythm never faltered. Until midnight

on this, the eve of the carnival, they would be the throbbing heartbeat of the island. In less than a day, the dusty streets would be filled with artists, collectors, revelers. And the curious—come to experience the exotic and mysterious.

"With Jericho's experts." Beau scarcely realized she'd spoken. Nor did she notice her brother, as he paused in the foyer, reconsidering his late night out.

Rick had never seen Beau like this. Restless, edgy, quick to laugh. Quicker to sober. In the week he'd been home, they'd talked, but with Beau falling into inattentive silences. At first he thought it was only horror of the murders. Now he knew it was more.

While he watched, she drifted through the drawing room, a wineglass nearly slipping from the fingertips of one hand, the other touching familiar treasures. Yet staring blankly, seeing none of them. Wherever her thoughts, they weren't of Cahill's Bluff and its ancient memories. And company was the last thing she needed.

On the verge of the front veranda, he glanced back, wishing he could ease this mood. But it was not he she needed. With a check of the service hall, assuring Opal was in the house standing discreet watch, he stepped through the doorway, leaving his sister alone, in the anguished solitude she'd chosen.

Beau had been alone most of her adult life. Surrounded by family and with the loving care of Tabby and Opal, a part of her remained inviolate. It was that part the drums touched, awakening a fever.

In this struggle with her own demons, though finely tuned to her brother, she never knew he was there. Never felt his uncertainties.

In her private conflict, the troubled, silver gaze looked but did not see. For once, concerns of a giving heart turned inward. Aimlessly trailing her palm over her father's favorite chair, a quiet, plaintive lament echoed the chaos of her thoughts. Once, touching the beloved heirlooms would bring comforting memories. But not tonight, with the drum of ritual filling her with a strange malaise.

"Stop!" She railed against the rite that had always been a part of her life. Exotic to many, it had been simply familiar to Beau. Until tonight when it evoked this alien restlessness as exhilarating as disturbing.

Raking a hand through loose curls, she stood, body rocking, head down. As the veil of her lashes shielded her eyes, she wished she could close her ears and her heart as easily. Yet she knew she wouldn't. Couldn't.

"Is that what I want?" Her question rang hollowly, lost in the unchanging timbre of the drums.

Drawn to the open door, Beau looked beyond the back veranda to the garden. The sky was black. Blacker than her mood. Even the full moon riding the horizon, couldn't light the hopeless darkness of an unnamed longing. No matter how many times she tried to put it behind her, to concentrate on the tragedy among her people... With a pain filled moan, she abandoned the futile thought.

Every thought was futile when the throb of the night became the throb of her body. With the rhythm trapped in her brain, pounding like a migraine.

Her head bowed, she touched her forehead with the frosted wineglass. Smoothing the gathering moisture over her skin offered little surcease. Drawing an unsteady finger down her throat, she found the mimicking pulse, and felt the subtle contracting created by a swallow of wine.

Her breasts lifted in a breath. Their turgid tips, unfettered by the wisp of clinging lace, brushed against the rough silk of her negligee. A sensation so erotic, she flinched and a cool drop of wine trickled like a lazy tongue into the shadowed cleft.

Stunned, she made no move to wipe it away. Instinct whispered it would be, should be this way with a lover. The graze of silk, his suckling kiss. The wine, the path of his sweet, marauding caress. The beat of the drums, the pounding of his heart and the clenching of his body exquisitely in tune with hers.

A lost breath became a shudder as the hypnotic beat writhed in her. As the monotony of its rhythm salved muscle and nerve with bittersweet yearning.

The wine fell from lax fingers. To the music of shattering glass, like a willow in the wind, she began to sway. As she moved from the lighted house into the night, her bare feet were only a whisper over timeworn walks. In the cold light of the moon, her body was an undulating flame burning too hot.

Cahills never danced. Never once, throughout the Moon Dancers' history. Only true believers took part in the secret ritual celebrating the waxing of the moon. Only they paid tribute to its influence.

But long ago, Tabby told stories of a beautiful woman, with eyes like the sea, and hair like the night. A woman who turned from all she'd known to dance as the Moon Dancers, casting her spell over Roderick Beaumont Cahill.

Tonight, as her mother had done, in the seclusion of the garden, to the cadence of the drum, Beau danced. As Anna Bonnet had done, in the throes of its hypnotic magic, she would call love's name.

Raucous laughter boomed through the tavern as circumspect islanders shed the inhibitions of daily lives. Carnival approached with revelry and sacred ritual.

To the beat of the drum that never stopped, the tavern regulars talked and laughed at fevered pitch. Few remained untouched by the pervasive atmosphere. A rested Rick Cahill watched from the midst of the crowd, a grin at the ready, yet not a part of the celebration.

Kieran, alone, seemed to realize how uninvolved the playboy of Moon Dancers Island remained. Only he saw Rick's silence as contrary to his reputation.

Perhaps Israel felt diminished in Rick's company, or subdued by his magnetism. Whatever the reason, the normally ebullient and caustic tavern keeper was absorbed by his old friend. The blue-black gaze turned constantly to him. Watching.

Conscience? For his nocturnal intrusions into Cahill's Bluff? Dread, that Rick might learn of the fiasco?

Suspicion?

This was the element that didn't work for Kieran. Leaving more questions than it answered. How would one deal with the fear that a childhood friend was a murderer? Why, among the rumormongers, was it Israel who spoke first and most often?

Conscience?

Weary of the nagging concern, Kieran let his attention wander over the bar. Times Two was his loquacious self. In his captive audience there were familiar faces. Of the regulars, only Skip Hayes was absent.

In the clamor, there was the oblivion of forgetfulness. In the small increment of time, the islanders put the anguish of murder behind them.

Rick slipped onto a bar stool. The smile he flashed at Kieran was Beau's smile. The face and eyes were hers, with a touch of rugged male splendor. For all his good looks, Fionna Elliott Cahill's son could never be called pretty. He was too formidable for pretty. "Buy you a drink?"

"Sure." Sliding his empty glass away, Kieran waited for the bartender to pour another. The young woman had scurried over when Rick sat down, and was in no hurry to leave. She either had not heard the rumors, or didn't believe them, judging by her manner.

"Haven't seen you around The Bluff lately." With a smile, Rick thanked the bartender for his own drink. Turning to Kieran, he missed her violent blush. "Not since I interrupted your meeting with Jericho."

"I've been around." Kieran sidestepped the inherent question.

Setting his drink aside, lacing his fingers, Rick rested his folded hands on the bar. "Just not around my sister." In a tone so markedly casual it couldn't be misinterpreted, he murmured, "At least, not that she knows."

Kieran didn't acknowledge the last. Waiting for Rick to pursue it, he let his regard turn in another direction. He'd never seen the prodigal Cahill at close quarters, had never witnessed his ghastly, scarred hands.

Neither were pretty. But the right was the worst, with the first joint of two fingers missing.

Following the direction of a stare that shifted a little too slowly, Rick shrugged. "An old injury. Caught them in the winch of a sailboat when I was twelve." His smile was crooked. "My one attempt at playing Stede Bonnet."

"To Israel's Blackbeard?"

"How did you know?"

"Lucky guess."

But it wasn't a guess. Tabby had impressed upon Kieran that when either Beau or Rick was hurt, Israel would be involved. Yet he walked away unharmed. Skip was more fortunate than the Cahills, but never quite so much as Israel.

"Skip isn't here," Kieran observed in a calculated change of direction.

"He snagged a lucrative charter to Barbados. Missing the first carnival of his life. But business is business, if you're Skip."

They drank in silence, with Kieran waving away the hovering bartender when she would have refilled his glass. The rattle of a coin in the jukebox preceded a smooth baritone lamenting a lady's choice.

Kieran's glass was empty. But no emptier than he felt. "How is she?"

Rick faced him, every trace of the charming rogue vanished. In his place was a hard, deadly man, who saw far more than most. One who loved his sister, and would be ruin and destruction to any who hurt her. "As you've seen from afar, she's fine." After a weighted pause, he added, "Physically."

Accepting that Rick knew he'd watched, and watched

over, Beau for days, Kieran met the pinioning gray stare. "But…?"

"Do you care?"

"I care."

Rick made a derisive sound. "Judging by the past week, I wonder."

"Don't."

An unrelenting gaze probed one as unrelenting. Long seconds ticked by, neither giving ground. A muscle flickered in Rick's face. The ice, in eyes bearing little resemblance to those of a dedicated playboy, melted.

"She's lonely." He spoke in a low growl. "For the first time in her life, surrounded by those who have been her friends all her life, my sister is lonely."

Kieran knew the feeling, the gut-wrenching loneliness only one person could ease.

"Hurts, doesn't it?" At Kieran's sharp look, a grin altered Rick's face. "This business of being noble."

"More than I thought it could."

Taking up his drink, Rick contemplated it as if discovering the answer to an important question in the amber liquid. Draining it in one swallow, he turned back to Kieran as if annoyed to find him still there. "What's your problem, mainlander? Waiting for the spirit to move you?"

Kieran laughed, recognizing Tabby's favorite condemnation of procrastination. "Not anymore."

As he slid from the stool, a scarred hand caught his shirt. Rick's face had gone sober. "Do I have to say it?"

"That if I hurt her I'm dead meat?" Clasping the ruined wrist, Kieran pulled Rick's hand away. "If Beau were my sister, I'd feel the same."

"But she isn't your sister."

"No." Kieran's mouth lifted in a smile. A dimple marked one corner. "Thank God."

Heedless of possible plundering eyes, Kieran walked in shadow to the back garden. Though informal and intimate in its pleasing complement of wandering paths and eclectic plantings, he hadn't come to enjoy The Bluff's sculpture garden. Neither did he expect the shadowy splendor beneath the full moon. Gliding along the low wall that marked its boundary, he moved unerringly to the crested gate.

In the moonshade of a grizzled oak, he felt a quietude, only accentuated by the distant beat of the drums, and the lazy trickle of a fountain. He breathed in fragrance, the scent of antique roses, lilies, honeysuckle.

White flowers.

The fragrance of the woman who moved like an angel along the winding paths. If Rick was Lucifer, perhaps having the archangel's evil as well as his beauty, with her flowing garments and flying hair, Beau was his counterpart. And everything that was good.

A sound drifted over the din of the drums. A low hum that accompanied the rhythm of her steps. As she danced, her own melodic notes blended with the pagan pulse of the island.

A wisp of shrouding cloud drifted from the face of the moon. As she paused to cast away the inhibiting negligee, she stood poised in the untarnished spill of its light. The image of her body alternately hidden and revealed by the folds of her shimmering gown, forever branding his mind.

To music only she heard, turning on bare tiptoes, her back arched, her arms raised, she began to sway. At first only in nuance, a subtle homage to the drums. Then faster, with her body weaving, her hair spilling to her waist as her back arched and her hips undulated.

Moving with the pulsing rhythm, she turned, her body pliant, mesmerizing. With a toss of her head, her shoulders rolled, her breasts lifted drawing taut the fragile lace that covered them like delicate petals. Her nipples were rose-brown, pressed against the filmy bodice. Her flesh tawny, in contrast with the creamy hue of clinging illusion that fell from tiny threads to tangle around her ankles.

A sheen of moisture gleamed on her face and arms and breasts. Part the sultry air, part evocative exertions. The gown clung, and clung again, becoming translucent. Folding her arms at the back of her neck, she gathered her hair in her hands, sweeping it to the top of her head. Laughing, spinning, her body writhed as it drifted in dark disorder to her shoulders.

Her face was pale in the light, her parted lips the same rose-brown as the crests of her breasts. Lashes like velvet lay heavy and sooty against the flush of her cheeks.

She was exquisite. A pagan worshiping a pagan moon. A siren enchanting. A mystery.

A woman.

Spinning, her hair flying, the translucent gown clinging and transparent, her arms outstretched, in a low obeisance at his feet, Beau's dance ended.

His heart in his throat, Kieran was dumbstruck. With the rasp of his labored breath filling his ears, it was a millisecond before he was aware that the night was silent.

The drums had stopped.

He had only a moment to think. Then Beau was rising, her lashes fluttered and lifted. Silver eyes, heavy lidded and far lovelier than any he'd ever seen, regarded him steadily.

In the great hall of Cahill's Bluff a clock tolled the hour. The sound filling the garden. Midnight.

The magic of the carnival had begun.

Dark anxieties vanished, swept away in the flood of desire denied too long. Stepping past the gate, yet holding himself a little apart, he touched her, drawing the back of his fingers down her cheek as if she might break with the force of his need.

Catching his hand, turning her lips in his palm, she kissed the calloused flesh. Her lips moved, speaking as Moon Dancers had for more than a century. As her mother had, she called the name of the only man she had ever loved. The only man she would ever love.

"Kieran."

Before his name was finished, he was lifting her in his

arms, cradling her body against his. His lips brushed her forehead. "Beau Anna."

Though he'd called her name so many times before, she'd never heard it as he said it now. Never as if she were to be cherished. Never with unbridled excitement in his touch and his voice.

"Do you know what I feel? How I feel?" A question that said so little, yet so much.

"I know." Her lips traced the line of his jaw. Against her breast she felt the breath he dragged into starving lungs. He'd fought this, trying to keep the flame of desire from becoming wildfire that burned too hot. But the battle was lost. "Because I know, I danced. For you, only for you."

"Then, God help us." When he strode to the veranda and the open door of the drawing room, she buried her face in his shoulder. She heard the pounding of his heels over the foyer tile, and felt the flex and pull of his body as he climbed the stairs. Then the slam of her bedroom door shut the world away.

Suddenly she was on her feet, standing before him, with his fevered gaze on her. "I tried," he muttered hoarsely. "I wanted it to be better between us, without the shadow of fear."

Fluttering fingers covered his mouth. "It doesn't matter. This is our world. Just here, just tonight. Nothing can touch us, or spoil this. Unless we let it.

"Don't think. Except about me." Then she was on tiptoe, taking the kiss he would give. To seduce when seduction wasn't needed. She felt him shudder. He gathered her hair in his fists, his mouth opened over hers, hot, rampant, demanding.

As she moved, in response against him, her body a caress curling into his, he went very still. Then, his hands slipped from her hair to her shoulders, to brush away ribbons like cobwebs.

"Nothing," he growled against her mouth. "Nothing."

Half understanding, half reading the desire that matched

her own, Beau stepped away letting her gown tumble to the floor, leaving nothing hidden from him. When she would have returned to his arms he stopped her. "Let me look at you. I need to look at you."

Beau let her arms fall, and felt no reservation before the searching of his hungering gaze.

"You're beautiful."

"No."

"To me you are." His hands returned to her face, his fingers wandering the planes and angles. "Here, and here." His exploration took him from her temple, to her eyelids, to her throat, his lips following.

"Here." Palms cupping her breasts, he watched as her nipples tightened. When she arched into his caress, he bent to suckle. His tongue circling, teasing, rasping gently until she was weak and unsteady. It was only when he felt her reach out to him for support, that he swept her back to his arms.

Her bed was spartan, not a luxurious trysting place for lovers, but neither cared.

"You are beautiful you know. Here…" This time his smile was wicked, teasing, familiar. But as he continued his maddening forays, Beau didn't have time to think on it, or care.

She'd never needed a man's touch. Never wanted it as she wanted Kieran's. And as his palms skimmed down her ribs and over her hips, she never dreamed it wouldn't be enough.

Catching his hair in her fists, she dragged him down to her. Her dazed and glittering gaze blazed up to his. "Play fair."

"Fair?" He laughed softly, his tongue dipping into the hollow of her throat before he raised himself to look down at her. "What's fair?"

"You undress, or I dress."

Bracing his forearms on the bed, he framed her head in his hands. "Is that a threat, my lady?"

"A promise."

"Are you sure?" For a long while she couldn't answer. His lips were in the way. Teasing her with a skill that made her forget threats or promises. When he drew away again, he asked, "Now, my love, what were you saying?"

"I don't remember." But just as wickedly, she arched and stretched like a contented cat. Her breasts brushed against the fine cotton of his shirt, and her thigh against the sturdy cloth of his trousers. "Do you?"

"It's coming back to me."

"Soon?"

There was longing in her voice, beneath the breathless banter. Longing he couldn't resist. Not bothering with buttons he tugged his shirt from his trousers and tossed it away.

His shoulders were broad and corded and marked by a new scar. A light dusting of hair covered his chest. His belly was flat and ribbed with muscle. Fascinated, she touched him, letting her fingertips drift from his throat to his navel. "If either of us is beautiful, it's Mavis and Keegan O'Hara's second son."

"Men aren't beautiful, Cahill."

"You are," she murmured, opening like a flower to the sun as he accepted the offering of her kiss.

When he stripped away the rest of his offending clothing, she saw he truly was beautiful. She'd never understood that beauty and consummate masculinity could be the same. Nor that it could make her want him even more. Nor that when he came down to her, covering her body with his, she would be frantic for him. For his kiss, his touch. The merging of his body with hers.

"No, sweetheart." With a calming touch he brushed wild silk from her face and kissed the corner of her mouth. "We take this slowly, savoring every minute. There can only be one first time for us."

If she hadn't already fallen in love with him, she would have then. And trusting as she'd never trusted before, she gave her body to his care, and her heart to his.

Kieran was a tender and patient lover. Who took time to

discover that kissing the back of her neck set her atremble. That the lave of his tongue over a taut nipple drew shuddering gasps. He laughed in delight when he found the graze of his lips and the heat of his breath at the bend of her knee drove her to distraction.

When in that distraction she tumbled with him over sheets scented with flowers, he endured her discoveries. Laughing with her, teasing, responding. Until the coiling pressure began in the base of his stomach and spread to every nerve. Until he cried, "Enough, sweetheart! Enough."

When he reversed their positions, covering her, his body seeking entrance, he was trembling. As the heat of her enfolded him, he began to move. Slowly, letting her take him carefully, easily. Pacing himself with her, by her silent urging, stronger, harder, deeper.

Until she shuddered beneath him.

Until she cried his name.

The name of desire, the name of love.

And his body answered.

Twelve

Beau woke to the tantalizing fragrance of coffee. Without opening her eyes, she knew she was alone. She'd slept too long in a solitary bed not to recognize its emptiness.

Yet she would never be truly alone, so long as she had her memories.

Stretching, feeling the sensuous pleasures of the night in every muscle, she laughed her delight. So this was what it was like to love and be loved. To go with that love where there was only wonder. With memories nothing ugly could violate.

Opening her eyes, she found her room unchanged. Somehow, she thought it would be. Surely the whole world would be changed by what she felt.

Changed by Kieran, for having loved him.

"Kieran." In a soundless whisper she tried his name, wondering how it would feel on her tongue. Delighted, again, by the rightness of it, she tried it again. "Kieran."

"Here, love." He stood by the open door, a heavy laden tray in his hands.

He was dressed. But with his shirt unbuttoned. His cheeks were shaded by a day's growth of beard, and his hair bore evidence of the forays of her fingers. Closing the door he crossed the room, his shirt bracketing a body as exciting in the blaze of morning, as moonlight.

Aware of the carnal direction of her thoughts, she scrambled among the tumbled covers gathering a rumpled sheet to her naked breasts. "I thought..."

"That I'd gone?"

His eyes were bluer than the sky on a perfect day. The touch of that wondrous gaze filled her with longing she'd foolishly thought the night would quiet. "Jericho's experts will be arriving."

"On the first launch." Setting the tray down, he faced her. Her hair was tousled, her lips dewy. The sheet did little to hide the luscious body he'd discovered within a veil of lace.

"I assumed he would want to meet before then." She spoke of the day, and the carnival, when all she wanted was to lie abed with Kieran.

"He does." The clock by the bed confirmed the time. "In half an hour. Which means, my love, you have enough time for a quick shower, juice, coffee." He unfolded a napkin covering a basket. "And scones, compliments of Opal."

"Opal?"

"She was at the door, worrying that you needed energy." He grinned with all his teasing charm. "After last night."

"Opal knows?"

Kieran stopped, cup in hand. "Does that bother you?"

Beau said nothing.

Catching up the freshly laundered negligee that arrived with the breakfast tray, Kieran crossed to her. "Do you regret making love with me, Beau?"

"No." Taking his hand, she drew it to her lips, then her cheek. "No matter what happens, I won't regret our time together."

Kieran kissed her, long, slowly. "Nor I. No matter what."

His teasing turned regretful. "You'd best take that shower." Wrapping the negligee around her, he gathered it about her throat. "While I can still let you go."

The shower was hot, steamy, the pelting water eased delicious aches. Would she ever grow inured to this part of loving Kieran, she wondered. Would there always be the bittersweet yearning, then the pleasure and the pain that truly wasn't pain?

She laughed. "You're so head over heels, you're babbling in your thoughts."

"Talking to yourself, doc?" Before she could turn, his arms slipped around her waist, drawing her back against him. Leaving no doubt that he was naked and aroused. "I can think of something better to do."

Beau leaned her head back against his shoulder, her lips brushed his throat. "Such as?"

"Is that an invitation?"

Turning in his embrace, she laced her fingers at his nape. Water cascaded over them as she fit her body to his. "Is this?"

His caress strayed down a favorite path. "Quoting Times Two, indeed. Oh yes, indeed."

"Jericho…" Her mouth touched his, as she spoke.

"…can wait." He finished as he lifted her to him and joined his body with hers.

"The launch arrives in three minutes. The men and women I've engaged will be among the first wave of celebrants. You won't recognize them, so go about your schedule as I've asked." Jericho was dressed in civilian clothes. As were his men, giving the impression they'd come to enjoy the festivities.

"Remember," he cautioned Beau and Kieran. "No one but the three of us know this. I'd like to keep it that way."

Beau stirred restlessly, thinking how eerily quiet the Tea House was before its customers arrived. "Are you suggesting I not tell Rick?"

"Rick, Israel, Skip, Opal," Jericho said emphatically. "Anyone."

"Surely you don't think…" Beau looked from Jericho to Kieran. "You do! You think Rick might have done these awful things."

"Everyone's suspect, Beau." Kieran's face was bland, betraying no emotion.

"Rick hasn't been here at the time of any of the murders," she protested.

Jericho had been dreading this moment. Now his massive hand came down on her shoulder. "Beau, I'm sorry. I hoped it wouldn't come to this."

She was on her feet, challenging them. "Tell me how. Tell me why!"

"We know that Rick was never supposed to be here at the time of the murders."

"What do you mean, supposed? He wasn't."

"Then why were there reports that some of the islanders had seen him?" Jericho asked regretfully.

"Rumors!" Beau snapped. "You've reduced your investigation to rumors?"

"Sweetheart." Kieran left his seat to go to her. "Jericho is only doing his job. Not making accusations."

Beau warded him off, refusing to let him touch her. "Who are these people who, conveniently, always see Rick? Tell me their names."

"I can't." The sheriff's stern visage didn't change.

"Can't? Or won't?"

"Both." One gray gaze collided with another. Out of deference, Jericho was first to look away.

"I've heard enough." Crossing to the door, she looked back at both men. "I'll do my part in this little charade. To prove you're wrong."

When the door slammed behind her, Kieran asked, "Do you think Rick might have done this?"

"No." Jericho flexed his tired shoulders. "But I didn't think the Moon Dancers were involved, either."

Kieran focused on nuances. "Past tense. Meaning you do now?"

"Meaning it's possible." Jericho hesitated. Then, drawing a sheaf of papers from a briefcase, he tossed them on the table. "Take a look."

The papers were photographs. Kieran studied them

gravely. "Beads. Dried berries made into beads. What are they?"

"Amulets. Symbols of secret ritual."

"Let me guess," Kieran said bluntly. "Found at the scene of the murders. Maybe found later, buried in the sand by all the activity following the discovery of the bodies. Never made public.

"Right. But not just buried in the sand. There was one with Dinah." Before Kieran could ask, he said, "Tied around her forearm, under her blouse."

"A Moon Dancers' amulet," Kieran ventured, because it was logical.

"Right, again. A very secret amulet. According to Tabby, these assure safe passage to the next world."

"Who else would know the meaning of these charms?"

Jericho stared, unblinking, into Kieran's eyes. "Who better than someone raised by a Moon Dancer? Someone familiar with the ancient religion and its rites."

"One of the Cahills."

"Not the vague 'one,'" Jericho refuted. "Rick."

"The man who was never here, yet always here," Kieran suggested. "According to rumor."

"Sourceless rumor." Jericho's comment held traces of bitterness.

Kieran knew one source. "I wonder." At Jericho's puzzled look, he shrugged. "It's nothing."

"Has it occurred to you that if the Moon Dancers and Rick are being implicated, Beau may be in danger?"

"That's a stretch, isn't it?" Kieran kept to himself that he'd considered that likelihood long ago. Desperate people committed desperate deeds.

Jericho's stolid expression didn't alter. "Call it gut reaction. Something I never ignore."

"Neither do I, my friend." As he spoke, Kieran was on his way to find Beau. Intending to stick with her like a Siamese twin. "Neither do I."

* * *

It was the last day of the carnival. For the first time, Beau was glad to see it end. The celebration had always drawn a number of art lovers who knew that when the island stopped producing rice, it started producing artists and artisans. Some from the original populace, some migrated to the friendly shores.

This year, there seemed to be more adventurers and curiosity seekers than art lovers. Rick and Beau had been inundated by questions, running the gamut from gauche to bizarre, to cruel. In his charming way, Rick deftly turned the questions aside, leaving his interrogators uncertain their questions were answered.

Beau took the questions to heart, and was hurt by them. Finally, risking her ire, Kieran stepped in. When he realized she was grateful, rather than angry, he continued.

"Your last day to ride shotgun." Beau strolled by Kieran, down a thoroughfare of booths and displays. "In a few hours the carnival will be over."

"Sorry to see it end?" Kieran caught her hand in his.

"Not this year." Her lips quirked in disgust. "We've never had so many visitors, nor such terrible people."

"Ambulance chasers. Hoping for blood and murder."

"That's appalling."

"Human nature," Kieran said in gentle apology.

Changing the subject, Beau voiced a source of worry. "Tabby's exhausted. Everyone wanted a fortune told. Mostly they wanted her to give them the murderer's name."

"As if she knew, and hadn't bothered to tell Jericho."

"Speaking of Jericho, have you seen him?" She was searching the crowd that had begun to thin. "I wonder if he had anything positive from his experts. If they were here."

"They were here."

Beau turned a startled gaze to him. "How do you know?"

"Jericho told me." He offered a partial truth. When, in fact, he knew many of them, and had seen them. At this minute, Matthew Winter Sky was having his palm read on the veranda of the Tea House. Simon was buying a basket woven of sweet grass. There were others. Some he knew. Some he didn't. Simon's agent in place, for instance.

"Not to worry." His fingers moved over Beau's. A reassuring caress. "Tomorrow the cleanup begins. After that, everything will be back to normal."

Her expression grew bleak. "Nothing will be normal until the murderer is stopped."

"We'll catch him." Kieran's grip tightened as if with his strength, he could make her believe. "I promise."

"It's peaceful, isn't it?" Beau crossed the veranda to stand by Kieran. "When I look over the shore to the sea, I almost forget the ugliness of the last few months."

Gathering her to him, Kieran rested his chin on the top of her head. She was a perfect fit, made especially for him. "That first day here at Heron's Walk, I knew Norrie had his sanctuary while the rest of us poor souls were still searching."

"Maybe you'll find it one day," Beau said thoughtfully. "One not tainted with murder."

Turning her in his arms, he brushed a flying curl from her face. How many times have I done that? he asked himself. Smiling, he wondered how many more times he might, in the days to come.

"Do you think about your reason for coming to the island?"

Startled, Kieran drew a blank. Then he remembered. "The eligible bachelor bit?" He chuckled in wry self-mockery. "My reaction to it seems silly now. In a hundred years what will it matter? When there are lives cut short, what importance is there in a minor invasion of privacy?"

"When you go back to the real world, we'll both have a different perspective." He'd come for the summer. Summer was almost over. When she woke each morning, it was with dread. For each morning brought his departure a day closer.

"It's late." Twilight had begun to fall. In a matter of minutes it would be dark. "I should go."

"I think you should stay." Kieran drew her closer, wishing he could banish the melancholy note from her voice. "You could stay the night. If you will, I promise I won't bore you with sleep."

Beau laughed. In the worst of times, Kieran could always make her laugh. A few months ago, she wouldn't have realized how wonderful it was to have a lover with that rare gift. A few months ago, she never suspected he was more than a man for good times. She hadn't learned he was a friend she could count on in the worst and best of days.

A few months ago, she didn't love this man for all times.

I'll miss you, she thought as she looked up at him. And she knew she would miss him more than life.

"Hey!" He tilted her chin, his thumb straying to the softness of her underlip. "Why so serious? You aren't turning me down are you?"

"'Fraid so." Beau kissed the tip of his finger as it moved over her lips. "I promised Tabby I would stop by her house on the way home."

"Oh no, you don't! You aren't wandering this island in the dark. Not without me."

Beau chuckled. "I was counting on that. In fact I told Opal to make your favorite breakfast."

"You're a wicked, scheming woman, Beau Anna Cahill." Kieran kissed her temple and hugged her. "Wicked, indeed."

"But you love it, don't you." *And me?* The question was on the tip of her tongue, but she knew it was one she would never ask.

"Oh, yes I do love it. Indeed, I love it."

"Careful there, Buster!" Beau punched him playfully in the chest. "You must be spending too much time with Times Two. You're beginning to sound like him."

"Is that a bad thing…"

The shrill jangle of the telephone cut Kieran's remark short. With one final kiss aimed at the tip of her nose, he left her to answer.

Beau wandered to the end of the veranda, remembering

the day Kieran had come into her life. Wondering what their friendship would've been if Moon Dancers Island had been the sleepy little atoll it was once.

Hearing his footsteps she turned, expecting some foolish teasing remark. The expression on his face swept her smile away. "What's wrong? Kieran! What's wrong?"

"Where's Rick, Beau?" His face was stark, his lips limned with white.

"He said something about a date." Frowning, she tried to remember. But her mind had been too full of Kieran for Rick's conversation to register. "Yes. He has a date with Israel's bartender. Oh! What's her name?"

"Marsha," Kieran supplied.

"Yes! With Marsha." The look on Kieran's face took her breath away. "Why?"

"Someone attacked Marsha on the beach."

"Is she…"

"She's alive. By the grace of God, and Jobe's need to sleep off a drunken stupor. He heard her scream. When he screamed, too, her attacker ran away."

"Who? Why?" She scarcely knew what she was saying.

"It looks like whoever it was meant to kill her, Beau. In the same fashion the other girls were killed."

"You think it was Rick," she whispered in a voice ragged with fear.

"I don't know what I think. I just want to know where he is."

"Where is Marsha? Is she hurt?"

"Jericho says she's only scared."

"Jericho is here, on the island?"

"We were to meet later this evening. To discuss some new information on the killer's non-profile."

"If I'd agreed to stay the night, Kieran? What then?"

Without missing a beat, he replied, "Then Jericho and I would have met tomorrow."

"He would have stayed the night?"

Kieran smiled, though a little sadly. "Contrary to first impressions, Heron's Walk is a big house, sweetheart."

This time Beau didn't smile in return. "Has it ever occurred to you that Jericho has been, or could have been on the island when these terrible things happened?"

"Are you suggesting he committed murder?"

"No." She stared down at the floor, her eyes filled with fear. Her voice low. "I was making the point that proximity isn't the same as guilt."

"Oh, love." Kieran drew her back to him, rocking her as he would a hurt child. "This will work out. Somehow."

As he held her, watching the last reflected light of twilight fade from the sea, he wondered what would happen to them, if Rick Cahill was guilty.

"She came out of the darkness. She was big. So big. Her dress was long and her hair was flying and wild. Her face was painted." Marsha shivered, and the hysteria in disjointed observations mounted. "She was ugly. Garish. With lipstick smeared from cheek to cheek. She had a knife."

Dropping her face into her hands, her shivers became shudders. Jericho knelt before her, stroking her disheveled hair. "Take your time, Marsha. We're in no hurry. Just tell it as you remember it. Slowly, precisely."

When he moved his hands away, the frightened woman clasped desperately at them. Needing someone she trusted to hold on to. "She was insane. Her eyes were insane. She was a man."

Jericho didn't bat an eye at the last. In fact, Kieran suspected it was what he had been waiting for.

"A man dressed as a woman?" the sheriff asked gently.

As Kieran watched, standing a little apart with Beau, he knew Jericho was establishing her credibility. Separating fact from hysteria.

"She was a man." Marsha was adamant.

"That's good." The gender confusion fit with the little profiling they'd managed to assemble. But didn't explain the costume. "Can you tell me why you were walking alone on the beach in the dark?"

Marsha lifted her face to Jericho. Shadows cast by the harsh light of the tavern painted a pale visage as grotesque as the one she described. "I had a date with Rick."

At Beau's low groan, she paused. Then after a hard swallow, the words choking her, she continued. "I had a date with Rick. We were to meet at the Tea House. But he left a note for me saying I should meet him on the beach."

"Rick left the note?" Jericho questioned carefully. "You saw him leave it?"

"No," Marsha said, with a little life returning to her voice. "If I'd seen him, he wouldn't have had to leave the note, would he?"

"No, he wouldn't." The sheriff smiled, pleased by her spunk. "Is there anyone who might know about your date?"

"Anyone at the bar who cared to listen. I asked him."

Patting her hand, murmuring assurances, Jericho stood. His bleak gaze searched out Beau.

Before he spoke, she knew he would ask about Rick. With a slight tilt of her head, she beat him to it. "I haven't seen Rick since breakfast."

"When you see him, will you tell him I need to speak with him?"

"Jericho, you can't think Rick did this. Israel," she pleaded with the person who had known her brother longest. "Tell him! Tell him that Rick couldn't do this."

Israel shrugged and looked away.

It was Marsha who answered. "Rick didn't."

"How do you know?" Jericho was back at Marsha's side.

"She...he was ugly. But he had beautiful hands. With long fingers and manicured nails." She looked up emphatically. "Beautiful hands with perfect skin and ten manicured fingernails."

Jericho knelt at her feet again. "You're positive?"

"It's not likely I'll ever forget anything about this night. Is it, sheriff?"

"No, I think not." When he stood again, turning to find Beau sagging in relief in Kieran's arms, the man who was sheriff and friend was smiling.

"I didn't leave her a note," Rick was saying in a quietly adamant tone. "When I went to the tavern and Marsha wasn't there, I thought she'd stood me up. So I went to spend the evening with Tabby."

"Came to cadge a meal, is what you did, Rick Cahill." Tabby's laugh was a pleased cackle. "Tired of Opal's cookin', I guess."

"Just feeling sorry for you, is all." Opal got in her share of insult.

"You're both wrong." Rick looked around the Cahill dinner table. His gray gaze moved from the elderly ladies, to Beau, and Kieran, and Jericho. Then very deliberately returned to Kieran. "I'm just a nomad, who's glad to be home."

Lifting his glass, his gaze keeping Kieran's, he proposed a toast. "To nomads all over the world, may they find a home such as this."

Kieran's expression didn't change by so much as a flicker of an eyelash. But with the toast, he knew he'd been contacted by Simon's agent in place.

Dinner ended, and while Jericho entertained the ladies, Kieran wandered to the veranda. As he expected, it wasn't long before he was joined by Rick.

"Nice night." He spoke without turning away from his view of the garden. The garden where Beau had danced for him.

"Yeah." Hands in his pockets, Rick rocked back on his heels. "My favorite time of year."

"The time for nomads to come home?"

"Something like that."

Kieran abandoned the view that would never lose its fascination. He needed total concentration. "Simon told you I'm called Nomad at times."

It wasn't a question. No one else could have passed on the code name. Rick said nothing. Waiting for Kieran to take the conversation where he would.

"You asked Simon to send me here?" At Rick's nod, Kieran asked, "Why the subterfuge?"

"I knew the rumors and wanted my innocence proven. But by someone who didn't know me. Someone whose judgment wouldn't be consciously or unconsciously swayed by what I am. I've been investigating a South American drug running operation targeting this area of the coast. I thought they were on to me and the frame was their scam. I should have known better." Rick's smile, barely visible in the shadows of the veranda, held no humor. "They'd just shoot me."

"What do you think is going on?"

"God help me, Kieran. I wish I knew. The profile suggested the killer is a man with conflicts about women. Thin and far-fetched as it seemed, it was on target. But that doesn't tell us enough. There is one thing." Light from the open door underscored his worried look. "If I'm a target, it's possible Beau is too. I'm hoping you'll stick like glue."

"That's my plan."

"I thought so, I hoped so."

They talked on. About the island. About Beau. Neither discussed how Rick came to be a part of the clandestine and dangerous Black Watch. Kieran didn't need to ask. He didn't know the exact catalyst, but he knew it would be of a kind. Some injustice indelibly scoring the mind. A tragedy, personal, or totally unrelated. To a man, or woman, the agents recruited by The Watch had a story to tell. A story only Simon would ever know.

"The rumors." Kieran returned to a sore point. "Any sources?"

Rick was a while answering. "One. It surprises me."

"Israel Johnson. Your great, good friend."

"Great, good, and for a long time. I keep telling myself it's a case of misplaced concern."

"Damaging concern," Kieran retorted as he calculated the cost to Beau, in worry and anguish.

"With no ulterior motive."

"Maybe." Kieran reserved judgment, questioning the blind faith of old friendships.

"You're joking!" The minute the words left her lips, Beau knew how foolish they were. Jericho wouldn't joke about murder. "This monster has done this before? On the mainland?"

"Several years ago. Never with frequency nor a pattern that made the deaths appear more than random violence." Jericho's face was grim. The austere lines so rigid, it seemed any expression would shatter the bones beneath the copper hue of his flesh. "Thanks to greater investigative skills and better communication, a pattern emerges."

"These women..." Beau swallowed, but the tension in her throat wouldn't go away "...they were killed like the first two here?"

"Attacked on the beach. Throats slashed. Bodies washed in the sea. Then carefully placed for display." The sheriff stared at the trees visible beyond the door. The beautifully appointed drawing room hardly seemed the place to discuss the horror of murder. "His first were crudely done, though much the same." A grim face grew grimmer. "He got better."

"How does one get better at murder, Jericho?"

"Beau." From his seat near her, Kieran reached out to comfort her. "Jericho's only telling the truth."

"Kieran's right." Rick offered his own assessment. "We need to know this. You and I."

"We?"

When she looked from Rick, to Jericho, Kieran could scarcely keep from sweeping her from her chair to his lap.

He wanted to shield her from this knowledge, but knew she must hear and understand.

"You think the murders on the mainland were rehearsals. A monster perfecting his craft, before coming to the island." Her hands had rested loosely in her lap. Now they curled into fists. "Why? What does he want?"

"We don't know, Beau." Kieran took her hand in his. Very carefully, he opened her fingers, lacing them through his. "But we intend to find out."

The anguish in her face tore at Kieran like a scream. Anger at a heinous creature escalated.

Beau stared down at their joined hands, her fingers tightened. When she lifted her gaze to the waiting men, she had judged and accepted the situation. For the sake of the young lives taken by this creature, she would do whatever would be required of her. "What can I do?"

Kieran relaxed. He'd never loved Beau Anna Cahill more than he did in this selfless moment.

With an impatient huff, Beau blew dust from her face. "It would help if we knew what we're looking for." Fanning a sheaf of yellowed pages between her fingers, she sneezed, then laughed at her foolishness. "Once I thought it was marvelous that the Cahills were such impulsive recorders. But I don't think anyone needed to save for posterity the fact that Emily Cahill nee Summerfield's wedding train was seventeen feet long."

"Seventeen?" Kieran returned a trunk to the space it had occupied in the attic for close to a century. "You must have misread it."

Beau held the tablet for his inspection. "Here it is in sepia and yellow. Seventeen feet."

"Must be a misprint."

"Cahills don't misprint."

"They don't?" Kieran stood. Ignoring his creaking knees and slipping an arm around Beau's waist, he brought her up with him. "When this great search is done, I'd like to see that dress. If it's still around."

"Do you doubt it? Considering this—" a gesture indicated the mountain of papers and books they'd searched "—I wish we'd discovered some motive for all that's happened." Disappointment crept into her voice. "A week of this, and nothing to show for it. I worry that if we don't hurry, there will be another young woman. One who might not be as fortunate as Marsha."

"We need a break."

"Kieran, we don't have time."

"We don't have time not to take a break. So, we take the afternoon off, blow the cobwebs out of our hair and minds, then we come back to the search refreshed."

Beau smiled wanly. "Is this a con?"

"Just a fact, my lady. Just a fact."

"There's either an echo in here, or Times Two is hiding among the trunks and files," Beau drawled with the beginning of a real smile.

"Then it's settled."

"It is?"

"Sure." Kieran swooped down to kiss the sooty tip of her nose. "What would you like to do? Choose something you haven't done in a while."

Beau realized Kieran was right. He needed a change as much as she. "A ride."

"Not the Island Buggy! Please."

"Horseback." She paused. "You do ride, don't you?"

Kieran looked doubtful, but game. "A little."

Thirteen

"You ride a little, huh?" Beau wrinkled her nose at him, as he reined the black stallion to a halt by her mare.

"A little is all I seem to have time for."

"Ahh, you were speaking of time in your disclaimer."

There was laughter in her eyes, and color in her cheeks, and Kieran found himself enchanted all over again. The break was a good idea. Riding, even better.

For an hour they'd splashed across creeks, and dodged trees. Even outraced a wandering alligator, as Beau led him deeper into the interior of the island. She'd ridden in a haphazard path, yet he never questioned that she had a destination.

"Care to tell me where we're going?" His horse, aptly named Blackbeard's Ride, shied at the sound of a strange voice. With an expert hand, Kieran settled him down.

"I'd considered a place, before we began. Now that I know how you ride, I'd like to take you there."

"I'll go anywhere with you, Beau." To hell and back, if necessary. "Lead the way. I'll be right behind you."

The way she took him was convoluted and arduous. When they splashed across a wide but shallow stream, Kieran realized they were on a separate island. One that was deeper rather than long, with a narrow strip of shore. Expecting Beau to turn to the east and the sea, he was surprised when she urged Jezebel, her feisty mare, through a thick growth of myrtle. Once past that narrow access, the trail widened.

Twisted trees grew stunted and sparse, yet years of fallen leaves covered the ground. Moss hung thick and low, causing

Kieran to lean in his saddle. Heat rose from the ground in sultry waves broken by sporadic breezes. The scent of loam lay heavy in the air.

Kieran wasn't ready for the clapboard church hunkered in a clearing. The path gave no warning sign of travel. Then he knew. The old, unpainted building was no longer used for worship. Nor had it been for a long while. Yet its steps were in good repair. Its shutters hung in perfect alignment by wind scarred windows, and the tin roof was newly painted. Even the hinges of the rough and splinter studded door were oiled and bright.

He didn't need to ask who was responsible for the good repair. Taking care of people and things came with the territory of being a Cahill.

Dismounting, with Jezebel's reins looped through her fingers, Beau walked across the churchyard. "I haven't been here in months. I'd forgotten how lovely the old church is."

"You don't check behind the crew that sees to its upkeep." Kieran matched his step to hers.

"There's no need. The crew would be too frightened of Tabby's wrath to do anything less than their best."

Kieran could relate to that. "Why did the church fall into disuse?"

"Changing topography. Time, tides, storms." Beau led him to a small cemetery enclosed by an iron fence. "This was part of the main island until a hurricane ripped lives and land apart. For longer than I can remember the stream we crossed was deep and wide. An obstacle that made it too difficult for the islander to worship or bury their dead here."

"With accretion the stream grows smaller," Kieran observed.

"Yes. If it continues, one day, two parts of an island will be reunited."

"At the risk of being torn asunder in another place, by another storm."

Beau met his steady gaze. "It's the lot of the islander to live and die and change by the whim of tide and storm."

Kieran knew Beau was thinking of her mother, who died from injuries caused by such a storm. He looked out over the neatly kept burial plots. Some were lined with shells gathered from the shore. Others were covered with grass or sand. The headstones were old and darkened, the wooden crosses and boards were splintered. None tipped over or tilted. "Are there Cahills here?"

Beau nodded. "Along with the freemen. But no one since early in this century, when the storm split the island."

"Is the church locked?"

"There's a key kept in a box by the door."

Kieran grinned. "Keeping out honest folk?"

"Maybe."

Beau led the way across what had once been a walk of broken shells. Now they were so deeply pounded into the ground by hundreds of feet over time, they resembled tabby.

The key rattled in a lock that opened easily. The door swung inward without creak or groan. Sunlight filtered through the frosted glass of arched windows, turning dust motes to fireflies.

But the dust drifting from the aged ceiling was the only dust apparent. The interior of the church was in perfect order, and scrupulously clean.

"My compliments to the repair crew," Kieran murmured.

Beau stepped into the church in bewilderment. "The crew didn't do this."

"How do you know?"

"The interior of the church was never painted. My father chose to keep it as it was. I've honored his wishes."

"Someone else had other ideas." Kieran ran a finger down a stark white wall. "Whitewash."

"But who?" Beau spun, trying to remember the church as she'd seen it last. "The pulpit has been repaired. There was a split in the base."

"Not anymore."

"The pews have been waxed. The hymn books are in their

holders. They were packed in metal trunks in the choir room years ago.''

"Maybe we should check the choir room,'' Kieran suggested.

"Maybe we should.''

More than an hour later, Beau was sitting in the choir room with the third of six massive leather-bound volumes in her lap. "We were told these records were lost in the storm. Where have they been all these years? Who returned them? Why has he done all this?''

"Someone with family buried here?''

"That could be any of us.'' Beau enumerated, "Tabby, Hattie, Norrie, Skip.''

"You didn't mention Israel. No family for him? I've heard the tale of the enterprising rumrunner. Beyond that, he seems to have sprung out of thin air.''

"Israel has recent family buried in the cemetery on the main island, but none here. Unless they lie in unmarked graves, with their names recorded in the lost records. I do know that some left the island and others were lost at sea.''

"Running rum.''

"I suppose. The only family I've ever known, or heard of, was his grandmother, who had returned to the island and lived in the tavern that had fallen into disuse again. She was a virtual recluse. Everyone, my dad included, thought she was the last of the line. Then, one day she left the island, and returned with a baby. Israel. No one knew she'd had a child, or grandchildren, and she never explained. She died while he was in college.''

"Not a prolific family. Nor a close one.''

"No, but she was the reason Israel came back to the island. He remodeled and reopened the tavern because it was the only home he knew, and a part of the heritage she gave him.'' Smoothing a hand over the stained cover of the book she held, Beau voiced a thought that had been troubling her. "You're suspicious because of his silly tantrum.''

"Tantrum?" Kieran considered it a hell of a lot more serious. A hell of a lot more dangerous.

"Israel's always been this way. When he sees his control slipping, or feels an encroachment on what he considers his territory, he reacts in the extreme. The drinking complicated matters."

"Is this the friend speaking, or the psychologist?"

"Both," she admitted. "But mostly the friend."

A friend who needed to shed her rose-colored glasses. Kieran realized he wanted to shake her, then kiss her. On the heels of that, he questioned his own attitude. "Son of a gun," he growled. "I'm jealous!"

"Kieran."

Steeling himself for her comment, instead he found her sifting through another trunk.

"Look." She held a book up for his inspection. A very small book, when all the others had been tomes of records and dates, dealing with the church and its members. Their marriages, births. Deaths.

"What is it, love?" Love. The word had come easily from the first. It had begun as a teasing endearment. Now it was the element of truth.

"A journal. Of a young island boy."

"Which island boy?" Kieran had grown familiar enough with the families that he might associate the author with someone he'd met.

"It doesn't say." From her place by the open trunk, she looked up at him. "If you don't mind, I'd like to read for a while."

It never occurred to Kieran to suggest she take the book home. Everything within the perfectly ordered church seemed to belong only to it. "I'll look around while you read."

"Thank you," she said, and meant it. That he respected the church and its contents as much as she, strengthened the bond they shared.

Kieran busied himself with the remainder of the trunks, and it was apparent someone had opened them recently, meticulously dusting covers and smoothing folded pages. The island had acquired an archivist of the first order. Norrie?

No. Whoever had done this labor of love, had been here recently and often. And would surely return. A chill he couldn't explain trickled down his spine as he thought of that return. "Sweetheart..."

As he began, she looked up at him. Her finger marked her place. "He's done all the things we did as children. Wade the creeks, bait the 'gators. He describes an old boulder washed in by a storm. He played pirate there. Pretending it was his lookout."

That stone was long gone. Washed away by another storm. Over the years other stones had taken its place, becoming the pirate's watchtower of other children. Skip and Israel, Rick and Beau had clambered across their share of stone pirate ships.

"He sounds like a happy child." As Beau had been after her sixth year, Kieran remembered.

When she didn't answer, he wasn't surprised. She was engrossed again in childhood adventures time never changed.

Once he heard her murmur, "He has a girlfriend." Then, laughing, she amended, "Lots of them. He could be Rick's twin, born a century before."

She was still reading when he left to take a walk. He had traversed the beach several times over and was standing on shifting sand, watching the rising tide, when a sixth sense caused him to turn. Beau stood just beyond the sand, surrounded by creeping vines and sea oats. The journal was in her hand. Tears streaked the dust on her face.

In the worst of times, even when her eyes misted with tears, Beau never truly cried. Uttering silent concern, with visions of biting snakes and spiders, he hurried to her. "Darling, what is it? Are you hurt?"

"It isn't me." She offered the journal. "It's the boy. He was only having fun, exploring his newfound masculinity. But she loved him."

As he took the journal, she explained. "The overseer's

daughter, and not suitable at all. They both knew it. But the last night of the carnival she danced for him.''

As Beau had danced for Kieran. A dance no man could resist.

Before he began to read, Kieran knew the outcome. It was an old story. A carefree boy maturing into a dashing young man, fair of face and body, exhilarated by the discovery of his prowess. The lovestruck, not-quite-acceptable girl, desperate for his attention, ripe for what he thought were games. Wonderful, scary games. But only that. She was never more than a dalliance. An adoring childhood companion, with whom he could perfect his wit and charm. In his innocence he never meant her harm, never thought beyond the moment of sexual conquest. Never considered the consequences. And even as he'd dallied with the girl, he'd fallen in love, truly in love, with another girl. Someone more suitable.

As he read on a cold chill swept the heat from the day. ''A child.''

''Born of the night she danced.'' Fresh tears brimmed in Beau's eyes. ''She must've been so afraid.''

''And he, torn between guilt for what he'd done and the call of a world so new to him.'' A rare breeze ruffled the pages that counted down to disaster. Holding them back, Kieran read on. Of pressures and threats, of coercion and guilt. And a desperate marriage, conducted in secret in the little church. With only the minister present.

Seeds of tragedy, irrevocably sewn.

The happy boy had become a terrified young man with a secret and improper wife, a bastard child, and a very proper fiancée.

Terror turned to desperation.

Desperation to murder.

Beau watched as Kieran sank to the trunk of a fallen oak. The journal clutched in a white-knuckled hand, as the account deteriorated into a disjointed ramble of fear and madness as the young man wrote of luring his new wife to the church, then the cemetery.

"He killed her." Kieran spoke the inevitable. "Here among the graves. Then he took her to the beach. He sat there with her for hours, covered with sand and bathed in her blood."

"Because he couldn't believe what he'd done," Beau whispered, for to speak it aloud was too appalling.

"'Stirring from my stupor, at last, I took her to the sea. To wash the blood from her.'" Kieran looked up, reciting softly, "'To make her pretty again.'"

The tide lapped at their feet. A gull cried like a child, and the day seemed darker when he began to read again. "'Then I laid her on the sand, to rest. And left her the gift of the Moon Dancers, to bring her safe passage into a better world.'"

Marking his place with a faded ribbon, Kieran closed the book. For a long while, he didn't speak or look at Beau. When his gaze lifted to hers, he read the sadness and the horror she felt. For the confused boy. For a poor young girl. And the knowledge that he'd read a description of the murders on Moon Dancers Island.

Opening the journal, he read again. Even in remorse, the boy's fugue of terror and madness was not done. Like a gruesome specter from the night, he roused the minister from his bed in the little parsonage behind the church. First to confess his sin, then to do murder again. Silencing the only witness to his lust, and the weakness of pride.

"'Taking the minister's body and his meager belongings to the boat the church provided, I rowed far out to sea. With an ax I smashed the hull. Then, leaving the boat to sink, I swam to shore.

"'It was so far. The sea was so rough, I thought I would die. I hoped I would die.'" Kieran looked away from the journal to a sea as calm as a lake. "'But I did not.'"

Beau had stood, a silent, unmoving observer. Now she crossed the dune, to sit by Kieran. He touched her face. Letting his fingers linger at her temple, he measured the beat of her heart.

Long ago a young girl died here on this shore. Now her death was being reenacted. But for what purpose? Why did he feel so strongly that Beau was in terrible danger, and time was running out?

Hoping the answer was in the journal, he opened the fragile, yellowing pages and, with Beau, returned to the shocking story.

A peculiar calm entered the writing, as if he told the tale of someone else. Reading the young man's stoic plan to go on with his life, letting the islanders believe the minister had killed the girl and run away, they knew a part of him had died that night with the girl.

"'I pray that someday my God, and the deities of the Moon Dancers will forgive me.'" Kieran's bleak gaze moved to the scrawled signature at the end of the damning revelation. "'Christian Cahill, first and favored son of Charles Cahill.'"

The next page and the pages that followed were blank. The story of a happy boy who grew into a handsome young man ended with this twist of tragedy. When Kieran would have laid the heartbreaking account aside, Beau said in a hushed voice, "There's more."

Taking the book, turning to the last page and an entry written by Charles Cahill, she read the words of a grieving father, who spoke of suspicions and then discovery of the awful thing his son had done. She read his admission that he couldn't give Christian to the sheriff, and instead, banished him from the island, forbidding him to ever return. Then, under the guise of another reason, he made generous restitution to the girl's family, and found the father more promising employment far away from the island.

"'As for my own punishment...'" Her voice broke as she read the words of the benevolent patriarch of Cahill's Grant. When she began again, she spoke precisely, but with pain in every inflection. "'As for my own punishment, I must deny myself my grandchild—the son of my favorite son.

"'And what greater punishment, I ask my God, than to lose both?'"

Closing the book, Beau folded it to her breast.

"What greater punishment, indeed." Kieran's low comment was nearly lost in the lazy wash of a sea that had kept its secret for longer than a century.

Rising, Beau held her hand to him. "I have something to show you."

Hand in hand and silently they climbed the small dune that separated the shore from the interior of the island. Kieran wasn't surprised when she led him to the cemetery rather than the church.

With a mild creak the heavy iron gate swung open. Stepping through, without hesitating, she threaded her way through the graves, so many of which seemed tiny. Babies, perhaps much loved, desperately wanted, yet lost. When another had caused only tragedy.

Stopping before a grave in the oldest part of the cemetery, Beau gestured to the small headstone with its engraving nearly worn away. "Hannah Desmond."

"The overseer's daughter."

"Charles Cahill took care of her grave for years. He came here regularly. So long as he was able, he wouldn't let anyone else do what was needed. In his will, provisions were made for the care to continue. He charged each of his sons, and their sons, and any who came after, to continue as he had. No one ever knew why. It was a mystery he took to his grave."

"Without understanding, each generation did as charged," Kieran said. "Because that was and is the Cahill way."

"It's all we've ever known."

"What of Christian?" With the Cahill penchant for meticulous records, there would be something of the boy. In her study and love of the family history, Beau would know.

"Shortly before Charles's death a monument was erected here, in memory of Christian, saying he'd been lost at sea." Beau's smile was melancholy. Her eyes were dark and shielded from the brightness of the day by the veil of her lashes. "Maybe it was true. Maybe not. But his soul was lost here by the sea, long before it claimed his body."

Kieran didn't comment. None was needed. "There's no monument."

"Like the parsonage, it took the brunt of the storm and tide that split the island. It was never found. When the church was abandoned, no one but the crews came here. Christian and Hannah were forgotten."

"Except by the Cahills."

"Even we never understood, until now."

She was tired, Kieran could see it in the angle of her shoulders, and in the shadows beneath her eyes. By the cant of the sun, he knew the afternoon was at its cusp, ready to slip into twilight. Laying a palm at the nape of her neck, he drew her to him. "Let's put the journal back where it belongs, sweetheart, and go home."

The word, home, slipped off his tongue as easily as the endearment. Most of his time was spent at The Bluff, now. With trips made to Heron's Walk for changes of clothing and to check on the house and grounds. His days and nights evolved around Beau. And keeping her safe.

"The tide's rising. If we don't want to swim the channel, we'd best get moving."

Beau nodded and lifted her mouth to his kiss. A long while later, they walked arm in arm to the horses.

The low rumble of masculine voices greeted her as she skipped down the stairs. Pausing at the last riser Beau identified the varied intonations. It had been a long while since all the men she loved shared the ritual of breakfast at The Bluff. Now all were here.

With one more.

One who made her hurry to the breakfast room and lifted her heart at the sight of him.

He lounged in his chair at the head of the table. The place Opal had set for him each morning since the first day she'd wakened to find him on the veranda, drinking coffee he'd made for himself.

Though the day was still young, sunlight filtered through the trees and in the fall of its reflected glow, Kieran looked fresh and rested. His dark hair, still damp from an early swim in the sea, fell in gradual disorder as it dried in the mounting heat. While he listened to the jovial conversation that had been missing from The Bluff's breakfast table for so long, his tanned fingers toyed lazily with the delicate handle of his cup.

Watching from the doorway, Beau remembered the touch of those gentle fingers. Their lazy, maddening caress at her breasts. The smile that vanished as his eyes darkened with passion.

With her own fingers curling against the need to brush a dark lock from his forehead, she stepped into the room.

Kieran was first to see her. First to rise in the courtesy the others had long forgotten as she'd become one of the gang. "Good morning, love."

Drawing out the chair by his side, he seated her, while Rick and Skip and Israel struggled, shamefaced, to their feet. When Kieran's hand lingered at her shoulder, she touched it with her own. "Good morning."

And it was. Beau was happier than she'd been in a long time, laughing with her brother and her friends. Listening to Skip's latest adventure with the eccentrics who seemed drawn to his charters. Seeing the natural camaraderie between the islanders and Kieran. Watching the easing of tensions in Israel.

It would have been a perfect day, if three young women had not died senselessly. If she'd never discovered the journal of Christian Cahill. Never learned his tragedy.

"You aren't hungry?"

Kieran's question and his hand covering hers drew her back from the path her thoughts had taken. "Not yet." She gave him the smile he could always elicit, no matter how dark her thoughts. "I slept so well last night, my stomach hasn't realized it's morning yet."

At her mention of the night, his look turned tender. His eyes darkened in memory of the hurting and beautiful woman who had come to him, needing desperately the surcease she found only in his love and passion.

"Later?" His fingers stroked hers. Their touch a promise.

"Please." The subtle stir of desire turned the single word breathless, and flagged her cheeks with color, as the desultory conversation around the table ceased.

It was Rick who drawled, "I'm not even going to ask what that was all about. But I'm not fool enough to think it has a damn thing to do with grits and eggs."

"On that fine note, I'll say my thanks to Opal and hie myself to the barn." Israel tossed his napkin on the table. "The groom asked me to take a look at Jezebel. She was wheezing this morning."

As irascible as he was with people, Israel was the soul of kindness with horses. For that, and for this morning, Beau could forgive him any ill temper. "I'll go with you."

"Sure." Israel grinned. "Jezebel's easy. A pat on the forelock and a cube of sugar, and she might accept your apology for the drenching you gave her yesterday."

"Drenching?" Skip set his cup down and turned a questioning look to Beau. "Swimming on horseback again, sweet Beau?"

"Crossing the channel from the church, near high tide," Kieran answered.

Skip's curious expression altered to a frown. "You went to the old island?"

With something in Kieran's look warning her to be cautious, Beau said casually, "Giving Kieran a quick tour of the island."

"Then you didn't spend much time there." Skip looked from Kieran to Beau. "You didn't go into the church?"

"We didn't have a lot of time," Beau evaded.

Skip tossed his napkin on his plate and stood. "Next time

you go, be careful. Steer clear of the steps to the sanctuary. At least until I can clear away the den of pygmy rattlers the crew found camping under them.''

"Rattlers!" Even knowing there were no snakes under the church steps, Beau shuddered. Little in the world frightened her as much as snakes. "Then I don't think I'll be returning for a while.''

"Maybe not," Israel drawled. "But if you're going with me to the barn, you'd best hop to. I was due at the tavern ten minutes ago.''

Before the tramp of their footsteps faded, Skip excused himself muttering vaguely about a troublesome engine again. When they were alone, Kieran turned to Rick. In succinct terms he described the day at the church. The perfectly ordered interior, the dusted books. The journal and the story it told of Christian Cahill.

"Whew!" Rick whistled softly. "Then what we have is a copycat.''

Kieran looked at him sharply, his eyes narrowed.

"Hey, man!" Rick lifted his shoulders in question. "Surely you don't think the similarities in the murders and Christian's deed are coincidental.''

"It isn't that. When you said the word copycat, it triggered something. Something I should remember." His fist closed over his napkin, crushing it in his palm. "Something.... Damn!" His look was frustrated. "It's gone.''

He would remember. Rick knew Kieran's reputation well enough to know the elusive thought would eventually be assimilated in that orderly brain. "Don't sweat it. Let it rest. It'll come to you.''

"Yeah," Kieran growled. "But soon enough?''

Rick sipped from a full cup. Scowling when he found it cold, he set it down. "If we just had one lead.''

Any who thought this Cahill was only a charming playboy would be shocked at the transformation Kieran saw. "Rick, what did you think of Skip's reaction to our visit to the small island?''

"Everybody knows how much Beau hates…" A hard gray stare met unwavering blue. "Except there were no snakes."

"Not at the steps."

"He was making sure Beau wouldn't go back."

"Why?" The blunt question was Kieran's response. "What does Skip have at stake here?"

"Nothing. None of this makes any sense. Except that maybe there were snakes. Once."

"Beau says he has family buried on the small island."

"Like the Cahill name, the name Hayes peppers the town and the cemeteries." Rick's grin was grim.

"What of the maternal side?" Kieran left the table to stand by the window. But today he didn't notice the land sprawling beyond the glass. "Were the wives and mothers islanders?"

"There's one person who would know."

Kieran turned from the window. "Tabby."

Jezebel stood quietly. The labored breathing the groom described was easing. Israel returned to Beau. "She'll be fine. Let her take it easy for a few days."

"What is it?"

"From the look of her leg, a Man-of-War got her. There's swelling, and sting marks. The breathing must be delayed anaphylactic reaction. It's late, but it happens. Jeremy will continue bathing the wound in vinegar."

"Man-of-War? They aren't that common here."

"Common enough. It only takes one, Beau. I wouldn't swim her across the channel again."

"We didn't swim. The tide wasn't that high."

"Whatever." Israel shrugged. "Still, I wouldn't risk it again."

"I guess I shouldn't."

"Kieran's seen the island." Handing the vinegar bottle to the groom, he took Beau's arm and led her from the barn. "Why would you go back?"

"No reason." To change the subject she said, "You missed your calling, Israel. You should have been a vet."

"Nah." He chuckled. "You know the only animals I tolerate are horses."

He drew her to a halt by the corral. Leaning against the fence, he stared down at her for an uncomfortable minute, then looked away.

Watching him in profile, Beau realized familiarity had blinded her. Over the years she'd forgotten how tall and blond and handsome Israel was. The perpetual tan made his blue eyes darker, rather than lighter. She wondered if it were possible they were truly navy.

"He's the one, isn't he?" His arm braced against the fence, he waited for her answer.

"Maybe."

"Maybe?" he chided. "Our innocent island girl sleeps with a man and says maybe? Won't wash."

"You know me pretty well."

"Better than I know myself, obviously." Israel looked at her then, the quirk of his lips somber rather than a smile.

"Are you all right now?"

"Ahh, you know how I've always been, Beau. Never know I want something until someone else has it." He touched her cheek briefly. His dark eyes glittered with some emotion Beau couldn't interpret. "I'm sorry it has to be this way. I wish…"

With a shake of his head, his hand closed into a fist, his knuckles drifted down her jaw to her chin. "In this case the best man won." Drawing a deep breath he straightened away from the fence, and glanced at his watch. "But win or lose, I have to go, or Cookie will be nuts."

"Israel…"

"Don't." He stopped her protest. "There's nothing to say. What's done can't be changed. What happens next was set into motion longer ago than either of us can know." He didn't touch her again, but his look was somber. "Thank Opal for the breakfast. When Skip and I dropped by, we didn't intend to do more than see how you were. But sharing a meal, with all of us there, was like old times."

Beau stood through the polite speech with the feeling that Israel was saying more than she understood. Then she attributed it to embarrassed rambling for his behavior on the nights he'd been drinking. "You'll come again soon?"

The grin he flashed was the old Israel, yet a little off kilter. "Sooner than you expect. Now, there's a lucky man in the house who must be wondering what's keeping you."

With one finger he tapped his forehead in a salute and took the back trail that led to the village. He disappeared into the underbrush before Beau turned, and with a brooding look in her eyes, hurried into the house. To Kieran.

Fourteen

"Hannah Desmond? Yes, my grandmother told me of her."

"What did she tell you?" Jericho leaned forward intently.

The old woman lifted her meagerly sighted eyes. "That she loved a man and danced for him." Her mouth twitched sadly. "She caught a baby. A son, born in nine months, a bloody birthing on a night of the full moon."

Caught a baby. A term Beau had heard all her life. One still used by the islanders to name an illegitimate birth.

"She died. Murdered," Tabby continued. "The night the minister of the old church disappeared. There were rumors of other men. Hints that it was her father. Or a Moon Dancer, because of a talisman found with her. But there was no proof. After a while, with the abandoning of the old cemetery, she was forgotten."

"What happened to the child?" Kieran kept from his voice his certainty that a son descended from that tragic union stalked the island.

"He was taken away. Hannah's father was a proud man, glad to leave behind his daughter's disgrace. But my grandmother feared for the boy. Raul Desmond was as brutal as he was proud. He hated all the child represented. Making his lot worse, the grandmother, a whining slattern, would surely pass on her family's insanity."

"Your grandmother feared for the boy." Jericho spoke with flagging hope. "She didn't know what happened after the Desmonds left the island."

"Her sight, like mine, was imperfect." Tabby was stoic in

regret that she couldn't give the information needed. "No one heard of them again."

Struck by inspiration, Beau took the gnarled hand in her own. "Can you see? Do you know?"

Scarves of Tabby's turban fluttered around frail shoulders. "I know only what she told me."

Beau pressed her hand. "I'm not asking about the past. I mean now. Surely there were children. The son or daughter of a son or daughter."

Beau hoped Tabby would respond with answers she didn't realize were significant.

Across the table, Kieran and Jericho waited in the sepulchral quiet of the Tea House. Within an hour, the small structure would be teeming with diners drawn to the island in spite of the murders. Or because of them.

Jericho spoke gently. "We think there might be a son, a descendant of Hannah's. If there is, do you know where he is?"

Tabby turned from one to the other, straining to see more than vague shapes. "He's where he's been from a babe."

Beau caught a trembling breath, asking the question that must be asked. "Where is he?"

"Why here, on the island. Of course." Scarves swirling, she nodded toward the tavern. "He lives there."

Israel.

Simply identifying Hannah Desmond's lost descendant wouldn't constitute proof of murder. But two among them had no doubt.

Beau was stunned, not sure what she believed.

Jericho was grim in bitter anger. At himself for being blinded by friendship. At Israel for his betrayal, and the terrible acts he'd committed.

Kieran was angry, but only at himself, for not pursuing an instinct so overwhelming. But he was puzzled by Tabby. Her gift of sight was real, yet she'd lived among those involved, knowing Israel's heritage, yet hadn't seen more than that he was a user.

For one moment this strange phenomenon made no sense. But only for one. "Tabby, when we saw Blue, you said one of the island children mutilated him."

"I remember."

"You told me something about that child, but you couldn't tell me his name then. Can you now?"

"No!" Her denial was uncompromising. "Beau never told me, and I can't see him."

"Can't?" Kieran asked kindly, for she was fragile as glass. "Or won't let yourself."

Jericho added his soft persuasion to Kieran's. "We have to know. Even if it implicates someone you love."

"I can't see!" The ancient seeress was adamant.

Kieran believed she'd locked herself away from something too painful. "Then tell us who you fear it was. Please. Lives are at stake."

Tabby hesitated, her age scarred face a mournful mask.

Understanding this must be told as the seeress believed it, Beau added her own plea. "Please, Tabby."

An unsteady hand passed over a dark face. Fingers pressed at sunken temples willing away excruciating agony. Then she laid splayed hands on the table. Tabby's decision was made.

"Rick."

The only reaction was Beau's startled gasp, cut short by a warning shake of Kieran's head.

If she heard it, Tabby didn't acknowledge the sound. Now that she told the story, it would be finished. "When Beau Anna brought the fawn to me, she never said what had happened, or who had done this terrible thing. But she was so upset, I understood."

Kieran believed in Tabby, yet this didn't fit. Sure some piece of the puzzle was missing or misinterpreted, he played a hunch to the hilt. "You couldn't see the boy, Tabby. But you told me something about him, something very important. Will you tell Jericho?"

The old woman was so withdrawn, he thought she wouldn't answer. When she spoke, after a time, her voice was weak. "I couldn't see the boy. I can't see him now. But I've seen that he's the one." Her face crumpled, her sightless eyes were dead. "He didn't want to do it at first, but he had to. Something made him."

"Something made him?" Kieran's voice was soothing, coaxing. "What did it make him do, Tabby?"

Tabby didn't blink or shift from her rigid posture. A gust of wind could have shattered her. "He hurt the girls."

"No!" Beau had listened in horror, her cry was for the agony of this beloved old woman who had shut herself in darkness, hiding an unbearable fear. In her shock, Beau understood. She'd witnessed this powerful force among the parents of her small patients. Denial, the subconscious protection of love.

Tabby hadn't allowed herself to see, because she feared the killer was her beloved Rick!

Taking an unresponsive hand back into both of hers, Beau spoke a child's secret, guarded for most of a lifetime. "Rick didn't attack the fawn that day, Tabby. It was Israel."

Israel, the child, of a child, of a child of Hannah Desmond and Christian Cahill. Who, by right of parentage and terms of the entailment of Cahill's Grant, was as entitled to his heritage as Rick or Beau.

Who, by the aberrations of his maternal lineage, was quite possibly, even probably, insane.

The missing piece. Kieran, who hadn't known his fists were clinched, sagged in relief.

"He was a cruel child." Tabby's voice splintered the hush shrouding the table. "Whenever Rick, or Beau Anna, or Skip were hurt, he was always there. Always unscathed. Israel never fell from rigging. Never caught a fish hook in his neck. Never found a burr under his saddle, or a rattler in his boot."

Tabby's shoulders slumped. "I should have known. I should have seen."

"It isn't your fault..." Beau's compassion was rejected abruptly, by the slash of a staying hand. Murky eyes lifted to her and seemed to pierce her mind and soul.

''Where is he?'' Tabby's demand was a desperate whisper. ''Where is Rick?''

''He stayed home. Thinking he shouldn't be a part of this, because of the rumors.''

''*He's* there!'' Fingers contracting like claws, Tabby's voice failed, the words only shapes on her lips.

Jericho, last to arrive for their meeting was first to react. His chair crashed back, his big body straightened in a purposeful move. ''We'd better hurry. Israel was taking the path to The Bluff when I arrived.''

Kieran was only a blink of an eye behind him, pausing to stop Beau. ''No, love. Jericho and I can handle this.''

She took his hand away, but clutched it tightly before releasing it. ''Rick's my brother. I have to be there.'' Looking from Kieran to Jericho, frightened, but determined, she explained. ''No matter what he's done, nor what he's thinking now, I've been part of Israel's life for as long as either of us can remember. If he'll listen to anyone, it will be me.''

''No.''

''She's right, O'Hara,'' Jericho cut in. ''Even if she's not, we don't have time to argue.'' His look was grave. ''We may be too late already.''

Kieran hesitated only another heartbeat. Jericho was right. But he'd wanted to spare Beau what they might find. ''All right.''

At the cost of a precious second, he bent over Tabby, kissing a tearstained cheek. ''You've done your part. Now, win or lose, the rest is up to us.''

Jericho added his agreement, and Beau whispered, ''I love you,'' against a withered cheek.

The tumult of running footsteps died away, the Tea House was empty. Except for Tabitha Hill, who sat silent and alone, at the edge of twilight.

''Dear God!'' Jericho groaned as he absorbed the chaos of the drawing room. Nothing was in place. Nothing was undamaged. Blood splashed wall and floor.

So much blood.

Kieran's first reaction was to reach for Beau. "If I know Rick, he put up a hell of a fight and as much of this is Israel's blood as his."

Hoping her knees would hold her, Beau stepped away from his embrace. "Where's Rick?"

"*He* took him."

Whirling, Beau came face-to-face with the housekeeper. "Opal! I thought you'd gone visiting in the village."

"Did." Her red head moved crisply and a painful flinch revealed she regretted the move. Her cheek was swollen and bruised. Blood from a cut on her mouth stained her chin and dried on her dress. "Came back early to bake Rick's favorite pie. Met them on the back path."

No one questioned that she spoke of Rick and Israel. "Rick was hurt. When I tried to stop them, *he* did this to me."

Still no one questioned that it was Israel who struck her.

Beau led the housekeeper to a chair as she continued in a rush, "Must've knocked me silly. When I came to myself, I'd bled like a stuck pig." Casting her gaze about the room, her damaged lips curled in grim satisfaction. "From the looks of this, so did he."

"He?" Beau asked desperately.

"Rick bashed his blond head, split it from forehead to crown." Opal cackled in glee. "Nothing bleeds like a head wound."

"But Rick was…"

"Hurt, but not too bad. Maybe drugged." Opal gestured toward a broken glass. "What on earth got into Israel? He looked as crazy as he acted."

"I think maybe he is, Opal. He has been for a long time." Beau knelt before her. "Would you like me to call Tabby?"

Opal patted Beau's hand. "You three best be on your way. I can call Tabby myself."

"Where was Israel taking him?"

"From the direction he headed, could be anywhere. My guess would be the old church."

Beau wasted no time wondering how Opal arrived at that conclusion. As the housekeeper finished speaking she was rushing toward the stables. The trip to The Bluff had been accomplished by an all-terrain vehicle Jericho brought to the island. With the tide coming in, it would be useless in the channel.

Kieran was at her side, Jericho a pace behind. Three horses were saddled, with rifles in scabbards. Mounted and anxious, after a terse request that Jeremy look in on Opal, Beau wheeled her horse toward the trail, urging him into a gallop.

The tide was in and rough. They would have to swim the horses across.

Leaning on the pommel, Jericho studied the current. "Could be dangerous. No chance of surprise, unless we split up. One of us acting as decoy."

"Israel will be expecting me," Beau interjected. "That's why Opal is still alive. She was to be the messenger. Long enough to entice me to the small island."

Kieran knew she was right. He knew that if this went as Israel planned, no Cahill would survive. Before he was done, neither would Opal, or Jeremy, and especially Tabby.

"I should go in alone." Beau quieted her horse with a touch. "The two of you can come later, when he's distracted."

"Won't work." Kieran was adamant. "Israel may be insane, but he's the most logical lunatic I've ever seen. He wouldn't believe for a minute I'd let you come alone." He stroked her cheek, his thumb caressed the softness of her throat. There was tenderness and concern in a stormy blue gaze that brooked no argument. "We go together."

In minutes, their plan formulated, Jericho watched as Cahill and O'Hara rode into the deadly current of high tide. It wasn't until they climbed, drenched and dripping on the opposite shore that he turned his mount and galloped toward the sea.

"Easy." Kieran soothed his horse as he dismounted. Turning, he caught Beau as she slipped from the saddle. He held her, his gaze reaching into hers. "You'll be careful?"

Beau nodded.

"Remember, the man who has Rick isn't the man who was your friend. You can't expect him to react as he would've. Israel's gone over the edge. He's walked that fine line for a long time, slipping once in a while. This time he's gone too far. He won't come back. He can't."

Kieran realized he was telling her things that as a psychologist, she knew better than he. But he had to be sure loyalties of the past didn't blind her to the truth. "We do this just like Jericho said. Right?"

"Like Jericho said," Beau agreed.

"Are you ready?"

Beau squared her shoulders and stepped away. "As ready as I'll ever be."

"Beau." When she looked at him, lovely in his eyes, and in the rosy hues of the beginning of twilight, he didn't say what he intended. This wasn't the time to tell her what he should have long ago.

Not the time to distract her with declarations of the love he'd spoken time and again in a look, a touch, an endearment. Yet never the words.

Never, simply, I love you. I have since that first misty day on the beach. I will forever.

No, this wasn't the time at all. But soon.

She wouldn't die today. Or any day. If it meant his life instead, she wouldn't die.

When he called her name, she'd stopped. He willed his mouth to open, and his tongue to speak, but he hadn't the words. The safe, encouraging words. In the end he only smoothed her wild hair from her face and kissed her temple where her life's blood pulsed.

"Luck."

Touching the place his lips had lain, her smile melancholy, she turned away to go to Rick.

The church was a hulking shape hidden from all but the most discerning eyes. No light broached the thickening shade. Footsteps, muffled by a blanket of leaves, were only a whisper. One could almost think it an ordinary walk, in an ordinary place, on an ordinary night.

But as they approached the cemetery with the fence casting long shadows, and stones painted in flickering light, the spectacle that awaited them was ghastly.

"Copycat," Kieran whispered. "He warned us. He wanted us to know."

That Israel had slipped beyond the realm of reason was unquestionable. He stood among the graves an unfamiliar figure—tall, the lines of his body blatantly masculine, and his hands stained with blood. He'd dressed for the occasion in an exquisite dinner gown of bright, flowing georgette. His blond hair hung about his face and brushed the tops of shoulders so wide they threatened the ruffled seams of the fragile fabric.

His face had been painted by a skilled hand. Mascara darkened long lashes. Cheeks highlighted by a sweep of blush accented bone structure any cover girl would envy. No lipstick smeared ear to ear. His mouth, lightly touched with gloss, and framing perfect teeth, tilted in a ghastly, lovely smile as he watched their approach.

Beau scarcely spared a glance for the beautiful horror that had been her friend. It was Rick, sprawled against an age blackened stone who riveted her concern. The brother she loved as if he were part of herself was pale, and bloody. And lifeless.

"Israel!" She gripped the iron pickets of the gate, challenging the specter above the flare of candles scattered among the graves. "What have you done? Rick never hurt you. Those young women never hurt you. Neither have I."

If he heard her, or noticed Kieran standing a pace behind, Israel didn't respond. Instead, the lovely face creased into a simper as he wiggled his fingers at his handiwork.

"How do you like your party? And the church?" His voice was breathless. As feminine as a bass tone could be. "I did this especially for you and Christian, you know." He eased his weight from one foot to the other, the sway of his skirts awkwardly effeminate. "I found the lost records in the tavern years ago when Norrie remodeled. When the time was right, I brought them here. This is where they were. Where they belong. I wanted to make everything as it was."

Beau listened, hardly aware of the heat, or the darkness. Only Kieran, standing a pace behind, reminded her it was truly a sane world as she listened to the mad babble with a breaking heart and cold fear lying like a stone in her chest.

"I killed the snakes under the steps. Since we all know how sweet Beau hates the crawly things. Skip would move them. But I killed them." The painted mouth formed a contrived moue. "But you remember, don't you, Beau, that I like to kill things?"

The knife flicked down, slicing Rick's cheek. Beau's choked cry was quieted by Kieran's warning touch.

Israel was too caught in his delusion to notice.

"Everything's ready," the singsong falsetto continued. "The church, Christian. You, me." His voice sank to a wheedle. "So come to the party, Beau. Sweet Beau."

"I don't feel like a party, Israel."

"Don't call me that awful name." In wavering candlelight his eyes were fierce. Lunatic. "I'm Hannah."

"Why?"

"Because my grandmother told me that one day I must become her. Since I was a little boy, she made me promise. She made me do things." His voice faltered, and for one small ration of time, Beau saw the Israel she'd known. The Israel she loved.

"I didn't want to rig the winch to hurt Christian's hands." The deep voice slipped from the broken falsetto and back.

"She said it was right you and Christian suffer for what you did."

"It was Rick's hands you nearly destroyed, not Christian's. Christian's dead, Israel. He has been for longer than a century. Before he died, he suffered for what he did to Hannah."

"I told you my name is Hannah."

"But you're not, you're Israel. Rick isn't Christian." Beau tried to make him hear and understand. "Why do you have to hurt him? Why the young women here on the island, and the mainland? They had nothing to do with what Christian did."

"I had to practice. Grandmother says we can't get better at what we must do unless we practice. I had to learn not to be sick with the blood."

"Your grandmother's dead, like Christian. You don't have to do what she said anymore."

"I do. Or she beats me." Clarity flickered in eyes that were magnificent in madness. "You didn't know, did you, Beau? No one ever understood why I always wore a shirt when the rest of you were nearly naked. After a while it was easier, doing the things she wanted.

"And the girls?" Israel laughed softly. "After a while, I liked that too. I liked the smell of their blood. Hearing them plead as Hannah must have pleaded was funny. I wanted to hear it more, but grandmother said I had to restrain myself, until you and Christian."

As he excused and explained murder so matter-of-factly, Beau realized there was no hope of reasoning with him. The best she could do was keep his attention focused on her until Jericho was in place.

"Have you been drinking, Israel?" She tried the ploy out of desperation. "You aren't rational when you drink."

An eerie sound meant to be an indulgent chuckle rippled in the night. "I wasn't drinking those nights I came to you. I never drink. Not ever." He laughed again. "Lover boy knew it. He's a smart one. He knew I'd only washed my mouth out with the stuff and poured it on my clothes.''

"Why?"

The pretty mouth twitched in an ugly smile. "To drive him away. But lover boy wouldn't go. He's a faithful sort. He'd make a good dog.'' A taunting glance slanted at Kieran, who didn't react.

Shrugging aside the failure of his insult, Israel turned again to Beau. "It's too bad you won't have a chance to hang on to Rover. But then, you won't be here to hang on to anything."

A flash of something in the woods behind Israel caught Kieran's peripheral vision. Jericho, working his way into position.

"Easy," he murmured in an undertone. "Just a little longer, love." He wanted desperately to take this chore from her. But one wrong move could send Israel into a killing rampage.

Helpless, he stood apart, knowing the agony she suffered. The terror for her brother. Terror he'd known many times over through the years. But the worst had been when Patience was nearly lost to the Bay. He would've done anything that day, and had, for his sister. What frightened him now, was his certainty that Beau would do the same for Rick.

"Patience, love. Jericho's almost there. Then we'll get Rick."

"What's that?" Israel glared at Kieran. "What are you telling her? What scheming tricks are you planning?"

"It's nothing, Israel," Beau assured. "Kieran's only worried about me. He doesn't understand that you really wouldn't hurt me. Do you remember the time I cut my foot and you carried me home?"

"Hush!" Israel slashed the knife through the air as if he warded off her reminder. "I don't want to hear this. I won't. Nobody thought I'd done anything so wonderful. It got me a beating."

"I thought what you did was wonderful. I'm sorry your grandmother was so cruel."

"Hush. I'm tired of talking. Time to do what I was born to do." Glittering, mad eyes raked over Beau. A lecher's smile, made more grotesque by his feminine accoutrements, tilted his lips crookedly. His fingers curled in a coaxing gesture. "Come here, Beau. Come to me."

"No!" Kieran snarled. "She isn't coming."

Israel laughed. "Wanna bet, Rover? I can make her do anything."

Israel pressed the knife to Rick's throat, drawing blood.

"Don't!" Beau's plea carried over graves clearer than a shout. "Please."

"You don't want me to hurt your precious brother?"

She stood mute, afraid she would choose the wrong words.

"Then come here." Long fingers coaxed.

"Beau, no." Kieran dared not move. "You can't change anything. Wait for Jericho."

"What's that?" Israel peered at them. "What's Rover telling you?"

"Nothing, Israel." As the knife cut deeper into Rick's throat, she lifted the latch.

At the risk of sacrificing Rick, Kieran lurched forward. "Wait."

Looking from his hand to his face, she asked quietly, "If this were your brother? Your sister?"

She waited.

Kieran's grasp tightened desperately. Then, teeth clenched, a harsh breath tearing at his throat, his hand fell away.

Beau held his gaze for only a moment before she stepped through the gate.

Ignoring Israel, she went to Rick. Kneeling by him among the graves, folding her fingers around the blade of the knife, she moved it from his throat. Blood dripped from her hand and down her arm, as she looked up into eyes empty of anything save madness. "I won't let you do this. You aren't Hannah. Rick isn't Christian."

With the sound of her voice, Rick roused from his drugged stupor. Thinking only that this was Beau, and she mustn't be hurt, he reached clumsily for Israel as the knife ripped through her fingers and targeted her throat.

In the space of a faltering heartbeat, in a tableau that would forever be branded on three sane minds, Israel lunged for Beau, a gunshot cracked out of the darkened forest, and Kieran exploded through the gate and over graves.

A vicious backhand sent the wounded, charging Israel sprawling. His bloody, blond head smashed into Hannah Desmond's tombstone with the sickening thump of a broken melon. Blood pumping from Jericho's bullet stained the shoulder of the elegant dress. Slowed to a trickle. Then stopped.

As quickly as that, it was over.

Assuring that Israel would never harm anyone again, leaving Rick's care to Jericho, Kieran went to Beau. Lifting her from a grave, taking her bleeding hand in his, he wrapped it in his handkerchief.

Then holding her at arm's length, he looked at her, his heart in his eyes. "Fool woman. Brave, wonderful woman."

Then he took her in his arms.

"It's over, my love. Your island's safe again."

Epilogue

Mist lay in hollows, and curled around oaks. But the sky was bright, promising a good day.

Beau stood in the doorway of her bedroom. The veranda stretched before her, and beyond that, the island. Her home.

Her sanctuary.

Kieran called it that the day they met.

Leaning her head against the door, she remembered. Some of it like a dream. Some a nightmare.

On bare feet she crossed to the balustrade to catch a glimpse of the village. The streets were quiet. But soon the shops would open, and Tabby would take her place at her special table in the Tea House. Children would play in the streets, on the beach and by the wharf, hoping to sneak aboard Skip's new sloop.

Once the tavern would have been the center of activity. But after it burned, mysteriously, no one expressed interest in rebuilding. Only the back gate garden survived the heat. Though, even it died from neglect.

Times Two developed a taste for tea, and now Miss Emily came with him each day for the libation and fellowship.

No one forgot the murders, or the loss of Israel. But no one dwelled on the sadness of those days. Even Tabby had forgiven herself for not having seen the trouble brewing.

Like Beau, she'd learned that love does strange things. Good and bad.

Like Beau, she knew now that the awful thing Israel did to Blue and so many wild animals on the island, were expressions of rebellion against his grandmother, not inherited insanity. They were mute, distorted cries for help no one heard. In the end, his gentleness with horses became his twisted penance.

Israel loved her. Beau knew he loved them all. Rick, Skip, Tabby, Opal. Because he loved them, he'd warned her. He'd warned Kieran. Hoping someone would stop him.

Then his love got lost in the madness.

They knew now that none of it had to be. Neither the cruelty, nor the tragedy. The boy Leila Johnson brought to the island that day so long ago, was a stolen child. Not a Johnson at all.

What could he have been, if so many things had been different? What would he have been?

Kieran's arms slipping around her were the first warning that he'd wakened. As he drew her against him, it was like coming home again, to her own private haven.

"You're thinking of Israel, aren't you?" His breath whispered against her ear. The hard strength of his body molded hers.

Folding her arms over his, she held them to her breast. "I'm sorry. You must be tired of this mood."

Kieran laughed. "Moods are to be expected given your condition, aren't they?" His caress strayed to the swell of her abdomen. "Considering that I'm responsible for the condition, I should accept my share of the blame for the mood. But if you'll come back to bed, I think I can change it."

Beau turned in his arms. "Are you forgetting all we have to do today? What with your parents coming. Patience and Matthew. Valentina and Rafe."

"Ty and Merrill, and Devlin," Kieran finished for her. "While you're counting, let's not forget Norrie and Jericho and Rick."

"You're making fun," Beau scolded. "Because I'm excited about Tabby's celebration. It isn't everyday someone admits to being a century old."

Kieran kissed her, and nuzzled her throat. Touching the fluttering hollow with his tongue, he felt her shiver, and grinned, knowing he'd won. "It isn't every day a husband can lie abed with his wife." His hands moved again to the bulge of her early pregnancy. "And bask in the wonder of his prowess."

"Ahh." Beau linked her hands at his nape. "Maybe I should call you one-time O'Hara, since that's all it needed."

Taking her hands from his neck, he kissed each palm. "What you call me, Mrs. O'Hara, is love."

Later, as she lay in his arms, Beau counted her blessings. The greatest of which was Kieran O'Hara. A man for an hour. A man for a day. A man for all time.

One day, she hoped Rick would find what she had. One day, when he settled down. The day she really knew who her brother and her husband really were. What they really were. And how the man called Simon figured in their lives.

But for now, the unanswered questions didn't matter. All that truly mattered was that Kieran loved her, and he would never leave her.

"You're smiling." Rousing from the lethargy of their lovemaking, he leaned over her. "Tell me what's so amusing."

"Nothing." Beau chuckled. "Just thinking that I should get dressed. The mail launch should arrive soon."

"You want to meet the mail launch?"

"Umm-hmm. I heard another magazine is starting a new series. Something called 'A Prince of Guys.'"

"Why would you be interested?"

Running her fingers through his hair, letting them drift from the black mane to the scar that marked his shoulder, she smiled innocently. "Considering what I found among the *Prominence* bachelors, what *would* I find among the princes?"

"Witch!" Kieran tumbled her on her back, covering her body with his. "Princes aren't half so much fun as reformed bachelors."

"No?"

"Nooo," he drawled, and the wicked teasing she loved danced in his eyes.

Reaching for him, for the man who was her sanctuary and the keeper of her heart, Beau whispered, "I know."

Later again, as she drowsed in his arms and remembered again, she murmured, "Kieran?"

"Umm?"

"You never saw the seventeen foot wedding veil."

"No problem. Our daughter can wear it."

"What if this is a boy? He'd look pretty silly in it."

"Then we'll make a little girl."

"Oh."

"Now," he drawled. "Is there anything else?"

"Well, I was wondering."

"Yeah?"

"Why do you think Jericho wears a gold band?"

"I don't know. Why don't you ask him?"

"Maybe I will."

"But not right now."

Beau laughed as only Kieran could make her laugh. "No. Definitely not right now."

* * * * * *

Here's a preview of next month's

—World's Most—
Eligible Bachelors

Rance Phillips
the sexy cowboy and secret father from
COWBOY ON THE RUN

by

Anne McAllister

It was the tour bus that did it.

One minute Rance Phillips was entirely focused on the dark red Simmental calf he'd roped and thrown to the ground, tying it for branding amid the sound and fury of bawling mother cows, bleating calves and the cussing and whooping of half a dozen cowboys.

And the next moment everything stopped.

The low diesel drone in the background, which had seemed like no more than the result of a shift in the wind bringing the sound of truck engines on the highway a half mile distant, suddenly grew very loud indeed.

"Will you look at that," J. D. Travers, his foreman, said.

Instead of branding the calf, Shane Nichols, who was wielding the iron, stood up and did just that.

His brother, Mace, who was supposed to be vaccinating, straightened, too. He took off his hat and said, "Now I've seen everything."

And Cash Callahan, who was turning baby bulls into steers, looked up, dropped the knife and whistled. "Whooo-eeeee."

"What the hell—" Rance demanded. He tightened his hold on the calf. "This isn't a Sunday school picnic, you know. Pay attention!"

They *were* paying attention. Just not to him. Disgusted, Rance finally looked up to see for himself what was going on.

A tour bus—a *neon pink* tour bus—was pulling to a stop just beyond the confines of the corral. Before he could say a word, the door on the bus opened and a horde of women spilled out.

"Ho-leee," Shane breathed.

"Maybe I *haven't* seen everything," Mace mumbled.

"Look at those mammas!" J.D. grinned as the women—all of them young, most of them pretty and not one of them dressed appropriately for a branding—advanced toward the corral. They seemed oblivious to the cattle, but they were evidently looking for something—or someone. Their eyes darted from this cowboy to that one.

Then one of them pointed straight at Rance. "There he is!"

Oh, no. He didn't believe it. *Refused* to believe it!

But no sooner had they spotted him than they made a beeline in his direction.

Rance said a very rude word under his breath. He let go of the calf and, as it bolted, he looked around for a bolt-hole of his own. There were none. The women descended en masse.

"Oooh! Rance! My name's Jolie, Rance."

"Ah, Rance. You're even handsomer than your pictures!"

"Rance, baby! You probably don't remember, but my mother and yours—"

The babble of female voices was deafening. The women were getting closer, swarming over the corral fence.

Rance straightened up and took one more desperate glance around, saw the astonished and bemused faces of his friends and knew there was no hope for him. He had to stand his ground.

So he did, but he was furious. For the past few months—ever since that damned article in *Prominence Magazine* had named John Ransome Phillips IV "one of the world's most eligible bachelors"—Rance's life hadn't been the same.

He had always had women batting their lashes at him. A few, here and there, had simpered and cooed. As he'd grown to adulthood, Rance had to admit that he'd become accustomed to seeing heads turn occasionally and hearing muffled female giggles when he looked their way.

But he'd never in his life get accustomed to this!

Everywhere he went now, women ogled him. They turned up in his law office, they followed him down the street. If he went into the grocery store, they trailed him down the aisles. If he ran into town for baling wire, women stampeded into the hardware store. They brushed up against him and wiggled their hips in front of him. They tucked their phone numbers into his pocket and patted his rear end!

Lately they'd begun turning up at the ranch. Last Monday evening he'd answered the door, expecting his tax man, and found instead a blonde in a miniskirt whose car "just happened to break down" in his driveway—no matter that his "driveway" was a gravel drive five miles from the nearest paved road.

One Tuesday after a harrowing day in court, during which most of the onlookers were females more concerned with ogling him than with following the case, he'd found another hopeful female already there sipping a margarita on the porch while she chatted with his father!

"You're encouraging them!" he'd accused John Ransome Phillips III.

"Me?" His father had flattened a hand against his chest and stared in wide-eyed innocence at his son.

On Wednesday morning he discovered a brunette in the barn when he went out to do chores. She'd been there all night, lying in wait.

"Proving I'm devoted," she told him as he hustled her to her car. "The article said you wanted your wife to be 'devoted,'" she quoted the magazine as he shoved her in and slammed the door. He didn't bother telling her that they hadn't even interviewed him. They'd talked to his father.

His father had apparently told them he liked apple pie. So many of those had turned up in the mail over the past four months that the post office was getting a little testy about the smell of rotting apples in their delivery vans. Rance told them they didn't need to bother delivering the pies, but the postmaster had cited some obscure regulation, assuring Rance that the pies had to keep coming.

Of course, half a dozen enterprising women hadn't bothered with the postal service. They'd shown up with their pies in person.

He felt hunted. Stalked. "I need a restraining order," he told his father.

The older man blinked. "Against half the human race?" Then, at Rance's stony look, his father suggested cheerfully, "You could get married. That would put a stop to it."

Silhouette

SPECIAL EDITION

Stories of love and life, these powerful
novels are tales that you can identify with—
romances with "something special" added
in!

Fall in love with the stories of authors such
as **Nora Roberts, Diana Palmer, Ginna Gray**
and many more of your special favorites—as
well as wonderful new voices!

Special Edition brings you
entertainment for the heart!

SILHOUETTE®

Desire®

Do you want...

Dangerously handsome heroes

Evocative, everlasting love stories

Sizzling and tantalizing sensuality

Incredibly sexy miniseries like **MAN OF THE MONTH**

Red-hot romance

Enticing entertainment that can't be beat!

You'll find all of this, and much *more* each and every month in **SILHOUETTE DESIRE**. Don't miss these unforgettable love stories by some of romance's hottest authors. Silhouette Desire—where your fantasies will always come true....

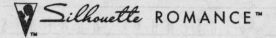

Silhouette ROMANCE™

What's a single dad to do when he needs a wife by next Thursday?

Who's a confirmed bachelor to call when he finds a baby on his doorstep?

How does a plain Jane in love with her gorgeous boss get him to notice her?

From classic love stories to romantic comedies to emotional heart tuggers, **Silhouette Romance** offers six irresistible novels every month by some of your favorite authors! Such as…beloved bestsellers **Diana Palmer, Annette Broadrick, Suzanne Carey, Elizabeth August** and **Marie Ferrarella,** to name just a few—and some sure to become favorites!

Fabulous Fathers…Bundles of Joy…Miniseries… Months of blushing brides and convenient weddings… Holiday celebrations… You'll find all this and much more in **Silhouette Romance**—always emotional, always enjoyable, always about love!

WAYS TO *UNEXPECTEDLY* MEET MR. RIGHT:

♡ Go out with the sexy-sounding stranger your daughter secretly set you up with through a personal ad.

♡ RSVP yes to a wedding invitation—soon it might be your turn to say "I do!"

♡ Receive a marriage proposal by mail—from a man you've never met....

These are just a few of the unexpected ways that written communication leads to love in Silhouette Yours Truly.

Each month, look for two fast-paced, fun and flirtatious Yours Truly novels (with entertaining treats and sneak previews in the back pages) by some of your favorite authors—and some who are sure to become favorites.

YOURS TRULY™:
Love—when you least expect it!

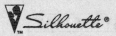

Silhouette®

FIVE UNIQUE SERIES
FOR EVERY WOMAN YOU ARE...

♥ *Silhouette* ROMANCE™

From classic love stories to romantic comedies to emotional heart tuggers, Silhouette Romance is sometimes sweet, sometimes sassy—and always enjoyable! Romance—the way you always knew it could be.

SILHOUETTE® *Desire*®

Red-hot is what we've got! Sparkling, scintillating, *sensuous* love stories. Once you pick up one you won't be able to put it down...only in Silhouette Desire.

Silhouette®SPECIAL EDITION®

Stories of love and life, these powerful novels are tales that you can identify with—romances with "something special" added in! Silhouette Special Edition is entertainment for the heart.

SILHOUETTE·INTIMATE·MOMENTS®

Enter a world where passions run hot and excitement is always high. Dramatic, larger than life and always compelling—Silhouette Intimate Moments provides captivating romance to cherish forever.

♥ SILHOUETTE YOURS TRULY™

A personal ad, a "Dear John" letter, a wedding invitation... Just a few of the ways that written communication unexpectedly leads Miss Unmarried to Mr. "I Do" in Yours Truly novels...in the most fun, fast-paced and flirtatious style!